Duets™

Two brand ... D0810823

Delightful Lori Wilde delivers a very special
Double Duets this month featuring
THE BACHELORS OF BEAR CREEK, a miniseries
about four fervent bachelors that began in Blaze
with #30 *A Touch of Silk*. This author always
"brilliantly weaves together lovable characters,
charming scenes and a humorous story line,"
say reviewers at *Romantic Times*.

Duets Vol. #80

Talented mother-and-daughter writing team
Jennifer Drew is back with a mouthwatering story
about a pastry chef wronged by a reporter, who then
sets out to get his "just desserts." Susan Peterson
serves up the quirky, delicious *Green Eggs & Sam*
about a sheriff named Sam, a sexy redhead and a
puzzling case of foul play—or is that fowl play?

Be sure to pick up both Duets volumes today!

Don't be scared.

She was no longer meek little Cammie Jo, but fearless Camryn Josephine, up for whatever life might throw her way. And she was loving her new self.

Mack was studying her, his eyes hot. So hot, her clothes stuck to her body. Everywhere his gaze landed she seemed to burst into flames.

His gaze slid from her eyes to the bridge of her nose.

Ka-pow.

Her nose burned.

Hungrily he examined her lips.

Ka-bang!

Her mouth became an inferno.

Visually he caressed her jaw.

Ka-blewy!

Her chin was toast.

Wait a minute, where was he going with that naughty stare?

Ka-bam!

Her breasts erupted in sparks.

Help! Call 911. Get the fire department here pronto. Camryn Josephine was in nuclear meltdown!

For more, turn to page 9

Whoaaa, baby.

A giant skunk, who upon closer inspection looked like Pepe Le Pew, was stalking after a provocatively dressed redhead. The young woman appeared to be whopping the skunk over the head with his own tail.

Jake grinned to himself as he started down the dock to the ship. He would hate to see the redhead's sassy patooty hauled off to jail for first-degree skunkslaughter.

"Need any help, folks?" Jake drawled as he approached the couple.

"I've never seen this skunk before in my life," the woman said as she laid a hand on Jake's shoulder, and his pulse beat faster. "Could you do me a favor?"

"For you, Blue Eyes, anything."

"Make him go away."

Jake looked at Pepe and lifted his shoulders. Reaching out, he took her hand and escorted her down the dock, a sense of pride swelling his chest. He felt oddly possessive, and the feeling startled him.

This could be the start of something special....

For more, turn to page 197

HARLEQUIN DUETS

ISBN 0-373-44145-2

Copyright in the collection:
Copyright © 2002 by Harlequin Books S.A.

The publisher acknowledges the copyright holder
of the individual works as follows:

SEXY, SINGLE AND SEARCHING
Copyright © 2002 by Laurie Vanzura

EAGER, ELIGIBLE AND ALASKAN
Copyright © 2002 by Laurie Vanzura

This edition published by arrangement with Harlequin Books S.A.

® and TM are trademarks of the publisher. Trademarks indicated with ® are registered in the United States Patent and Trademark Office, the Canadian Trade Marks Office and in other countries.

Visit us at www.eHarlequin.com

Printed in U.S.A.

Sexy, Single & Searching

Lori Wilde

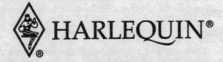

HARLEQUIN®

TORONTO • NEW YORK • LONDON
AMSTERDAM • PARIS • SYDNEY • HAMBURG
STOCKHOLM • ATHENS • TOKYO • MILAN • MADRID
PRAGUE • WARSAW • BUDAPEST • AUCKLAND

Dear Reader,

Once upon a time, I was a very shy girl. I couldn't speak to a boy, much less look him in the face. I didn't go out on my first date until I was nineteen, and it was a total disaster. The guy didn't even kiss me, and I was puckered up and ready.

The idea for Cammie Jo's story came to me one day when I was recalling my painful youth. I would have given *anything* for a magic potion or a charmed amulet that would have allowed me to be brave.

So Cammie Jo is especially dear to my heart because she is a part of me. But Cammie Jo was lucky. She had the treasured wish totem to help her over her shyness. Me, I had to do it the hard way, one step at a time. But now I'm happy to say I'm far from shy and living my dreams writing romance novels for Harlequin.

I hope you enjoy reading Cammie Jo's story. If it gives just one woman the courage to face her fears and go for her heart's desire, I'll be happy.

Don't miss out on the other heroes in my BACHELORS OF BEAR CREEK miniseries. Read Jake's story next in this very volume and coming in the fall from Blaze see what happens to Caleb and Meggie.

I love to hear from readers. Visit me at my Web site— www.loriwilde.com—or write to me at loriwilde@yahoo.com.

Happy reading!

Lori Wilde

Books by Lori Wilde

HARLEQUIN BLAZE
30—A TOUCH OF SILK *Bachelors of Bear Creek, Bk. 1

This book is dedicated to Jackie H.—
Goddess of all goddesses.
You pulled my hiney out of the fire.
Thanks for reminding me to protect the magic.

Prologue

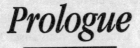

WILD WOMEN WANTED! Do You Have What It Takes To Become A Wilderness Wife?

Cammie Jo Lockhart sat cross-legged on her bed, her laptop computer pushed to one side, staring down at page 110 of the glossy women's magazine in her hand.

She should be working on her dissertation, she really should, but the photograph of four very eligible, very shirtless Alaskan bachelors provided a more provocative lure than ''The Role of the Personal Computer in the Development of Archive Retrieval.''

She had been fascinated with the June issue of *Metropolitan* since her copy had arrived in her post office box in mid-May featuring the bachelors' advertisement and the accompanying essay contest sponsored by the magazine. The winning entry would receive a two-week, all-expenses-paid vacation to Bear Creek, Alaska.

The trip was what interested Cammie Jo. The blue-jean clad, bare-chested hunks were just an added bonus.

Soon, the winner would be announced. Too bad

she'd been too chicken to enter. Cammie Jo sighed, her gaze lingering on the picture she'd committed to late-night fantasy. Quinn Scofield, wilderness guide. Caleb Greenleaf, naturalist. Jake Gerard, B&B owner and last but not least, Mack McCaulley, bush pilot. All four were heart-stoppingly gorgeous but time and again, her eyes were drawn to Mack.

What a man, what a man, what a man. The guy was so hot her fingers scorched just turning the page to read about him.

He was everything she had ever wanted but could never have, with his sensual cleft chin, short dark-brown hair, sun-kissed cheeks and deep chocolate eyes. He had a defiant expression on his face as if to say, "I'm not scared of anyone or anything." Something in his brave countenance called to the squeaky mouse inside her.

A rap at her door had her stuffing the magazine under the covers. She didn't want her aunts in on the secret that Cammie Jo, serious academician, had a soft spot for a frivolous women's magazine featuring silly articles on sex and love and romance.

She pushed her thick, black-frame glasses up on her nose, tucked an escaping hank of dishwater blond hair back into the loose bun piled atop her head.

"Come in."

The door opened and her three great-aunts,

whom she shared a home with near the University of Texas in Austin, peeked their heads in.

"Guess what?" Aunt Coco asked in a teasing singsong.

"It's so exciting." Aunt Hildegard's blue eyes, the same color as Cammie Jo's, twinkled.

"You won!" Aunt Kiki squealed and clapped her hands, unable to stand the suspense any longer.

"Won?" Cammie Jo blinked. "Won what?"

"The contest."

"What contest?"

"The one in the magazine you love so much. You know, the one with the bachelors. The one giving away the free vacation."

"But I never entered the contest," Cammie Jo protested, realizing she was busted.

A sinking sensation plunged into the pit of her stomach at the same time a strange euphoria said hello to her heart. She thought of the brief passage she'd scribbled on a piece of scrap paper and tucked between the folds of the magazine, never meaning to send the thirty-words-or-less essay.

I want to go to Alaska because I'm very timid and more than anything in the world I long to be brave. If Alaska can't save me, nothing can.

"We found your entry and sent it in for you."

"No." Cammie Jo shook her head.

"Yes." Her aunts nodded in unison.

She would give anything to see the place of her intrepid mother's birth, but she was terrified of flying, nervous around strangers, fearful of new situations, scared of wild animals, anxious when she got too far from home and apprehensive about making a fool of herself.

"I can't."

"We accepted for you. The plane tickets arrived in today's mail." Aunt Kiki handed her an envelope. "You leave tomorrow."

"I can't leave tomorrow!"

"Yes you can," Hildegard interjected. "We already packed your bags. And I had your contact lens prescription renewed."

"But I don't like wearing contacts."

"You need to play up your assets, dear. I even ordered a new color for you to try. Emerald green."

"I didn't write the entry because I was husband-hunting. I just want to visit Alaska."

"And now here's your chance." Aunt Kiki winked. "You're out of school for the summer, you have no excuses."

"I have to finish my dissertation."

"Which isn't due until October."

Cammie Jo shivered and stuffed her hands into the oversize pockets of her gray, shapeless jumper. "You guys know I'm too shy to travel. Fear kept me from mailing the essay myself."

"But you want to go, don't you?" Hildegard coaxed.

In the answer to that question lay the central paradox of Cammie Jo's life. In spite of her inherent timidity, in spite of her natural reserve around people, in spite of the fact she spent her days cocooned in the cozy academic milieu of a graduate assistant, Cammie Jo longed for adventure. She craved to be brave, but deep inside she was nothing but a bashful wimp.

Her aunts exchanged glances.

"It's time to tell her," Aunt Coco said.

"Tell me what?"

"About the treasured wish totem," Hildegard replied.

"The treasured what?"

Aunt Hildegard nodded at Coco. "You're right. Fetch the amulet."

Cammie Jo worried her bottom lip with her teeth while Coco disappeared. After a few minutes she returned with a gray metal lockbox and key.

Aunt Hildegard whispered, "When your mother realized she wasn't beating cancer, she gave us this necklace, but made us promise not to let you have it until you were mature enough to handle the powerful magic."

"What magic?" Cammie Jo didn't understand.

"Open the box," Hildegard urged. "There's a letter from your mother."

Her fingers trembled as she flipped open the lid and stared down at the whalebone necklace resting there. Attached to the bone beads was a hideous totem carving.

"Uh, gee," Cammie Jo said, overcome with an urge to wash her hands. "It's…"

"Vulgar. We know. But the totem's crudeness

is beside the point.'' Aunt Kiki placed a hand on her shoulder. ''Read the letter.''

Cammie Jo unfolded the yellowed notepaper. Her mother's delicate script jumped out at her.

My dearest darling daughter,

By the time you read my letter many years will have passed since I held you in my arms.

I am passing on to you the only thing of value I have to bestow. The treasured wish totem has magical properties beyond the reasoning mind, but the power is very real. I instructed your aunts not to give you the necklace until you were old enough to know your heart's desire. Whatever you wish for will come true. But there are conditions. You only get one wish for a lifetime, you must keep the necklace on your person and you must not tell anyone about the secret.

The doctors told your father and I that we could never have children. I wished on the totem for a beautiful, healthy baby, and look what I got!

Think about your wish long and hard, then ask for it. Believe, my darling and the world is yours!

Love forever,

Your Mother.

Blinking back tears, Cammie Jo reread the letter three times. ''Omigosh.'' She turned the necklace over in her hand. ''Omigosh.''

Her mother had worn this odd jewelry, had believed in its peculiar magic. Well, if the necklace worked for Mama, maybe it would work for her. Cammie Jo steeled herself, then slipped the ugly thing over her head.

The totem rested between her breasts and a strange warmness, as if it had been lying in the sun instead of stored in a lockbox for fifteen years, heated her skin through the material of her blouse.

"Should I make my wish now?"

"No!" her aunts exclaimed.

"You must wait," Hildegard cautioned, "until you know for sure what you want most. Once the wish has been made there's no going back."

"Remember, you can't tell anyone else about the totem or it will defuse the magic." Aunt Coco shook a finger.

"And don't forget," Aunt Kiki admonished. "Be careful what you wish for, because you *will* get it."

1

"FIRST TIME IN ALASKA?" Mack McCaulley asked to make conversation.

It was three twenty-seven on a gorgeous Tuesday afternoon in late June, and they had been in the air for fifteen minutes. His passenger had yet to utter a single word. He was beginning to wonder if she was mute.

The petite young woman wedged beside him in his Beaver floatplane, dubbed *Edna Marie* after his beloved grandmother, bobbed her head.

An overabundance of clothing—upturned coat collar, turtleneck sweater, wool knit toque—almost swallowed up her round little face. And what the clothing didn't obscure of her features, the thick glasses did.

When he had picked her up at the Anchorage airport, she'd reminded him of a nearsighted marshmallow, so swaddled was she in goose down. She had dressed for a winter in Antarctica, not a balmy sixty-degree day in Bear Creek.

No telling what kind of figure she possessed beneath the many layers. Not that he was interested.

Actually, she seemed more Caleb's type. Quiet,

studious, introverted. Mack could tell with one glance she was much too timid to make a good Alaskan wife. At least for him. He considered fortitude the number one quality he required in a mate, and this woman was about as brave as bumbling deputy, Barney Fife, from the old *Andy Griffith Show*.

She had inched into the plane, clutching at whatever handhold she could find as if she believed the metal might collapse beneath her insignificant weight. And when he'd placed a hand on her shoulder to help steady her, she'd gasped out loud at the casual contact.

What? Had she thought he would ravish her on the spot? Maybe he should tell her he always toasted his marshmallows before eating them.

In the ensuing moments since takeoff she had been staring at the floorboard, her hands clenched in white-knuckled terror.

"Uh-huh," she spoke so quietly, Mack had to tilt his head and lean in her direction to hear. She had taken so long to respond he'd almost forgotten the question.

Thank heavens not all the women who'd shown up in Bear Creek following their advertisement in *Metropolitan* magazine were this uncommunicative. Mack smiled at the thought of his last fare. A foxy redhead with a killer figure who'd pressed her cell phone number into his hand and whispered, "Call me."

Now, she'd seemed very adventuresome.

Mack exhaled audibly. Yep, he and his three friends were in for a hot, hot summer.

Er…better make that two friends. Quinn was already spoken for, having courted and caught Kay Freemont, the beautiful reporter *Metropolitan* magazine had sent to cover their story.

And this particular bachelor's curiosity was not piqued by the geeky lass beside him. He would be more than happy to dump her at Jake's B&B and head back to Anchorage for another bunch of bachelorettes. His next passengers were sorority sisters from the University of Las Vegas. Those women had to be livelier than this one.

And he craved liveliness in his mate. He wanted an exciting wife who would embrace Alaska with all her heart and soul. A best friend. A woman who loved long dark winters and relished active sunny summers.

To Mack, fearlessness was the ultimate aphrodisiac.

In his pocket, he kept a "wife" list—an itemization of his future spouse's ideal qualities. The list reminded him not to get sidetracked by a pretty face or a sexy body that turned out to have a couch potato soul, as he had in the past. As the last surviving McCaulley male he was serious about getting married and having kids. And he was very specific about what he wanted.

"But my mother was born in Alaska," Miss

Marshmallow whispered after a silence so long he jumped when she spoke. "She was a bush pilot like you."

He almost didn't catch the last bit. "For real?"

The woman bobbed her head.

"Where's your mother from?"

"Fairbanks."

Well, that explained her overdressing. Fairbanks, nearer to the Arctic Circle, was much colder than the southern coastal region.

"So you're an Alaskan by proxy." He smiled. Poor thing. He felt kind of sorry for her. He had a sneaking suspicion if he yelled "boo" too loudly she would faint dead away from fright.

"I guess so."

"Your mom let you come here all alone?" Mack could have sworn she wasn't any older than sixteen.

"Both my parents passed away when I was a kid."

Way to go, McCaulley. Open mouth, insert size thirteen-and-a-half boot.

"Oh, wow. I mean, I'm sorry."

She shrugged. "It's okay. You didn't know."

"Did your folks die at the same time?"

"No. A car crash killed my dad when I was six."

"That must have been terrible."

She nodded. "My mom was so grief-stricken she didn't take care of herself. The doctors refused to say losing the love of her life caused her cancer to grow, but I know better. She and my dad were true soul mates. She even gave up Alaska and her life as a bush pilot for him.''

''Your mom sounds like a hell of a woman.'' Too bad the daughter hadn't inherited any of her mother's moxie.

''She was.''

''So you're an orphan.''

''My three doting great-aunts raised me. So I never felt like an orphan. But I miss my mom.''

Her voice had gotten stronger as she spoke. She had the cutest little drawl. Mack had flown enough tourists in his day to pinpoint her heritage as Texas. Or maybe Oklahoma.

''It's nice. That you're not all alone, I mean.''

Geez, he sounded like an idiot. Good thing Miss Marshmallow *wasn't* potential mate material. With these brilliant and insightful comments falling from his silver tongue, she would drop him like a stone and he couldn't blame her.

''How about you?'' she ventured in a whisper. ''Are your parents still alive?''

''My father died last year. My mother?'' He shrugged, not wanting to talk about his childhood. ''She left me and my dad when I was eight. Couldn't handle the Alaskan winters any longer. She lives in Georgia with husband number five or six, I forget which.''

''Do you ever see her?''

"Not much. She hates Alaska. Says the wilderness scares her." He rolled his eyes. "She doesn't have much staying power when it comes to relationships."

"Maybe you should reach out to her. She could be lonely."

Mack hooted. "She's invited to a different party every night. I seriously doubt she's lonely."

"She hurt you when she left, didn't she?"

Mack angled her a look. "Funny," he snapped. "You seem too shy to be the nosy type."

"I'm not. I mean...oh drat...how much longer until we reach Bear Creek?" she mumbled.

He'd cut her off short. Not very nice of him. Especially when he recognized that conversation did not come easily to her. But he didn't want to discuss his erstwhile mother.

"About thirty minutes," he said more gently.

"Oh."

"Name's Mack, by the way." As a way to apologize for his rudeness, he stuck out a hand. "Mack McCaulley."

She stared at his palm and hesitated a moment before slipping her slender hand into his, then pulling away as fast as she could.

What? Did he have cooties?

"I know who you are. I recognized your picture from *Metropolitan* magazine. Page 110. The four of you guys are sitting around without shirts on."

"Ah, the infamous ad."

She stared at his chest then, as if recalling how bare he looked in that confounded advertisement and her cheeks darkened to bright crimson.

"You've got the advantage because all I know is your last name." He tapped his log book lying on the seat between them. "What's your given name?"

"Cammie Jo."

Had she said Tammie Jo? He couldn't be sure, she had such a soft tone, but the name suited her. Old-fashioned, sweet, innocent. For no good reason, he had the strangest urge to wrap his arm around her to protect her from the big bad world.

"Pleased to meet you."

"Pleased to meet you, too."

She smiled and met his eyes at last, although she immediately glanced away again. But that rapid-fire smile did dazzling things for her—let's admit the facts folks—rather plain-Jane face.

Mack returned his attention to business as they neared the mountain range that almost surrounded Bear Creek. Like most of the numerous mountains in Alaska, this cluster had no official name, but the locals called them the Tlingit Peaks for the original natives who'd inhabited the area.

He angled the nose of the floatplane upward as the majestic blue hunks of snowcapped jagged rock drew nearer. She sucked in her breath with an audible *whoosh.* Turning his head to look at her once more, Mack discovered she had her eyes clenched shut.

"Afraid of flying in small planes?"

Cammie Jo nodded and swallowed hard. "Any planes."

It had taken a strong dose of Aunt Hildegard's home-brewed chamomile tea and a meditation tape to even allow her to set foot on the dawn flight from Austin to Dallas/Fort Worth and then on to Anchorage. If she hadn't wanted to see Alaska so badly, nothing would have persuaded her aboard.

And planes weren't the only things that frightened her. Top on her list of phobias? Making small talk with handsome strangers. And not just any handsome stranger but the very bachelor she'd been fantasizing about.

Being here with him was too cool and too cruel. Out of all the bush pilots in Alaska, how had she ended up with the object of her affections?

Of course she hadn't the faintest notion of competing with other women to become this man's wife. Because of her shyness, she feared she would never find her true love the way her mother and father had found each other.

How she wished she was gutsy enough to flirt with him.

Ha! That would be the day.

She knew Mack wasn't impressed with her. Men never were. He'd barely even glanced at her when she'd sidled up to where he'd stood in the airport, holding a placard with her last name written in a bold masculine hand.

But what about the treasured wish totem nestled in the bottom of her handbag, waiting for her to come to a decision? What if the necklace worked? She could wish for anything.

Bravery.

A husband.

True love.

Wishing doesn't make it so, Cammie Jo. There's no proof the necklace is anything more than suggestive jewelry.

No proof at all, except for the letter her mother had penned to her on her deathbed.

How she wanted to believe in the mystical power.

Mack's gaze on her was disconcerting. Frankly, everything about him disconcerted her.

His outdoorsy, masculine scent when she was accustomed to delicate, feminine aromas like lilac and lavender and rose. His husky masculine voice when the dulcet, ladylike murmurs of her three aunts most often graced her ears. His stubble-darkened jawline when she was used to…well, okay, so Aunt Kiki did have a bit of a five o'clock shadow, but not when she regularly used her depilatory cream.

Anyway, he represented an alien creature, from the corded muscles of his wrists and forearms to his disheveled brown hair to his proud aquiline nose.

And in his presence Cammie Jo was as tremulous as a bunny rabbit at a hoot owl jamboree.

She turned her head to look out the window, but the closeness of the mountains in conjunction with the smallness of the plane unnerved her almost as much as the man beside her. She shifted in her seat and tried to cross her legs, not an easy feat in the many layers of puffy clothing she wore.

Accidentally, she kicked the handset mounted on the dash. The two-way radio slipped from its mooring and crashed to the floor of the plane.

Shy klutz, thy name is Cammie Jo.

"Omigosh. I'm so sorry." She reached for the handset at the same time Mack leaned over and their heads cracked together.

"Ow!"

"Ouch, ouch, ouch." She rubbed the bump on her noggin. Mack was wincing and doing the same.

"I'm so sorry," she apologized again. Without thinking, she reached out to touch the red angry welt forming on his forehead but he drew back.

"I'm okay." His voice was gruff; his gaze fixed on a spot outside the windshield.

Mortified, she shrank into her seat.

Remember why you came here, she scolded herself. *Not for love, not for romance, not to snag yourself a handsome bachelor but to face your*

*fears, visit the land of your mother's birth and to
have a grand adventure.*

And if she couldn't face her darkest dreads?

Cammie Jo gulped. She would no doubt end up
single for the rest of her life, living in the same
old house in Austin, teaching college and pining
for what might have been.

No. She refused to hide from life any longer. So
what if she had embarrassed herself in front of Mr.
I'm-Too-Sexy-For-My-Shirt Bush Pilot. Big deal.
She would live. No point putting the guy on a ped-
estal.

She might not be sexy and brave and graceful
and totally feminine from her head to her toes, but
she was whip-smart. She had maintained a perfect
4.0 GPA all through undergraduate school and a
3.9 during her graduate studies in information science.

So there. *Pffttt.*

She warmed to the subject. Who was he anyway? Sitting there looking so accomplished, so
tough. Her own mother had been a bush pilot. How
hard could flying a plane be? The guy wasn't a
brain surgeon or nuclear scientist. In fact, if she
wasn't so scared of flying, she could become a
pilot if she wanted.

Oh yeah, dead easy to be courageous inside her
own head.

On the outside was another story.

Do something brave, stare out the window, study the landscape. Imagine you're piloting the plane.

Cammie Jo forced herself to look out the side window and wished she hadn't.

The mountains were so very close and it looked as if Mack flew straight at them.

Her breath took its sweet time strolling from her lungs. Her pulse crescendoed in her ears.

I won't look away, I won't, I won't. I'm brave. I'm strong, I'm invincible. I'm intrepid Camryn Josephine.

The nose of the plane dipped. The wing wavered. Startled, Cammie Jo's eyes widened.

Was this normal?

She peeked over at Mack. He looked calm and controlled, but of course he would. He was the pilot. He wasn't supposed to let on if things were bad.

The plane dove down, down, down in a rapid descent, falling into a small valley hidden between the massive mountains. She stared at the control panel, some gizmo spinning wildly as if they were in deep trouble.

Calm down.

But she couldn't. Her stomach scraped the roof of her mouth. The sheer face of a mountain lay mere yards away. She spied trees and other vegetation and hey, was that a mountain goat?

Down, down, down. Almost at a ninety-degree angle. It couldn't be normal to slip in so steep.

Something had to be malfunctioning. She fisted her hands, fought for self-control and failed.

Aiyeeh! We're gonna crash! Mayday! Mayday! Oh, shoot, I didn't want to die a virgin.

Freaked out of her wits, Cammie Jo spun in her seat, unbuckled the belt, dove sideways and plowed her head into Mack's lap.

Seconds later, when the plane leveled out and it became clear they weren't crashing, Cammie Jo realized she had her face buried snugly in a strange man's crotch.

2

"CAN I HELP YOU with something, Sugar Plum?"

Mack struggled hard not to laugh. His restraint was evident in the tightening of his thigh muscles, the wheezy quality of his voice rumbling from his chest. Chagrined, Cammie Jo's head bobbed up as quickly as it had gone down.

She gulped. You could have fried an egg on her cheeks, they were that hot.

She wanted to explain, but just ended up mumbling incoherently, "I...bub...er...mum...ah...I..."

Desperately, she swiveled around in her seat, snapped her seat belt back in place and forced her gaze on the toe of her boot.

"Bear Creek usually makes a strong impression on people as we fly down in through the mountain pass. Some folks sigh. Others giggle with delight. I'll have to admit no one's had quite the same reaction as you."

She was horrified at what she'd done. She could never face this man again. She would wait out the rest of her vacation in the B&B, then find herself another bush pilot to fly her back to Anchorage. She buried her face in her hands.

"We do go in at a steep angle," he said, all traces of humor disappearing from his tone. "I should have warned you. I can see where your first up-close-and-personal view of the mountain might be scary."

Oh great! Now he was feeling sorry for her. She didn't know which was worse—being seen as a joke or a tragic figure.

"We're landing on the water." He leaned over to point out her window, bringing with him the scent of his soap and the foreign—at least to her unsophisticated nose—aroma of delectable man. "Just to forewarn you."

Well, duh. She could have figured that out from the pontoons attached to the landing gear. Where was Mr. Reassuring Tour Guide when the plane was aiming straight for the mountain. Hmmm?

Cammie Jo spread her fingers and peeked out at the little town circling the bay. A couple of docked cruise ships and a plethora of other floatplanes were parked next to planked piers. She spotted salmon boats and kayaks paddling up smaller tributaries, while sailboats sluiced gracefully through the cove.

She forgot to be scared as Mack circled the inlet and curiosity vanquished her shame. She dropped her hands for a better look and studied the neat row of rustic houses and storefronts bordering the main avenue.

Bear Creek was gorgeous.

A rush of emotion swept over her. An odd sense of belonging. Even though she hadn't been born here, even though she'd yet to set foot in this place, the bedtime stories her mother had told her about the magnificent state of Alaska bubbled up in her consciousness.

She felt as if she'd come home.

I'm having my first adventure, she thought, amazed. *My first real honest to gosh adventure.*

Now, if only she could work up the courage to try kayaking herself or salmon fishing, or maybe even join a group of hikers headed into the mountains.

She wanted so much and frankly, the intensity of these new desires alarmed her.

Mack set the floatplane down in the bay. A teenage boy waited on the dock to tie it up when they coasted to a stop. The teen helped her out of the plane, then took her bags from the cargo hold.

"This way, miss," he said.

Cammie Jo looked at Mack. "Aren't you coming?"

His eyes when they met hers were gentle. "I've got more passengers to pick up in Anchorage. Jimmy Jones will drive you to the B&B."

"Oh, well then. I guess this is goodbye."

Should she offer to shake his hand? Should she tip him? Cammie Jo juggled her carry-on bags and her purse, but by the time she got her hand free, Mack had already turned back to the plane.

Her heart told her stomach to scoot over because it was coming right on down. Her earlier euphoria at seeing Bear Creek dissipated.

He had already dismissed her. Out of sight, out of mind.

"Miss?"

Cammie Jo gave her attention to the smiling young man carrying her heavier luggage up the pier toward a vintage yellow touring car with Taxi printed on the door in bold black lettering. Already a few other passengers were seated inside.

"This way," the teen prodded.

Okay, well, fine. She didn't need Mack Mc-Caulley to guide her through town. She would survive just dandy on her own. That's what grand adventures were all about.

Right?

She struggled up the walkway. Her bags were too darned bulky and she tripped over a raised plank. Falling down didn't hurt much—she was wearing lots of padding—but the giggles from inside the taxi skinned her pride.

And when she glanced back over her shoulder she saw that not only had Mack witnessed her third humiliation of the day but he was shaking his head to himself. Tears sprang to her eyes. Blinking them away, she pushed her glasses up on her nose.

I'm tough. I'm tough. I'm tough, she mentally chanted but she knew she was seriously deluding herself.

Jimmy, seeing for the first time she had taken a

spill, rushed over to help her, but it was too late. What little courage she'd managed to drum up evaporated. Then, when she found herself settled into the taxi with four women so beautiful they could have stepped from the pages of *Metropolitan* magazine, Cammie Jo's spirits joined her heart and her stomach in the bottom of her boots.

The women didn't bother to introduce themselves. Since she certainly wasn't comfortable initiating conversation with sleek-haired cover model types, she just leaned back against the seat, closed her eyes and pretended to nap on the quarter-mile journey to Jake Gerard's bed-and-breakfast establishment positioned smack in the middle of town.

The lobby of the B&B was packed with additional attractive women and tons of ruggedly handsome men chatting them up. No one noticed her. She felt like a holey old gym sock stuffed in a drawer full of sexy lingerie. Now Cammie Jo remembered why she rarely ventured away from the world of academia.

Cammie Jo inched over to the front desk. She recognized the guy behind the counter as another one of the bachelors. He smiled at her.

"Hi, I'm Jake."

Too shy to speak directly to such a handsome man, she rummaged through her purse for the reservation confirmation slip the magazine had mailed to her.

At first she couldn't find it. Jake's scrutiny made

her sweat. Perspiration pooled in the hollow of her neck, then slid slowly down her breasts.

Ack! She had too much junk. She moved aside her hairbrush and her wallet. And there was that ugly amulet taking up so much room.

"What's that?" Jake pointed to the totem.

Highly flustered, she pretended not know what he was talking about. "Oh, that's a roll of peppermint candy."

"Not that." He pointed blatantly at the necklace, but she chose to pretend she didn't understand.

"That's my lip balm."

"No, no, the other thing."

"What other thing?" When all else fails, play dumb.

Jake's eyes were glued to the totem. Why wouldn't he stop staring at it? For goodness' sake, it was embarrassing enough just having the item in her purse.

"Looks like an Aleut fertility totem to me. Very powerful stuff."

"It's not." She snatched the necklace from her purse and jammed the unsightly thing into her pocket, safely out of Jake's line of vision.

"Better be careful with it," Jake warned and then winked. "Fertility totems possess potent magic."

When she realized he was flirting with her, Cammie Jo's face heated. She ducked her head and kept digging through her purse. Her hands shook. Finally she found the piece of paper and passed it across the desk to him.

He read it and said, "Welcome to Bear Creek, Camryn Josephine. We're so glad to have you. Congratulations on winning the contest."

Cammie Jo nodded. Her aunts had entered her under her full given name and that's how the magazine had made her reservations. Except it seemed they'd forgotten the Lockhart part. Never mind. Josephine was her mother's maiden name, and she liked using it. Besides, she wanted to get away from this desk as quickly as possible.

Jake handed her a key. "You've got the best room in the house. Number 12. Your luggage will be delivered shortly."

"Thank you," she mumbled.

"Oh, and if you want to sign up for any excursions, just let me know. *Metropolitan* is picking up the tab."

"Excursions?"

"You know, salmon fishing, mountain-biking tours, that sort of thing." He eyed Cammie Jo. "Although you might prefer something a little less strenuous. There's a guided hike of the Tongass National Forest scheduled for tomorrow morning at seven." He handed her a brochure. "Are you interested?"

Cammie Jo nodded, anxious to get up to her room where she could regroup. "Sounds fine."

"Good. I'll book you."

Keeping her gaze on the floor, Cammie Jo scur-

ried through the mob of people gathered around
the staircase. She was wandering down the corridor, searching for room 12, when she saw the dog.

A Siberian husky.

Cammie Jo stopped, caught her breath.

She loved dogs but because of Aunt Coco's al-
lergies, she'd never been able to have one. She put
her bags down and sank to a crouch.

"Come here," she cooed.

In an instant the dog was at her side. Cammie
Jo rubbed the pooch's belly.

"I see you've met Jake's dog, Lulu."

She hadn't heard him approach. She whipped
her head up to see Mack grinning down at her.

Her heart did this crazy gymnastic thing.

Say something, stupid.

But her tongue lay cemented to the floor of her
mouth. She couldn't think of one intelligent thing
to say. So much for being a Mensa member. Nervously, she stuffed her hand in her pocket and her
fingers glided over the totem.

*I wish I was brave enough to have a real con-
versation with this man.*

Mack squatted beside Cammie Jo and scratched
Lulu's ears.

Lulu moaned in ecstasy.

He rocked forward. His knee bumped into Cammie Jo's. If he didn't move away soon, she would
be doing a bit of moaning herself.

Pant, pant, pant.

Her right hand rubbed the dog's belly. Mack's

left hand scratched under Lulu's chin. He tilted his head and grinned at her in the muted hallway lighting.

"She's adorable," Cammie Jo ventured, keeping her gaze firmly focused on the husky.

"She's a big old thief is what she is," Mack said, with obvious affection.

"Not her," Cammie Jo protested. "She's too sweet."

"Don't let her looks deceive you and don't leave anything you prize laying out. Lulu's a kleptomaniac."

"Surely you exaggerate?"

He shook his head. "Nope. She steals whatever she can get her teeth on. Jewelry, candy, socks, pens, car keys."

Lulu whined and gave them an I-was-framed expression, as if she knew her thieving habits were the topic of conversation.

"Yeah, we're talking about you," Mack assured the dog. He stood and leaned nonchalantly with one shoulder against the wall.

Cammie Jo glanced up and realized she was eye level with the zipper of his blue jeans. Unnerved, she shot to her feet.

Mack's eyes met hers.

She gulped then blurted, "Uh…what are you doing here? I thought you had to pick up more passengers in Anchorage."

"I do," he said.

Her hurly-burly heart lub-dubbed. Had he come

looking for her? But why would he do that? His presence seemed so intimate, so cozy, so wrong. And yet her blood was singing through her veins like a chorus of Christmas carolers.

"Why are you here?"

"I found something under the passenger seat of my plane. Thought this might have fallen out of your luggage."

"Oh?" She arched an eyebrow. No telling what she might have dropped in her haste to get away from him. "What is it?"

From his pocket he withdrew a thin scrap of scarlet silk and stretched it over his palm.

Cammie Jo pushed her glasses up on her nose and stared at what he held in his hand.

A pair of thong undies.

How in the world did women wear these silly things without getting a permanent wedgie? Just the idea of putting them on made her squirm with discomfort.

"Although," he continued, "this type of under-garment doesn't really seem your style. I thought it might belong to one of my previous passengers. I feel like Prince Charming going door to door try-ing to find the Cinderella that fits these panties."

Normally, she would have been embarrassed witnessing a handsome man handle dainty undies, but the smug look on his face irritated her to the point where she just snapped. He was so certain she was a boring fuddy-duddy, that she would never wear something as brazen as this—which of course she wouldn't, but he had no right to make such an assumption about her—that Cammie Jo fibbed.

"Yes, they are mine." She snatched the panties from his grasp and thrust out her jaw, daring him to contradict her.

The expression of surprise on his face made her feel something she'd never felt before. Boldness? She prodded the emotion. No, not quite boldness, something saucier than mere audacity.

She rested her hands on her hips. His eyes tracked her movements. He gazed at her as if trying to picture her in that thong. He shook his head as if he couldn't even visualize it.

Cammie Jo notched her chin upward and looked just above the top of his head. A trick she'd learned in graduate school when she had to give lectures to undergrads. Don't make eye contact and you'll be okay.

"What did you think? That I wear white cotton, high-waisted granny panties?"

Which was indeed exactly what she had on beneath her clothes. Aunt Hildegard did everyone's underwear shopping during the twice-a-year white sales, and Cammie Jo had never cared enough about the issue to buy her own panties. But she would roll over and die before she would admit such a thing to Mack, who thought he had her pegged right down to her choice of lingerie.

"I never said that." A speculative note crept into his voice and in that moment Cammie Jo was able to label the amazing new sensation churning inside her.

By gum, she was feeling *cocky*. Puffed up with pride and ready to take whatever he dished out.

"I'm much more than I appear on the surface, Mr. McCaulley. Still waters run deep."

"Apparently so." He seemed a bit taken aback.

"Thong undies are just the tip of the iceberg."

"Is that so?"

"Yes it is."

"Okay, then. I believe you. They're your panties. Mystery solved."

"Anything else?" she sassed. She was astonished, pleased and giddy with the thrill of her newfound bravado.

"Nooo. Guess that's it."

It was only later, after he'd sauntered away, that Cammie Jo realized from whence her unexpected bravery had sprung.

The treasured wish totem resting in her pocket.

3

ONCE SHE WAS safely ensconced in her room, Cammie Jo took off some of her layers of clothing and moved to stare out the window overlooking Main Street.

People crowded the road, wandering in and out of the shops and restaurants. Honestly, she hadn't expected so much activity. Crowds made her nervous.

Everything makes you nervous. Like good-looking bush pilots.

A sudden rap at the door startled her so much she almost fell off the window seat.

Was it Mack?

Holding her breath, Cammie Jo crept to the door. Rats! No peephole. And no chain.

Timidly, she cracked the door open and peeked out. A gorgeous woman who looked like the actress Charlize Theron stood there smiling at her, a pen and notebook in her hand.

"Hi," she said.

"Uh, hi," Cammie Jo responded, impressed with the woman's smartly tailored clothes and flawless skin.

"I'm Kay Freemont with *Metropolitan* magazine, and I'm the one who picked your entry to win the free vacation. I'd like to interview you if I may."

"Oh." Cammie Jo opened the door wider. "Come on in."

Kay stepped into the room and Cammie Jo closed the door behind her.

"Did you come all the way from New York just to interview me?"

"No." Kay's smile crinkled the corners of her brown eyes. Cammie Jo realized that even though Kay looked very worldly and sophisticated, she was only a couple of years older than her own twenty-five years. "I live in Bear Creek now."

Cammie Jo gestured at the window seat, not all that comfortable with playing hostess. She glanced over at the totem, which she'd placed on the dresser after that scary-but-thrilling encounter with Mack in the hallway. She wasn't quite sure if she was ready to handle the consequences of wearing the necklace.

"Thank you." Kay sat by the window while Cammie Jo perched on the end of the bed.

She ran her palms over the tops of her thighs, a habit of hers when she was nervous or uncertain.

"Relax." Kay's smile deepened. "This won't hurt a bit, I promise."

"I've never been away from home before," Cammie Jo confessed.

"Alaska can be overwhelming, even for a world

traveler,'' Kay assured her. "I first came here in February. Talk about overpowering.'' She shook her head. "So tell me, Cammie Jo, why are you interested in becoming a wilderness wife?''

"What?''

"You did enter the contest hoping to meet the bachelor of your dreams, didn't you?'' Kay sat, pen poised over notebook waiting for Cammie Jo's response. "Although I've got to tell you, Quinn's no longer on the market.'' Laughing, Kay held up her left hand to show off a diamond engagement ring. "We're getting married next month.''

"Hey, that's great.''

"So.'' Kay lowered her voice. "Which bachelor are you interested in?''

"Can I be honest with you?'' Cammie Jo shifted on the thick comforter.

"By all means.''

They talked for a long while. Cammie Jo told her about her great-aunts, and how their attempts to shelter her had resulted in Cammie Jo being afraid of her own shadow.

"So getting married is really the last thing on my mind,'' Cammie Jo said. "I need to stretch my wings and fly. I need to discover who I am before I'll ever be ready for marriage. I hope that doesn't disqualify me from the free vacation.''

Kay shook her head. "Your reasons are your own. You won the contest fair and square. If you're not interested in any of the bachelors, that's fine. I don't think they will suffer. Ever since the article ran women have been arriving in Bear Creek by the hundreds. It's a modern-day gold rush but instead of gold, the hunt is on for eligible men.''

No kidding. Cammie Jo had seen the hordes of women strolling the streets of Bear Creek.

Kay smiled. ''The bachelors, in conjunction with the magazine, are throwing a party tonight at the community center across the road. Seven o'clock and you're the guest of honor.''

Cammie Jo ducked her head. ''I'm really not much on parties.''

''Now, now, didn't you come here to overcome shyness? A party is a great way to start.''

''But I don't have anything appropriate to wear.''

Kay looked her up and down. ''You're a few inches shorter than I am, but I'm betting we're the same size. What about shoes? What size do you wear?''

''Six and a half.''

''Hey, me too. Imagine that. I'll bring over a selection of dresses and shoes. Then I'll help you do your hair and makeup.''

Two hours later, after Kay had returned to create Cammie Jo's metamorphosis, she stepped back from the mirror so Cammie Jo could see the results.

''Ta-da!''

Cammie Jo stared owl-eyed. No. It couldn't be.

This wasn't her. Her pulse thundered. Her head spun. Kay was a wizard with a makeup brush.

"I can teach you how to do this for yourself if you want."

"Oh, yes," Cammie Jo breathed.

The woman staring back at her was a complete stranger.

This woman was beautiful.

Her eyes were not Cammie Jo's normal blah blue but a deep shade of emerald-green, converted into something mesmerizing by the colored contacts. Her round chipmunk cheeks had disappeared. Instead it seemed as if she possessed high, sculpted cheekbones. Her lips were full and pouty; her skin as luminous as dew-kissed blades of grass.

And her hair.

Oh, her once plain brownish-blond hair! Now, it hung down her back in a myriad of loose, shiny curls. She sucked in her breath, totally stunned by the transformation.

"Wow," she whispered. "Wow."

"That's what every bachelor in Bear Creek will be saying. I'll leave you to get dressed. Gotta go change myself and meet Quinn at the community center. Come on over when you get ready."

"Okay." Cammie Jo nodded. "Thanks for everything."

"You're welcome."

Once Kay had gone, Cammie Jo hugged herself, feeling simultaneously excited and scared. First a total makeover and now a party? Her? There would be lots of handsome men in attendance. Shivers pushed down her back. And a lot of beautiful women to compete against.

She thought about having to make conversation with strangers—it had been hard enough talking to Kay, but the woman had a journalist's flair for drawing people out. The very idea of chit-chatting with people she didn't know made her want to flee screaming into the wilderness.

And yet, she wanted to go so much.

Make a wish and you can have your heart's desire.

She moved toward the dresser, picked up the necklace and wrapped one hand around the totem, tentatively rubbed it with a thumb and squeezed her eyes tightly shut.

"Please," she whispered. "Grant me my most treasured wish. Make me strong and brave. Take away my fears, vanquish my shyness, free me from my own insecurities."

She slipped the necklace over her head, gave a sharp "eek" of surprise at the unexpected warmth. The totem had certainly seemed to work when she'd sassed Mack in the hallway. Plus, Jake said it was an Aleut fertility totem and it possessed potent magic.

Truth be told she had the sudden urge to stand up straight, throw back her shoulders and yodel from the rooftop, "Look out Bear Creek, here comes Camryn Josephine."

MACK COULDN'T GET enough of staring at the fine-looking women packing the streets of Bear Creek. When he and his three friends had taken out that ad, he had no idea women would appear like snow-flakes in winter.

He was loving the attention. As he'd hoped, the sorority sisters from UNLV had been a lot more fun than Tammie Jo Lockhart, although he suspected they'd had one too many cocktails on the plane.

One of the daring lasses had even pinched him on the butt when he'd unloaded their luggage. Mack wasn't sure whether he liked that or not. He preferred daring women, sure, but there was something to be said about respecting a man's private parts until you got to know him a little better.

He thought of tremulous Tammie Jo plunging her face into his lap when she believed the plane was crashing and Mack had to laugh. Okay, she had violated his private parts too, but not intentionally. She'd just been scared.

It was almost seven o'clock, and he was heading to the party Quinn and Kay had organized to celebrate the arrival of the contest winner. He wore a tuxedo at Kay's insistence and he tugged at the stiff, choke-a-man collar. She'd had the four bachelors outfitted from some place in Anchorage, and he hated wearing the monkey suit. Kay had told him to get used to it since undoubtedly his bride-to-be, whoever she was, would expect him to stand at the altar in one.

Mack almost said he wasn't marrying that kind of woman but quickly shut his mouth because that's exactly the kind of woman Kay was. And the last thing he wanted was to hurt her feelings.

But Mack's dream wedding would consist of something adventuresome. Like getting hitched in hiking gear atop a glacier. That's the kind of woman he wanted for a wife. Gutsy, courageous, up for anything. The exact opposite of what his weak-willed mother had been like.

His mind was wandering down this familiar but unpleasant train of thought when from his peripheral vision he caught a glimpse of a woman strutting down the sidewalk.

She moved like a regal queen. Confident, self-assured, poised. Her hair, a tantalizing caramel color, floated down her back in a spiral of curls that made Mack think of pecan taffy, and his imagination triggered his mouth to fill with the sweet, buttery taste of nutty candy.

An incredible black dress made of some soft clingy material hugged her curves snugger than a label on a wine bottle. The skirt had this amazing little tattered hem that fluttered like a handkerchief around the most sensational calves he'd ever seen.

She was perfect. Absolutely perfect.

His mouth went dry. His eyes bugged. His palms grew sweaty on the steering wheel.

Who in the thunder was she? He hadn't flown in any woman who looked like that over the last couple of days. He would have remembered. It must have been one of the other bush pilots. The lucky devil.

Her shoulders were thrown back, her head held high, her eyes fixed straight ahead. She stalked forward on four-inch heels like she owned the world. Instant admiration sprung in his chest. His kind of gal.

Wait a minute, what was that she was wearing around her neck?

Stunned, he stared at the lewd totem bouncing off her perky breasts and he was completely mesmerized.

So mesmerized, in fact, that when she stepped off the curb in front of him, Mack's foot accidentally hit the accelerator instead of the brake.

Good Lord, he was about to kill a dream walking!

He slammed on the brakes while simultaneously jamming on the horn. His tires squealed in protest at the sudden pressure and his stomach vaulted into his throat.

The woman turned to look at him, an expression of shocked surprise in her wide green eyes. Mack sprang from the front seat, rounded the hood and was devastated to see that he had stopped mere inches from her gorgeous body. His heart pounded so hard he feared it would jackhammer a hole through the bottom of his foot.

At first, she leveled him an insouciant stare, as if it were all his fault. Then she blinked and said in a voice that sounded vaguely familiar. "Goodness, did I step right out in front of you?"

"Yes," he said, feeling bashful as a boy for absolutely no good reason at all. "You did."

"Aren't I lucky that you have lightning-fast reflexes."

He couldn't stop staring at her. Couldn't reconcile her calmness with his own flustered state of agitation. Didn't she recognize that he had almost killed her? Or at the least given her a whoop knot bad enough to land her in the emergency ward.

"I'm sorry. I was so busy looking for the community center, I simply didn't see you."

His mouth hung open. He had a sudden desperate desire to touch her and it was all he could do to keep his hands to himself. "You're going to the *Metropolitan* party?"

She nodded.

"Me too. Come on." He reached out and took her by the hand. A shudder of yearning passed through him. How could one woman knock his world so completely out-of-kilter? He inhaled deeply. He couldn't let her see how much she affected him. Not now. Not yet. "Let's get you out of the road."

"What?" She blinked her big green eyes at him, and he was a goner.

"Let's get out of the road."

"Oh. Okay."

All right, so she wasn't a brainiac. Big deal. She possessed a figure to make angels cry hallelujah.

Um, McCaulley, what's number seven on your list? His conscience nudged.

Mentally Mack rolled his eyes at that nagging voice. Intelligence was number seven on his "wife" list.

He'd written down that trait for a reason. He had a tendency to get involved with beautiful but flighty airheads who thought putting down roots meant bleaching your hair.

Give this one a chance, he argued with himself. Just because she stepped out in front of his truck didn't mean she was dumb. Everyone made mistakes. Hadn't he hit the accelerator instead of the brake?

He settled her in the passenger seat beside him, then drove the short distance to the community center parking lot. Heads turned to stare at them when they walked up the pathway.

Where on earth had she come from? This exotic fantasy dropped into his tiny corner of Alaska.

You're not looking for a fantasy, pal. You're looking for a wife.

Shut up, already. I'm just walking her into the party, not getting down on one knee.

That was good because he didn't even know if this woman was interested in getting married. Or if she was even interested in him.

And then there was that...*thing* she had on around her neck. What in the hell was that all about?

"Name's Mack, by the way, Mack McCaulley." He stuck out his hand.

She studied him a moment. "Haven't we already met?" she asked finally in a breathy whisper.

"Oh no, ma'am. I would never forget a lady like you."

For some reason his statement caused her to frown in displeasure when he figured she should have been flattered. What had he done wrong? Could they have met before? He paused a moment to think. Nah. He would have remembered her.

"I'm Camryn," she said after a moment. "Camryn Josephine."

He grinned. "Like Cameron Diaz?"

"Pronounced the same but spelled differently."

"Still." He wriggled his eyebrows and hoped he was forgiven for whatever he had done to make her frown. "It's a very sexy name."

"Thank you."

He pushed open the door and escorted her into the community center. Kay and Quinn came over to greet them. Camryn leaned over and said something to Kay.

"You're kidding." Kay laughed at whatever it was Camryn had told her, then Kay looked at Mack with a disapproving gleam in her eyes.

What? Now it was Mack's turn to frown.

What on earth had he done, dammit? He hated being talked about behind his back. It brought back bad childhood memories from the time his mother had run off with another man. And from the time his first serious girlfriend had dumped him for a software program designer who pulled down a high six-figure salary.

"Am I missing out on a joke?" he asked Kay.

"You could say that," Kay demurred. "Do you have any idea who she is?"

"No." Mack snorted in exasperation.

"She's the winner of the *Metropolitan* magazine contest."

"No kidding."

Hmm, that meant she probably *was* interested in snagging a husband. The plot thickened. Mack looked at her with new possibilities but Camryn still seemed miffed with him for some reason. He wanted to make amends and quick.

Kay locked arms with Camryn and whisked her away before Mack could protest. "I'll bring your date back in a minute."

"I'm not Mack's date," Cammie Jo murmured to Kay once they were out of the men's earshot.

"He thinks you are." Kay guided her up a staircase to the second floor and pushed open the door to the powder room. She stopped in front of the mirror, pulled a comb from her purse and ran it through her sleek blond hair.

"No he doesn't. He doesn't even recognize that I'm the same person he flew in from Anchorage this afternoon. He thinks I'm some gorgeous creature."

Kay gave her an appraising glance. "Well,

sweetie, in Mack's defense, you do look like an entirely different woman.''

"It's irritating. When I was Cammie Jo he didn't give me the time of day. But as Camryn Josephine, he can't be solicitous enough.'' Cammie Jo folded her arms across her chest, felt the smooth sleekness of the totem against her forearm.

"That's men for you.''

"And that's precisely why I'm not interested in them. It doesn't matter that I have an IQ of 145. All that matters is that I look good in a dress.'' Camryn snorted.

"Don't judge them too harshly,'' Kay said. "You've got to remember in Bear Creek the men outnumber the women ten to one. That's why the bachelors advertised for wives. And the women that do live here are practical, rural women who don't have much use for makeup and designer clothes. This publicity-generated infusion of femininity has gone straight to their heads.'' Kay giggled conspiratorially. "Quinn's ape crazy over my collection of provocative stockings.''

"Promise me you won't tell Mack what I'm really like.''

"What do you mean?'' Kay applied a fresh layer of lipstick to her full lips, then passed the tube to Cammie Jo.

Cammie Jo swept her hand at her sexy outfit. "I'm not really beautiful and sophisticated and self-confident.''

"Don't be silly, of course you are. You just needed a little makeover."

Kay didn't understand. This transformation wasn't the result of a little blush, a push-up bra and a new color of contact lens. Only the totem could have wrought such a change, and she couldn't explain that to her new friend. For one, she didn't want to sound like a nutcase and for two, she certainly didn't want to chance defusing the magic by talking about it.

"Please, just don't tell Mack I'm Cammie Jo. Okay?"

"Sure, honey. Whatever you want." Kay squeezed her hand.

"Thanks."

"Now let's get back out there. We've kept the men waiting long enough."

They returned to find the party gearing up. More guests had filtered in. The band was playing some current, chart-topping country-and-western tune. Mack was standing near the front door, his eyes on her. He was resplendent in that tuxedo. Every little girl's dream date. In fact, he looked as if he could grace the top of a wedding cake.

Cammie Jo hadn't taken five steps toward him when she found herself surrounded by men. For a second, panic set in. Then she took a deep breath and reminded herself there was no reason to be afraid. She had the treasured wish totem, which she had decided looked less suggestive in plain view than tucked into her dress. She tugged on the totem and told herself not to get embarrassed. If they wanted to gawk, by George, let 'em gawk.

That ought to give Mack something to think about.

4

MACK STOOD BY the punch bowl glowering at
Jake, who'd scooped Camryn out from under him.
He glared while his best friend waltzed his dream
woman around the dance floor.

No fair! He had seen her first. Had almost ran
her down in fact, because he'd been studying her
so hard.

He admired Camryn's graceful movements. Enjoyed the way her dress swirled and flared around
her legs. A bullet of jealousy shot through him
when she cocked her head upward and smiled at
something Jake said. He shouldn't be jealous. He
wasn't much of a dancer himself. Let her have fun
with someone who didn't possess two left feet.

So why the burning sensation in his gut?

Camryn's hair fanned out, swirled behind her as
she danced. Mack found himself enchanted by that
twirling mane and he wasn't the only one. He spied
many covetous glances angling her way from the
numerous single men lined against the wall.

She might be pretty but it really wasn't enough.
Not anymore. Secretly, he was terrified of making
a grave mistake, of picking a woman too beautiful

and delicate to survive in his homeland. That's why he had the "wife" list.

Mack patted his breast pocket, then remembered he was wearing a tuxedo and had left his list at home. No matter. He knew the requirements by heart. His ideal woman would be brave, feisty, loyal, trustworthy, adventuresome, honest and intelligent. Just like his grandmother.

When Jake had seen his list, he'd retorted that what Mack wanted was a Boy Scout, not a wife. Mack had pondered on Jake's comment for a few days, then added: a sense of humor, likes to snuggle and doesn't mind being spoiled. He hadn't shown that part of the list to Jake. A man could only take so much razzing from his friends.

He didn't know if Camryn possessed all the qualities he needed or not. They'd shared a connection, a moment. Only getting to know her better would tell if their initial attraction was anything more than superficial sexual awareness. He didn't have time to waste on meaningless affairs. Been there, done that.

He'd just turned thirty-one and while he'd never heard of men having biological clocks, damned if he didn't hear this strange ticking in the back of his head.

He didn't want to be an older single parent like his father. Pop had been forty-two when Mack was born and in a wheelchair with rheumatoid arthritis by the time Mack was thirteen. He wanted to have his kids while he was still young enough to pitch a baseball and hike a mountain and shoot a hockey puck. Mack had learned that experiencing life to the fullest was the only way to live. Because you just never knew what the future held.

Well, buddy, you won't find out anything about Camryn standing here on the sidelines. Get out and get into the game.

The band switched tunes, going from a jazzy rock beat to a slow, dreamy waltz at the same moment Mack tapped his buddy on the shoulder.

"Do you mind?" he said to Jake, then to Camryn, "May I have this dance?"

Jake shrugged, nodded. Camryn smiled and held out her arms to him.

That's what he liked most about her, the way she met his gaze head-on. Clear and straight, with nothing to hide. She didn't act coy, nor did she present an overly aggressive demeanor like that grabby UNLV sorority sister. She was honest, open, flexible.

On the surface she seemed to be everything he'd been dreaming of when he placed that advertisement with his friends.

"Hi," he said.

"Hello." Simple, direct, no game-playing.

Camryn pushed a tendril of hair from her face and tried her best not to drop her gaze. Mack looked unbelievably handsome in a tux.

Don't be scared, she coached herself. *You've got the treasured wish totem around your neck and you're having the adventure of a lifetime.*

She was no longer meek little Cammie Jo, but fearless Camryn Josephine, up for whatever life might throw her way. And she was loving her new self.

Mack took her in his arms. Oh yes! He was all brawn and muscle and sinewy male.

Being held like this was an eye-popping experience for her, startling and novel. His body heat, so incredibly thermal, slipped into her skin roasting her from the inside out. His smell clobbered her senses, left her addled with yearning. Oh, she was falling too fast, stumbling too quickly out of her element and her normal comfort zone.

Dazed, Cammie Jo just stared at him. Her brain had turned to banana pudding.

"I'm not a very good dancer," he apologized.

Oh baby, I don't care.

Lucky for them both Aunt Kiki had once been a professional dance instructor, otherwise Cammie Jo wouldn't have known a fox trot from a fox hole.

Then she realized Mack thought she was staring at him because he'd just crunched her toe, but honestly, she'd barely noticed. She was concentrating on those sultry eyes that smoldered with a banked sexuality.

"I might not be much of a hoofer," Mack continued, and here his gaze roved downward to peruse her lower extremities with obvious appreciation. "But you've got legs just built for dancing."

In the past, she would have blushed at his compliment but tonight she accepted his appraisal as a matter of course. By gum, she did have rather nice legs. It was about time someone noticed.

Don't hide your light under a bushel.

One of her mother's favorite sayings sprang to mind. Even when she was little she recalled her mother worrying that she was too shy, too modest, too introverted by half, and she'd struggled hard to draw Cammie Jo from her shell.

"So," he said. "What do you do for a living, Camryn?"

Should she tell him the truth? Would he be impressed or turned off by an academic? But she couldn't lie even if she wanted to. She couldn't think fast on her feet.

"I'm working on my Ph.D. in information science. And I teach undergraduate classes at the University of Texas."

"Really? That surprises me."

"Why? Do I look dumb?"

"No, no. Of course not. It's just that information science seems like a profession that would attract an introvert, not a gregarious lady like yourself."

"You think I'm gregarious?"

Oh lovely, Cammie Jo. Tip your hand on the first day.

"Sure. You're so at ease in a crowd."

She almost laughed out loud. No one had ever paid her that particular compliment.

Mack was studying her, his eyes hot. So hot her clothes stuck to her body. Everywhere his gaze landed she seemed to burst into flames as if he possessed a kind of libidinous pyrokinesis.

His gaze slid from her eyes to the bridge of her nose.

Ka-pow!

Her nose burned.

Hungrily, he examined her lips.

Ka-bang!

Her mouth became an inferno.

Visually he caressed her jaw.

Ka-blewy!

Her chin was toast.

Wait a minute, where was he going with that naughty stare?

Ka-bam!

Her breasts erupted in sparks.

No, no, don't go any lower. Please.

Ka-sizzle!

Her abdomen caught ablaze.

He raised his eyes to hers briefly, then with a devilish grin he dropped his gaze to the lowest point yet.

Her pelvis. Oh her pelvis!

Whoosh!

Backdraft.

The Yellowstone forest fires had nothing on what was raging down there. Help! Call 9-1-1. Get the fire department over here pronto. Camryn Josephine was in nuclear meltdown.

They were moving around the dance floor, albeit not in time to the music. They could have been handcuffed together in solitary confinement, so oblivious was Cammie Jo to any stimuli other than Mack's dangerous eyes. The Occupational Safety and Health Administration should look into labeling those incandescent orbs with a high octane warning.

"Thirsty?" he asked when the band took a break.

She nodded, her insides nothing but vapor. No, not thirsty. Parched, scorched, desiccated.

"Let's grab some punch, get some fresh air."

"Sounds good," she murmured and was shocked to hear her own voice come out as seductive and husky as a whiskey-voiced blues singer.

He wrangled them a couple of glasses of punch and a few cookies and steered Cammie Jo to the back door of the community center. When the heavy metal fire door clanged closed behind them, she took a deep breath and looked up at the sky, surprised to find it was still bright daylight despite being past nine o'clock at night.

Summer in Alaska.

Cammie Jo gazed at the mountains in the distance and nibbled on an almond cookie to collect herself. The breeze blew cool against her skin and that helped soothe her feverish thoughts, until Mack came to stand directly behind her.

She could *feel* his manly presence.

Felt his gaze drop onto her body, her hair, every darned where.

Talk about sensory overload. If she didn't have

the totem, Cammie Jo would have run for the safety of the B&B long ago. Heck, let's be honest. She would never have left her room in the first place. She would be curled up on the bed sipping hot cocoa and watching old movies.

Bor-ing.

"Your punch," he said and held out a cup.

She took it from him and their fingers brushed. She concentrated on sipping to keep from meeting his gaze once more. Her core body temperature had to be a hundred and ten. She didn't think she could stand any more heat.

I'm brave. I'm strong. I'm courageous. Nothing but nothing scares me. Not even a man with Fourth of July rockets for eyes.

"You're very beautiful," Mack said, taking a step closer.

"Thank you."

I simply will not blush and I won't back up. I won't! Camryn would be accustomed to receiving and deflecting advances from amorous admirers, but Cammie Jo was not.

"I suppose you hear that all the time."

She affected a ho-hum expression. "Not as much as you'd think."

He took another step forward.

Her heart clattered like an aging engine on low-octane fuel.

"I'd like to get to know you better."

Cammie Jo couldn't help noticing the dimple

carved in his cheek and the provocative twinkle in his eyes. Was he asking her out?

"Really," she murmured.

"Yeah. I'll admit it. Out of all the women who've shown up in Bear Creek over the last couple of weeks, you're the only one who's really raised my interest."

"And why is that?"

He cocked his head and a sheaf of dark-brown hair shifted over his side part. "You're something of a mystery, and I love solving puzzles."

"Oh you do?" She couldn't believe how easily she was flirting, how she was matching his stare without blinking or turning red as a boiled lobster. She took a bite of cookie, ran her tongue along her lips for effect.

"I do." His eyes tracked the movement of her tongue.

"Well good for you."

"You're making fun of me."

"I'm not."

"Where did you come from, Camryn Josephine?"

He raised a hand and for one jumpy moment she thought he might touch her, but instead he reached out to brace his palm against the side of the building and lean in toward her. His scent was pure heaven. He was close enough so that she could see just how long and lush his lashes were. They looked supple as sable and softened his direct, inquisitive eyes.

"Out of the blue."

"I believe you," he murmured. "You're that unique."

She'd never been in such an intimate position and she found she loved being close to this glorious representative of the male species.

"How are you when it comes to adventure?"

"How do you mean?"

"Do you like the outdoors? Are you game for mountain biking and kayaking and salmon fishing?" He waited, and it seemed, held his breath.

Goodness, what was the correct answer?

She thought of the ad, visualized the caption underneath the picture.

Wild Women Wanted.

Could she be wild enough for this man? She moistened her lips with her tongue, tasted the too-sweet flavor of strawberry-banana punch mingling with the almond of the cookie she'd just finished.

"I'll take any adventure you can throw my way and eat it up with both hands."

He hissed in his breath as if his mind had conjured some very wicked adventures indeed. "Anything?"

"Anything," she declared, happy she had wondrous magic to help her keep that vow.

"Wait a minute." Mack was suddenly looking at her real funny, staring at her mouth.

Uh-oh. Had he finally figured out she wasn't really brazen Camryn, but shy Cammie Jo? A moment of fear licked through her before she remembered her wish.

Reaching out, he smoothed his thumb over the corner of her mouth.

Cammie Jo shivered. What was he doing?

"Cookie crumb," he said.

"Oh."

But the crumb was gone and he was still here, his face so very close to hers.

"Not so fast." His arm snaked around her waist and he pulled her flush against the length of his body.

Good thing there wasn't a maximum speed limit for pulses. She'd be liable for the highest fine imaginable.

Then he lowered his head and took her mouth with his own.

She was in heaven. But when he pressed his tongue to her closed teeth, she jumped back startled.

Mack blinked. His initial thought was one of complete surprise. Camryn Josephine knew next to nothing about kissing. But how could that be? Surely this hot, sassy babe had kissed dozens of men, if not hundreds.

Maybe she'd given him the weird, platonic-but-not-quite kiss because she was uncertain of her feelings. Mack scratched his head and looked down at her.

She was such a cute little thing. All curves and dips, so different from his own hard, angular body.

The woman might not be clear on her feelings, but he was clear on his. He wanted to taste more of her, go deeper, explore. See if she could indeed be the woman he was searching for.

He hooked his index finger under her chin, lifted her face up to meet his again. He watched the pulse in her neck jump with anticipation. Slowly, he lowered his lips to that throbbing beat and kissed her exposed throat with the lightest touch he could manage, heightening the anticipation.

Her skin was hot and getting hotter by the minute. The more his tongue laved over her rapidly pounding pulse, the faster it beat.

Mack felt her tremble. Her escalating excitement matched his own. Did her quest for adventure include those of the flesh?

He wanted her with a sharp spike of desire that stabbed straight through his groin. But letting lust rule his head was not the way to go.

No. As much as he might want to, he wouldn't drag her home to his bed. But he *would* sample another taste of those lips. Just to give himself something to think about.

He took her mouth in a heated rush. She gasped into him. She tasted so exquisite he almost groaned.

The feminine scent of her filled his nostrils. He felt her chest raising raggedly against his own. He threaded his fingers through that mane of golden brown hair, cupped the back of her head in his palm.

Camryn wriggled in his arms, every nerve ending in her body on full alert.

It was too much, too soon. She was in sensory overload and she couldn't absorb everything that was happening.

Yes you can, silly, you've got the totem.

She reached up to caress the necklace, to draw strength from its power. But when her fingers crept to her throat she felt nothing but her own skin.

Panic-stricken, she jerked away, leaving him looking dazed.

"What...?" he asked.

Cammie Jo stared down at her chest. The totem was gone!

Without it, she was not brave enough to kiss a virtual stranger. On her own, she was not the type to flirt and bat her eyelashes and volley innuendoes.

She was her old self. Vulnerable, scared and way out of her league.

In desperation, she cast her gaze to the ground, looking among the flowering lupine at their feet for her missing necklace. Her breath came out in frantic wheezes, as if she was an asthmatic in a room full of ragweed pollen.

"Camryn? What's wrong?" Mack reached out to put a hand on her shoulder.

His touch sent her over the edge. She had to get away. Had to leave before she ruined everything. Had to hide from him so he wouldn't see her for the timid spinster-in-the-making that she really was.

Later, after the party was over, she would come back and try to find the necklace. But for now every phobia she'd ever experienced was gelling into one major fear. That of being found out a fraud before she'd ever had a chance to really live her great adventure.

Get out. Get away!

"I...I can't do this." She spun on her heels and took off at a dead run.

"Camryn," Mack cried. "What's wrong? Talk to me."

She never hesitated.

"Wait!" His footsteps thundered behind her.

Clippety, clippety, clippety—stumble. Her ankle turned sideways in the impossible heels but she ignored the bite of pain and kept going.

Hurry, hurry. You've got to give him the slip.

Except she could hardly see where she was going with this darned hair bouncing free and unfettered about her face and she didn't know the area. She rounded the building at a dead-on sprint, hoping he'd give up the pursuit. For heaven's sake, if a man was running away from her she'd take the hint and not chase after *him*.

But Mack stayed right on her tail.

Was the man part bloodhound? Jeez Louise. Talk about relentless.

Where could she go to get away from him? She leaped over some shrubbery at the edge of the sidewalk. A well-dressed crowd was just walking into the entrance of the community center. Cammie Jo barreled past them, using human bodies as a shield between Mack and herself.

"Excuse me. I'm sorry. Didn't mean to step on your toe." She heard Mack apologizing but she never slowed, not for a second.

Lungs bursting. Stitch in her side. Throbbing ankle. She could endure all that but not a totemless face-to-face encounter with Mack.

Rabbit quick, she darted through the front door, spun past a startled Kay and clattered upstairs to the relative safety of the ladies' room.

Okay, don't panic, don't panic.

Lovely advice. About as useful as telling a hostess not to panic when she's got ninety-nine guests coming for Thanksgiving dinner in fifteen minutes and a hundred pounds of Turkey *à la Froufrou* just exploded in her brand new rotisserie oven.

Cammie Jo paced the tiled bathroom, arms folded across her chest. What to do? She couldn't stay in here all night.

Or could she?

Tempting thought, but considering the way he'd chased after her, Mack didn't seem the kind of guy to let things go without a fight. He would probably send someone in after her.

Rats, rats, rats.

And then her gaze landed on the window.

Hmmm. Small opening, but she was petite.

Cammie Jo climbed up on the sink and leaned

over to raise the window. She stuck her head out and peered down.

Yipes!

The ground was farther away than she expected. Never mind that directly underneath the ladies' washroom window sat a row of sturdy, metal, bear-proof garbage cans that looked as if they could skin a girl something nasty.

Cammie Jo pulled back, and mulled over her choices. She could take a header, or more precisely, a footer out the window, or she could face Mack again.

Which was easier to do?

She closed her eyes briefly and wished for the totem.

If wishes were nuts and cherries we'd all have a Merry Christmas, Aunt Kiki was fond of saying, although Cammie Jo had never quite understood the adage. Herself, she'd always wanted clothes and toys for Christmas, not nuts and cherries.

"Camryn?" Kay's voice called to her from the outer room. "Are you in there? Mack's looking for you."

Ulp. It was now or never.

Cammie Jo dangled her legs over the window ledge, took a deep breath and jumped, stiletto heels and all.

5

WHAT ON EARTH had happened to her? Mack wondered as he paced the corridor, hands clasped behind his back.

Damn his tendency to jump in with both feet when he wanted something, never mind that he could be barreling off a cliff.

He needed to amend his "wife" list. Under "likes to be spoiled," he was adding, "not a flight risk."

Kay reappeared a few minutes after she had gone inside the ladies' room to look for Camryn. Mack raised his head, and gazed at her expectantly.

"She's not in there."

"What do you mean she's not in there? I saw her go in with my own eyes."

"I checked all the stalls. No one is in there."

"You're covering for her," Mack accused.

"Why Mack McCaulley, are you calling me a liar?" Kay settled her hands on her hips and gave him a mischievous grin.

Contrite, he said, "No, Kay, of course not."

"I will tell you that the bathroom window was hanging open."

"You think she climbed out the window?"

Kay shrugged. "Looks like it. What did you do to her?"

"Me? I didn't do anything."

"Camryn's missing after slipping off alone with you. You Alaskans have the tendency to go after what you want pell-mell. Maybe you were moving too quickly for her."

"Then why didn't she just say so?" Exasperated, Mack jammed his hands in his pocket.

"You'll have to ask Camryn that question."

"Right. And how can I do that when I don't know where she is?"

"She's staying at Jake's."

Just forget her, McCaulley. There's millions more fish in the sea. Look around you.

But part of him could not so easily dismiss Camryn without a valid explanation for her behavior. And he really wanted to apologize if he'd upset her in any way.

He left the community center and walked across the street to Jake's B&B. He pushed through the door into the lobby, then went over to the front desk where he found the desk clerk, crotchety old Gus, sitting on a stool reading some true-crime paperback with a lurid cover.

"Hey, Gus."

Gus grunted and barely looked up from his book.

"You have a guest by the name of Camryn Josephine staying here. Would you tell me her room number?''

''We don't give out that kinda information.''

''Come on, Gus, you know me.''

''Yeah, and you're a rascal, McCaulley. I don't trust ya.''

''That was twenty-five years ago, Gus.'' The elderly man gave him grief about his long-ago transgression whenever he could.

''I gotta long memory.''

''Obviously. I apologize profusely. I was a terrible kid. Now would you at least ring her room for me?''

''You ain't got a chance with that one. She's too smart for the likes of you.''

''That's what you said about Quinn and Kay and you were wrong on that score, too.''

Gus snorted, put down his paperback and dialed Camryn's room. He waited a few minutes then hung up the receiver. ''She ain't answering.''

Gus went back to his book and Mack turned away.

Where could Camryn be? The woman had disappeared like smoke up a flue.

Sighing, he walked through the lobby and plunked down on a chair in Jake's great room where the guests and locals often congregated. Tonight, the room was empty save for that mousy woman with the Coke-bottle glasses.

What was her name again? Tammie Jo? Maybe she'd seen Camryn come through here.

He got up and stepped over to where she sat curled up on the sofa by the low-level fire. She was reading a copy of Jane Austen's *Pride and Prejudice*. Her hair was pinned to her head in that unflattering bun and she wore a fluffy pink chenille bathrobe and outlandish Bugs Bunny house slippers. Somehow he wasn't surprised at her silly get-up. There was a half-empty glass of milk in front of her and a plate of cookie crumbs.

Party on, Tammie Jo.

He perched on the edge of the heavy cedar coffee table in front of her. "Hello, there."

She kept her head tucked down, her eyes glued to her book. She was as bad as Gus. What was this? Blow off McCaulley night?

"Remember me?"

She nodded, still not glancing at him.

"You been sitting here long?"

She shrugged.

Was she so shy she couldn't even look at him? He recalled their encounter in the upstairs hallway. She'd acted pretty spirited then. Maybe it took sexy underwear and provocative talk to bring out the vixen in her.

"Would you happen to have seen a woman come through here? Tall. No wait, she had on really high heels." He looked Tammie Jo over for a moment. "Actually, she might have been about your size. She had on this really amazing black dress. She's got hair the color of pecan taffy and killer gams."

"Sorry," Tammie Jo snapped. "Didn't see her."

Okay. He'd handled that wrong. Apparently Miss Plain Jane didn't care to hear him rhapsodize about some other woman and how could he blame her?

Mack got to his feet without a second glance at Tammie Jo. "Thanks for your help."

She didn't reply, just kept her nose buried firmly in her book. *Hy-ca-rumba.* She'd come all the way to Alaska to sit on a couch and read?

Shaking his head, Mack left the B&B. Time to go home. He was done with chasing after his fantasy woman. At least for tonight.

HE STILL hadn't recognized her, Cammie Jo fumed as she combed through the lupines on her hands and knees outside the back door of the community center. It was after midnight, the sun had finally gone down and she had a pocket penlight clutched between her teeth.

Was the man as dumb as a post? Or was he so blinded by Camryn's supposed beauty he couldn't see that the blah woman right in front of him was the same one he'd been drooling over all night?

Or was the truth plainer than that? Had he instantly labeled Cammie Jo a nonsexual entity and dismissed her the same way men had been dismissing her for years? She knew the conclusion he had drawn about her. Baggy clothes + thick glasses + no makeup + books = a boring spinster woman.

The thought made her blood boil.

Men, the simple beasts. They were so swayed by appearances.

Take one push-up bra, a pair of colored contact lenses, high-heeled shoes, professional grade makeup and voilà—the cinder girl becomes a princess.

She was put out, disgusted, annoyed and still very attracted to that bothersome Mr. McCaulley.

And for some vexatious reason she couldn't stop thinking about him.

Or the way his lips had tasted on hers.

Why hadn't she simply come out and said, "Look, I'm Camryn. That's my real name but everyone's called me Cammie Jo since I was knee-high to a grasshopper."

Why? Because without the totem she was too damned shy to speak such things to him. And because she would hate to see the disappointment on his face when he realized she wasn't the hot, sexy babe he thought she was.

Well phooey on him anyway. She hadn't come to Alaska to snag a husband. Marriage was the furthest thing from her mind. She wanted adventure and plenty of it. She wanted to sample new foods, drink in novel sights, inhale fresh smells. She wanted to see moose and bald eagles and grizzly bears.

But she wasn't getting her wish unless she found the missing totem.

Just when she was about to give up, her hand hit something solid in the grass and she yelped with glee. Yes! The hiking trip to the Tongass National Forest was back on for the morning. Cammie Jo shone her penlight over the necklace, found where the string had broken, tied it into a secure knot and slipped it over her head.

Instantly, she felt stronger.

There. To heck with Mack. She was brave Camryn again and as long as she had the totem, nothing or no one was stopping her from having the time of her life.

CAMMIE JO woke at the crack of dawn ready for the hiking tour. She opened her window and breathed in the fresh, clean mountain air. She dressed, laced up her hiking books, double knotted the totem and slipped the necklace over her bulky azure sweater. She wasn't losing it a second time.

After several attempts, she finally got the contact lenses in her eyes. She tried her best to recreate Kay's makeup job, and she managed a serviceable replication. She brushed out her hair and let the curls trail down her shoulders as she'd worn it the night before. She checked herself in the mirror.

All right! Camryn Josephine was back.

She scurried through the lobby, apparently the only one awake in the whole place save for the elderly desk clerk who never looked up from the morning paper. Once outside, she found the street filled with passengers leaving the cruise ships for shore excursions. The restaurants were hopping, and the air was permeated with the tantalizing aroma of omelettes, bacon and strong coffee. She purchased orange juice and a blueberry muffin from a street vendor, then headed for the tour bus.

The bus that was to take them to the Tongass National Forest for their four-mile hike idled at a wooden park bench just a few feet from the B&B. Cammie Jo hurried over to find more than a dozen attractive young women and a few middle-aged couples already aboard.

She plunked down in the seat behind the driver. He looked familiar and after a few minutes of studying him she recognized him, not only from the party the night before, but from the *Metropolitan* magazine ad as well.

He was, quite frankly, the most handsome man she had ever seen, with coal-black hair and eyes the piercing blue of a glacier. He was probably the reason the bus was packed with so many single gals at this time of the morning.

Where as Mack was handsome in a rugged way, this man was handsome in the way of perfect Greek statues and paintings of heavenly beings. She found his beauty incredibly intimidating. On the dashboard in front of him lay a well-worn copy of a book by John Muir.

Caleb, she remembered. Caleb Greenleaf, the naturalist and apparently bus driver as well.

A few more women boarded—they giggled and flirted up a storm with Caleb before finding seats. Then Caleb rose to his feet and began to count heads. He consulted a clipboard. ''Looks like everyone's here except my assistant. He must be running late. We'll give him a few minutes because it's hard for me to lead a group of this size by myself.''

Everyone must have been pretty happy just to sit and eyeball Caleb because no one protested too much, although Cammie Jo heard someone behind her whisper, ''We've got to be back on the cruise ship by noon.''

At that moment, a man in a brown bomber jacket sprang onto the bus.

''Morning, folks,'' greeted Mack McCaulley. ''Sorry I'm late.''

A wave of forgiving female twitters sounded around the bus.

He held on to the grab bar and remained standing while Caleb closed the door and put the bus in gear. Mack picked up the microphone and held it to his mouth as if to start into the regular tourist spiel when his eyes lit on Cammie Jo.

They both inhaled in unison and their gazes welded.

Mack's sharp intake of breath crackled over the microphone.

Cammie Jo's heart slipped sideways in her chest. What was he doing here? Why wasn't he out flying his plane?

He recovered quickly, introduced himself and began telling everyone about the trip ahead. But Cammie Jo didn't hear a single word he said. Her mind was a frayed ball of twine unraveling at an alarming rate.

She wrapped a fist around the totem and began to breathe easier. It was okay. She was all right.

They arrived at the edge of the forest in under ten minutes and Caleb parked the bus. He gave instructions for the people to divide into two groups of twelve. One group was to go with him, the other group to follow Mack.

Caleb climbed off the bus and the tourists followed. Mack stayed rooted to the spot, his eyes never leaving her face. Cammie Jo hesitated, not knowing what to do.

Her pulse jumped like water droplets on a red-hot griddle and her tummy tugged to and fro with this swishy-swashy sensation like a washing machine set to agitate.

She shouldn't be scared. But then she realized the emotion wreaking havoc on her insides was not fear at all. But rather excitement tinged with something else. A feeling she'd never experienced with such intensity.

Sexual arousal.

The air between them was charged with more voltage than any high line wire. Every hair on her arm stood at erect attention.

Cammie Jo gulped. Hard. She was hot and wet and achy down there.

And then the bus was completely empty, save for her and Mack.

He trod slowly toward her, his boots echoing with a solid thud, thud, thud, that matched the crazy rhythm of her heart.

"I've got a bone to pick with you," he said.

Cammie Jo jerked her head around, looking for a way out. Not because she was afraid of this bundle of walking testosterone but exactly because she wasn't. She should have been scared to death because he was so close, so manly, so gosh darn p.o.'d at her. Instead she was turned on like a faucet twisted to full blast.

"No place to run, Sugar Plum." He was standing directly in front of her in the middle of the aisle, his big hands planted on the backs of either seat. "If you want off this bus, you'll have to come through me."

Was she even breathing? All she knew was that his smoldering dark eyes had pierced her clean through and pinned her in place.

Normally, she hated conflict. Avoided it at all costs. But now she possessed a newfound bravado.

"And what kind of bone do you have that needs picking?" she asked coolly, amazing herself with her impudence. "Chicken? Beef? Pork perhaps?"

Ha! He almost smiled. She saw it flit at the edges of his mouth before he gained control by frowning deeply.

"Why did you run out on me last night?"

"Mack!"

They both jumped.

Caleb rapped on the outside of the bus window and tapped at the face of his watch. "We're burning daylight, bud."

"Duty calls." Cammie Jo said with enough sugar in her voice to choke a honeybee.

"Don't think this lets you off the hook. Sooner or later you and I are having a long talk."

"Fine with me."

"Fine."

They stared at each other.

"You coming on the hike, then?" He inclined his head.

"Why, of course."

He stepped aside, gestured with a hand. "Ladies first."

Haughtily Cammie Jo rose, nose in the air, and started forward. She sailed past him, but then promptly tripped over her boot laces as she descended the bus steps, and sprawled face forward in the dirt.

IT WAS AN HOUR and a half into their three-hour hike through the spongy forest undergrowth and Mack couldn't stop looking at Camryn. He smiled whenever he recalled how she'd leaped to her feet after falling from the bus and dusted herself off before he could get to her. He'd made a move to help, but she'd glared at him so hard he'd stepped backward, palms up in a gesture of surrender. She was a feisty thing; an odd combination of half regal cutie, half fierce tomcat.

Proving beyond a shadow of a doubt she possessed quality number two on his "wife" list.

He halted the group from time to time to give minilectures on the flora and fauna. During these little breaks, Camryn assiduously avoided looking at him, pretending instead to be wildly enraptured with a skunk cabbage or chipmunks or wild blueberry bushes.

Apparently she didn't think he noticed when she cut her eyes surreptitiously at him. For his part, he stared at her boldly. He had nothing to be ashamed of.

Except she was a distraction to beat all distractions. Some nerdy middle-aged guy outfitted in the wrong kind of footwear kept asking him silly questions. Like, "Why are the Sitka spruce and the western hemlock the only variety of trees in the Tongass?"

"Because that's the way it is," Mack had finally snapped and he heard Camryn snicker. Was she laughing at him or the nerdy guy?

Caleb and his twelve adoring disciples were a quarter mile ahead of them in the forest. Mack brought up the rear in his group to prevent stragglers while Camryn had positioned herself far ahead of the pack, as if to put as much distance between them as possible by infiltrating Caleb's group.

Mack admired the way Camryn's trim little butt

swayed from side to side in those snug-fitting jeans. He loved watching her hair bounce about her shoulders as she walked and the way her sweater adhered to her breasts.

He recalled the moment when they were alone on the bus together and he'd been trying to intimidate her with his maleness, hoping to wring a confession out of her concerning her strange behavior the night before. Instead of being unnerved as he expected, he could have sworn he saw sparks of unmitigated mischief in her fabulous green eyes.

"Which kind of bone needs picking?" she'd drawled, all spunk and sass.

My bone, he'd thought but hadn't had the guts to say.

An unwitting image of that cute little butt of hers curving above his cupped palm jettisoned itself into his head and just like that, *boom!,* he got hard.

Taking a deep breath, Mack paused, put one hand on a tree and struggled to rein himself in.

"Oh!" someone up the trail cried and it sounded an awful lot like Camryn.

Mack's head came up just in time to see a flash of color as she tumbled down the embankment.

6

JUST CALL ME GRACE, Cammie Jo thought as she somersaulted head over heels down a steep slope into a mossy creek bed where she ended up sprawled on her butt. The totem might cure shyness, but it didn't seem to do a darn thing to exorcise a chronic case of klutz.

At the thought of the totem, her fingers flew to her neck.

Whew! It was still there.

Chagrined at her clumsiness, Cammie Jo shook her head.

"Camryn," Mack shouted, "are you okay?"

She squinted up at the top of the hill and saw Mack in silhouette, the morning sun at his back. She waved perkily. "Fine."

Cammie Jo heard him coming, crashing down through the mossy undergrowth like a bull elephant on the rampage. She was short-winded by the anticipation the sounds of those rescuing feet wrought inside her.

Mack was coming after her.

In a second, he was there, his arms going around her, lifting her out of the damp mud.

Her back was against his chest, she raised her head. His chin was at her mouth so unnervingly close, Cammie Jo forgot everything but the smell of his woodsy skin and how good his solid body felt. Rampant lust raged through her, startling her with the sheer magnitude of erotic sensations.

She wanted him. Hotly, desperately, madly. Here. Now. On the forest floor, in the woods, in the creek. With the squirrels and birds and rabbits watching. He was magnificent. He was sexy. He was...

Laughing at her.

"What's so funny?" she demanded, narrowing her eyes at him.

"You are, Sugar Plum."

"I'm not your sugar plum."

"No," he said, "I dare say you're not."

"Good. So stop laughing."

"I can't. You should see yourself. Miss Priss is a mess. Twigs in your hair, mud on your cheek, moss stains on your jacket."

"Who are you calling Miss Priss?"

"As if you didn't know."

"Where is everyone?" She plucked leaves from her curls and looked up at the embankment for signs of the other hikers.

"I sent them on ahead to catch up with Caleb."

"So it's just you and me?"

"Yeah." His voice was husky. "Alone."

Uh-oh, what was that dangerous look in his eyes?

"Why are you on this hiking trip? Shouldn't you be out ferrying tourists back and forth from the airport or something?"

"You don't want me here?"

"I didn't say that."

He cocked his head. "Ever since we ran the ad, Caleb's been swamped with unexpected business. Tuesday mornings are usually slow for me so I'm pitching in for the summer. Helping out a buddy."

"And getting a eyeful of the backsides of sexy young women."

"That too." His grin turned lopsided and he tightened his grip on her waist. "And your backside is the best I've ever seen."

"Liar."

He held up two fingers. "Scout's honor."

"You were a Boy Scout?"

"Uh-huh."

"I find that hard to believe." She also found it hard to believe that she was standing here in a dark forest alone with the sexiest man on the face of the earth.

"It's true."

"Guess I'll have to take your word for it."

"If I kiss you again, will you run away like you did last night?"

"No," she whispered.

"Why *did* you run away?"

"Er…because I had something in my eye?" That was no lie, she'd had contacts in her eyes.

"Then why did you climb out the bathroom

window and leave me with a broken heart?'' Dramatically he clutched a hand to the left side of his chest.

Cammie Jo snorted. ''Your heart wasn't broken.''

''But it was.'' His tone was light but the expression in his eyes told her she *had* wounded his pride.

''A girl's entitled to cold feet, isn't she?''

''Oh, so that's what happened.''

Somehow he'd shifted her around in his arms and they were no longer back to chest but chest to breasts and his face was right there, just waiting to be kissed.

''Are your feet cold now?'' he murmured.

''Well, they're pretty wet. I forgot to wear wool socks like they tell you to do in the guide books.''

He made a clucking noise with his tongue. Tsk. Tsk. She wondered what it would feel like to have him make that same sound inside her mouth.

''You'll never be a good wilderness woman with that kind of memory.''

''Nor by the way I skim helter-skelter down embankments.''

''True enough.'' He languidly plucked a twig from her hair, his rough fingers skimming through the silkiness of the loose strands. How many times had she dreamed of moments like these, of being held by a man like this? ''But I'm imagining you must have other skills that'd compensate for your lack of memory and balance.''

"You'd think."

They peered deeply into each other's eyes. Neither of them blinked or looked away.

"I'm only guessing," he said. "But yeah, I bet you've got a lot of hidden talents. Can you cook?"

"Nope."

"Sew?"

"'Fraid not."

"Good with numbers?"

"Sorry."

"Hmm, so you're completely without talents?"

"I didn't say that."

"Ah." His pupils widened.

"Keep your mind out of the gutter, McCaulley."

"How do you know where my mind's at?"

"That wicked twinkle in your eye."

With the cool air and the dimness of the forest floor contrasting with the heat and brightness of Mack's eyes, Cammie Jo's body came alive like a blossoming flower.

"I would like to kiss you," he said. "But I'm nervous about making the first move. Considering your cold feet and all."

"That's thoughtful of you."

"That's me, Mr. Thoughtful."

"Mr. Full-of-himself is more like it." She grinned.

"So what's it gonna be? Do we get up, climb out of here and go find the others or…"

"Or what?"

"You tell me."

She couldn't stand any more of this cat-and-mouse stuff. She wanted to kiss him and that's all there was to it.

Have an adventure. Live a little.

Cammie Jo wrapped her arms around his neck, sank to the ground and pulled him down on top of her.

CAMRYN WAS HUNGRY for him, oh yeah, but it was as clear now as it had been last night that she was no expert at kissing. And if she was a novice at kissing did that also mean she was a novice at lovemaking? Mack had trouble reconciling this—since Camryn was old enough and certainly sexy enough to have her pick of lovers—but he couldn't deny her inexperience.

When he moved his lips from her mouth to the tender flesh at the nape of her neck and then sucked lightly on her skin she just about came undone.

"What? What's that? What are you doing?" Her body tensed beneath his.

"Love bite."

"You mean like a hickey?" She sounded horrified.

"Sort of. If I sucked harder it would be a hickey. But giving hickeys in places people can see is immature. I wouldn't give you one without your permission."

"Oh, well, that's good to know."

"No one's ever nibbled on you like this?" He shook his head in disbelief.

"Nooo. Not quite like that."

"How 'bout this?" He nipped a trail up her neck to her ear, breathing in the intoxicating scent of spruce and moss and sexy woman, then slowly rimmed her ear with the tip of his tongue.

She shivered all over and goose bumps sprung up on her exposed skin. "Is that what they call a Wet Willie?"

"Uh-huh, do you like?"

"Er…actually no."

"I'm not driving you wild with anticipation?" No one had ever complained about his technique before.

"Personally, I prefer a Dry Herman."

"What's that?"

"No tongue in my ear!"

He chuckled. "You're a hoot. And I like your honesty. No more Wet Willies."

"Hey, down there. You two need any help?" Caleb's voice rang out in the forest, ruining everything.

Mack rolled off Camryn and got to his feet. "Nope." He shielded his eyes with his hands and looked up the embankment at the twenty-four people grinning down at them. "I think we've got everything under control."

"Is that what you call it? Are you two joining us for the trek home?"

"We'll be right there." Mack sighed. Just when

things were getting really interesting between them, well, except for the Wet Willie misstep. How far might things have gone if Caleb and company hadn't shown up?

Not too far. You don't have any condoms on you and it's a sure bet she doesn't, either.

They made their way up the hill back to the others, then finished the hike. Mack sat next to her on the bus ride back.

"How 'bout dinner tonight?" he asked.

"I don't know. I'm thinking not."

That surprised him. He'd expected her to say yes. "Those iceberg feet of yours again?"

"Something like that." She smiled, Cheshire Cat-like.

Mack said nothing. He was confused. Did she like him or not? Her kisses had said yes, yes, yes, but now her mouth was saying no, no, no.

"Okay, fine." He leaned back in his seat, folded his arms over his chest."

"Oh, why not," she said. "All right. I'll go out with you."

OH GOSH, what would she wear? Cammie Jo perused the dresses Kay had loaned her. They were all so beautiful, it was difficult to choose.

Lulu sat on the floor, thumping her tail and watching her try on first this one and then that one.

The totem kept getting in the way as she tugged the dresses over her head and finally, in exasperation, Cammie Jo pulled it off and laid the necklace on the bed.

She decided at last on a pale lavender silk skirt and blouse set. Humming to herself, she grabbed clean underwear from the dresser drawer and hurried to the bathroom for a long soak in the tub before getting ready.

An hour later, after she'd finished her bath and done her hair and makeup, she padded back to the bedroom in her bathrobe. She glanced at the clock. Seven-twenty.

She'd left the door open so Lulu could depart at will, and it appeared the dog had gone. Cammie Jo shut the door and turned to get dressed. She slipped on the skirt and blouse, wriggled into panty hose and heels, then reached for the totem.

It was gone.

Odd. She could have sworn she left it on the bedspread. Maybe she'd placed it on the dresser and had forgotten about it.

No. Not on the dresser.

A bit of panic began to rise inside her. She dropped to her hands and knees, searched under the bed.

No totem.

She fluffed the bedspread, lifted the pillows.

Nada.

She flung open the dresser drawers, ransacked the closet.

Zippo.

Oh jeez. Oh no.

Dread squeezed her heart as she remembered what Mack had told her about Lulu. The dog was a kleptomaniac.

And then she knew exactly what had happened. That Siberian husky had stolen her necklace!

She looked at the clock. Seven-forty. Officially time to freak out. She couldn't let Mack see her like this.

A quick glance in the mirror told her the truth. Her shoulders were slumped. Gone was Camryn's straight, confident posture. Her hair, which only minutes before looked perfect, was now a disheveled mop, rife with static cling. Her mascara had smeared, giving her raccoon eyes and in her worry, she'd chewed off her lipstick. She was a hopeless mess.

She had only one option. Cancel the date.

She searched in the bottom of her purse for Mack's business card with his telephone number on it. She punched in the number with trembling fingers and left a message on his answering machine, telling him she wasn't feeling well.

WHAT? SHE WAS breaking their date, blowing him off? Mack, wrapped in a bath towel and dripping water onto the kitchen rug, poked the answering machine button with an outraged finger and played her message a third time.

He called the B&B and asked for her room.

The phone rang. And rang. And rang.

She better damn well be in the bathroom tossing her cookies or she had a lot of explaining to do.

Forget her, McCaulley. A fickle woman isn't worth the aggravation.

Good advice, but his ego wouldn't let it lie. What had he done wrong? Mack fumed.

Women! He raked his fingers through his hair, stomped to the bedroom and got dressed. Maybe he would wander the streets of Bear Creek and find her cozied up with some other guy. Mack ground his teeth. And what would he do then?

No, better plan, go see if Jake wanted to grab a beer or two over at the Happy Puffin. It wasn't as if there weren't dozens of women in town eager to entertain the *Metropolitan* magazine bachelors.

Yeah okay, some of those women had numerous pierced body parts and tattoos and green hair but what the hey? Right now that's exactly what he needed. A night out with his vivacious buddy, flirting with any and every female in sight. That would cure his infatuation with Camryn.

Except drowning his sorrows in beer and female companionship wasn't really Mack's style. Deep in his heart Mack was a one-woman man. He wanted that happily ever after and he was scared it didn't exist. He was worried that he wasn't any better at picking a wife than his father had been.

Why did it seem he was attracted to gadabout types like Camryn?

Except she wasn't as fast and loose as she liked to pretend. Her naive kisses gave her away. He took a deep breath, held it a moment then blew it out in one long *whoosh*.

The fact remained—her tendency to play mind games aside—she was the epitome of his perfect mate.

Just stop thinking about her, will you?

Easy to say, not so easy to do.

He drove over to Jake's and forced himself not to search the streets for Camryn's graceful strut. He parked behind the B&B and went in through the back entrance. He heard voices coming from the kitchen, but at this time of day, that wouldn't be unusual. The door banged closed behind him, and he rounded the corner of the anteroom into the kitchen.

What he saw stopped him in his tracks.

There were Jake and Camryn sitting at the kitchen table, their backs to him, heads intimately close together, voices lowered in confidential tones. Camryn's hair was caught up with a barrette and pinned to the top of her head in a rather unflattering style, but that didn't seem to stop Jake. In fact, he reached out, patted Camryn's hand and muttered Mack's name.

They were whispering about him. Whispering just like people used to whisper when his mama left.

Mack's blood froze. Those old memories weren't what haunted him. Oh no. What gnawed his belly with a fire angrier than rotgut moonshine was the domestic picture in front of him. His best friend in the whole world snuggling up with the woman he was interested in.

They looked too cozy. Too damned cozy by half.

Spurred by a jealousy that took his breath, Mack trod across the kitchen floor and clamped a hand on Camryn's shoulder.

"Too sick to go out with me, but not too sick to flirt with Jake," he said in a hard voice that didn't even sound like his own.

Then she turned her head and Mack realized his mistake.

The woman wasn't Camryn.

She had the same caramelized sugar-colored hair but there the resemblance ended. Her eyes were lupine-blue whereas Camryn's were emerald-green, and those eyes in question were almost obscured by her thick glasses.

They both had similar features, yes, but Camryn had a sassy tilt to her head, a confident air about her. This woman's shoulders slumped. To top it off she was wearing an outfit that stylish Camryn wouldn't be caught dead in. A high-necked gray sweater and dull brown baggy corduroy trousers. She couldn't meet his gaze to save his life.

Miss Marshmallow.

Tammie Jo? Was that her name?

He frowned. Surely party-loving wild man Jake wasn't interested in this shy little thing. Not smooth-talking Jake who could bring the most beautiful of women to their knees with a mere crook of his finger.

"I'm sorry," Mack said and took a step backward. "My mistake. I was looking for another woman."

Cammie Jo glanced at Mack then quickly looked away again. A lump of dread and disappointment settled inside her.

Yes. He wanted Camryn Josephine. Not her, Cammie Jo.

But he must want Camryn an awful lot to come storming over here to find her. Cammie Jo's tummy fluttered.

"Well," Jake said, "I don't see any other women here, do you?"

"No." Mack snorted.

"Sounds like she's got your hackles up, whomever she might be," Jake continued.

Cammie Jo studied the table, afraid to look at Mack. *Please don't let him recognize me. Please don't let him recognize me. Why doesn't he recognize me?*

Was she so inconsequential as her dowdy, timid self that he didn't even notice her uncanny resemblance to Camryn? She knew with despair the answer to that question.

"You're right about that." Mack sighed and ran a hand through his hair.

"Is she worth the aggravation?" Jake drummed his fingers against the table. "I've rarely ever seen you this steamed."

Cammie Jo held her breath, waited for his answer. She tried her best to remain invisible, falling back on her favored technique of imagining herself part of the woodwork.

''She's gorgeous, Jake.''

''There are five hundred new women in town who fit that description.''

''She's got a body that won't quit.''

Cammie Jo arched an eyebrow, peered down at her form cloaked in her trusty shapeless clothes. He thought she had a great body? She couldn't stop a smile from creeping across her face.

''So what's the problem?'' Jake asked.

''She's smart and funny and brave as all get-out. I think she's double-booking dates behind my back.''

Cammie Jo's heart wrenched, and she bit down on her bottom lip. She hated knowing she was causing Mack pain.

''What's wrong with that?'' Jake asked glibly. ''I do it all the time. In fact, I've got four...count 'em, four dates lined up for the weekend.''

''I'm not like you,'' Mack said. ''I'm a one-woman man, and I want a one-man woman.''

Yes, Cammie Jo thought. *You only want one woman and she doesn't really exist.*

''Whoa, buddy, you just met this girl.''

''She's special.''

''Don't let your urge to get married cause you to do something rash. I know Quinn made falling in love at first sight look easy, but he and Kay went through their tough times. Don't, I repeat, don't leap into anything.''

"How can I? I can't even find her."

Cammie Jo couldn't stand hearing Mack agonize over Camryn.

Pushing back her chair, she pointed to the door. "I gotta...I was...I'm just gonna...go."

Mack turned to look at her and the expression in his eyes told the awful reality, he *had* forgotten she was even in the room.

7

"YOU'RE LATE," Jimmy greeted Mack the next morning when he arrived at the pier.

"No kidding."

"You're never late."

"I'm late today." Thanks to Camryn, he'd had trouble sleeping.

"Rough night out chasing women?"

Mack snorted. "Not hardly."

"Why not?" Jimmy grinned. "I was."

"You're only seventeen."

"Prime chasing age." Jimmy wriggled his brow. "Got to thank you guys for running that ad. I sure am enjoying the fallout."

"Maybe you should be enjoying doing your job. You fuel *Edna Marie?*"

"But of course."

Mack pulled a pencil from his pocket, consulted the clipboard Jimmy gave him and began running down his preflight check list.

"Got an add-on for the Juneau flight," Jimmy said. "You'll have a full house."

On Wednesdays Mack had a standing route ferrying tourists to the weekly Mendenhall river rafting excursion just outside of Juneau.

"Oh yeah?" Mack knew the UNLV sorority sisters were already on the docket. "What's the name of the other passenger?"

"Camryn Josephine."

He almost dropped his pencil. Dammit! He wasn't ready to face Camryn again. He needed time to get his defenses in place. She didn't owe him an explanation, and the fact that he even felt like she did, meant he was investing too much in her too soon.

Slow down. Chill out. Act nonchalant.

At that moment a vintage taxi pulled up to the dock and three women got out. The sorority sisters and Camryn.

His gut did this weird loop-de-loop thing.

The sorority sisters wore dark sunglasses and looked as if they'd partied too hearty the night before. They half supported each other in their stagger up the dock and managed weak giggles at Mack.

"Oooh." One of the sorority sisters—he thought it might have been the one who pinched his butt—moaned. "I think I'm gonna hurl."

"No, Deanne," cried her plump friend. "Not here. Not in front of Mack." Deanne's friend looked apologetically at him. "She had too many Jell-O shooters last night."

"Don't even say the word Jell-O," Deanne cried.

"You wanna go back to the room?" her friend Pam asked.

No! Don't leave me alone with Camryn.

"I've got airsick bags," Mack offered.

Deanne raised her sunglasses briefly and squinted at Mack. "I'll try to make it," she said.

Mack gave Deanne the front seat. He positioned Camryn directly behind him, thinking this would keep her out of his range of vision and therefore out of his mind during the short flight to Juneau.

Wrong!

He'd clearly forgotten about the sense of smell. Her succulent scent overtook the interior of the airplane and addled his brain.

In desperation, he began giving the tourist spiel, telling the women about the countryside, the glaciers, the weather. He chattered about everything and anything in order to keep from dwelling on Camryn.

Was he pathetic or what?

When they finally reached Juneau and Mack got out to escort them over to the bus that would take them to the rapids, Camryn motioned him to one side.

"May I speak with you a moment?" she asked.

It would be sweet revenge to say no, hop back into his plane and fly away but the truth of the matter was, he didn't want to do that. Plus, he was flying them back in four hours. No point in returning to Bear Creek. He'd planned to kill time buying supplies in Juneau.

He nodded, took her by the elbow and moved them to a secluded spot.

She seemed nervous, constantly worrying that totem necklace with her fingers. "I'm sorry I canceled our date last night."

"No big deal," he said, trying hard to keep his voice on an even keel. "I missed seeing you but if you were sick, then you were sick."

"That's the thing." She looked down at her hands, shifted her weight.

Ah, why did she have to be so pretty? Why did she have to suddenly look so vulnerable? Why did he have trouble convincing himself that this sweet-looking woman was nothing but a capricious heart-breaker? His heart gave a strange hop at the thought.

"I wasn't sick."

"Oh no?"

"No."

He waited.

She lifted her head, met his gaze with a brave stare. He had to give her credit, facing him like this.

"I canceled our date because I was scared."

"Scared?" He raised a skeptical eyebrow. He'd been expecting her to confess to a tête-à-tête with another man.

"You intimidate me, Mack."

"Me?" This surprised him. "How's that?"

Had she been in a bad relationship before? Was that why she was nervous about getting involved?

But if that were the case, why come to Alaska looking for a husband?

"It's not that I don't like you," she continued. "It's that I like you too much."

"That's a new one."

"I'm afraid of getting in too deep, too soon."

"Well, Sugar Plum, so am I. But the only way we'll know if this chemistry between us will lead anywhere is to explore it. You gotta take a few risks in this life if you want to get anywhere."

"I'm not sure I'm prepared for that."

"And having dinner with me would have been too much for you to handle?"

"Yes. No. I don't know."

"McCaulley!" A man from the river rafting tour bus called to him.

"They're probably ready to leave." Mack nodded.

"Probably."

He walked Camryn to the bus, feeling hopeful again about their budding relationship. It was up to him to convince her to stop guarding her heart so closely and take a chance. This thing between them might not work out, but oh, the potential if it did.

"We're short a river guide," the man at the tour bus said. "You used to be a guide."

"Yeah."

"What you doing for the next four hours?"

"Stocking up on supplies in town."

"Take a raft down the Mendenhall with us. We'll make it worth your while."

Mack hesitated.

"Come on," Camryn said. "Go with us."

He pretended to consider the offer but he already knew he was going. "All right," he agreed.

Thirty minutes later they were at the head of a glacier-fed river suited up in rafting gear and life jackets and bobbing down the river in a large rubber raft. There had been fifty people from other tour groups gathered there, and they were seated six to a raft.

Mack sat in the back, guiding the craft along with larger oars as the six passengers rowed with smaller paddles. It had been a long time since he'd done something like this and he found he missed it, even though his arms were already aching from rowing. He was out of practice, not the same strapping college student he had once been when he'd done this for tuition money.

He had to admit he was impressed with Camryn. He suspected she might be too much of a girly-girl to row but no, she wasn't afraid to get her hands dirty. She plunged right in, laughing at her own beginner's attempts then smiling brilliantly when she got it right.

"Look at me, Mack! Look at me!" she cried and turned in her seat to face him. "I'm doing it."

Her exclamation of pure joy dug a hole straight through his chest and sent a languid sensation like heated honey oozing through his veins. The warmth seeped into his body and buried deep in his groin, nearly disorienting him with runaway lust.

"Keep your eye on the river, Camryn," he said, his measured tone belying the emotional turmoil raging inside him. "We can overturn without warning."

Camryn turned back around and gave her attention to the water. The totem—which Jake had found in Lulu's doghouse and returned to her without ever learning how important the necklace was to her—lay flush against her skin under her woolen clothes, rubber rain gear and bulky life jacket. The necklace wasn't going anywhere this time, even if the raft tipped over in the rapids and they all got soaked.

And speaking of rapids, she could hear them in the distance, water rushing over rocks. Her pulse sped up. Yes! Another adventure.

"The water temperature is forty degrees, folks, so even though it's a warm day, I'm sure most of you aren't interested in taking a swim. Do as I ask and hopefully we'll get down the rapids without going in the drink," Mack announced when they reached the roaring, white-capped water.

Cammie Jo stared at the churning river. She wasn't the least bit scared. "Bring it on!" she cried.

"Here we go."

And then they were in the thick of it. Mack shouted out instructions, telling them when to row, when to hold off. Shouting first "go left" then "go right" as he needed weight to shift in the raft.

Rocks battered the rubber boat. They banged off the slick surfaces, bounced from one jagged outcropping to the next. Then they got caught in the swifter, deeper part of the river and they shot forward, disengaged like a car in a flume ride.

Except this wasn't some mild amusement park water adventure, this was the real thing. Honest to Pete white-water rafting.

Okay, so it wasn't the roughest white water around, but she was doing it! True enthusiasts of the sport would no doubt laugh their hineys off at the mildness of the Mendenhall. But dang it, until now the most daring thing she'd ever done in the water was to wade in the kiddie pool at the city park.

Some in their group were gasping with fear. Pam was actually crying. The man in front of her had a death grip on his oar, and his face had gone white as chalk.

Whoosh. Splash. Gurgle.

Cold water pelted her face. Cammie Jo threw back her head and hollered in her best Texas twang, "Yee-ha!"

And from the back of the boat came an answering, "Yee-ha!"

Grinning, she turned to see Mack looking at her. Impishly, Cammie Jo stuck out her tongue.

And in that flash of a second, with Mack's attention diverted, the raft plowed straight for a huge black rock jutting three feet above the river's surface.

"Look out!" someone shouted.

But it was too late.

Foom!

The front of the raft hit the rock and was airborne. It seemed as if a dozen things happened at once.

"We're all gonna die!" Miss Jell-O Shooter shrieked.

"Hang on, folks." Mack commanded, struggling to regain control of the boat.

Cammie Jo felt the weight of the totem against her chest and she laughed right out loud. "Wheeee!"

"You're crazy!" Miss Jell-O Shooter snapped at her. "You realize that, don't you?"

"Crazy about adventure that doesn't include slurping alcohol from gelatin desserts." Cammie Jo smiled.

The raft twisted in midair. The passengers were bucked from their seats. The next thing Cammie Jo knew, she was underwater.

But with her life jacket tied securely around her torso, she immediately bobbed to the surface, her hair plastered to her head, her clothes soaking wet.

The water was thrashing her against the rocks but it wasn't very deep here. Probably three or four feet at most. Except the current was so strong she couldn't stand up.

She glanced around, saw the raft was beached

against a group of rocks a few yards away. Mack was busy trying to snag people from the water and shove them ashore.

Cammie Jo grabbed on to a rock and sat watching him. She simply couldn't help herself.

Damn, but the man was spectacular.

He was like a battlefield general, ordering the stragglers to obey his commands. He lifted Pam from the water and carried her to dry land. His big forearm muscles bunched beneath the woman's weight, but he hardly looked affected by the effort. It was hypnotizing, the way he took charge.

He fascinated her.

She wondered what he was like in bed. Would he be so imperious there? She shivered at the image that thought aroused.

After lowering the plump woman to solid ground, Mack lifted his head. Cammie Jo realized she was the lone passenger still in the water and at the same time recognized he probably couldn't see her from her position behind the rock.

He stood on the shore and scanned the water, feet wide apart, hands on his hips, the cool Alaskan breeze ruffling his dark-brown hair. A worried frown cleaved his brow and he began to prowl the riverbank.

"Camryn," he called and she could tell he was having trouble keeping the worry out of his voice.

She raised up in the water so he could see her, hands still clutching the rock. His eyes met hers.

Cammie Jo couldn't look away. Didn't want to look away.

Then he was coming toward her, splashing waist-deep in the icy water, impervious to the cold and the swift currents. In that moment it dawned on Cammie Jo that her teeth were chattering and her nipples had turned to hard pebbles beneath her clothing.

The expression on his face was an odd combination of disapproval and concern. Cammie Jo felt the tiniest spurt of fear. Was he mad at her?

Then she realized it couldn't be fear. The totem was still attached around her neck. This alien feeling was something else.

Sexual arousal? Lust? Plain old-fashioned horniness?

She gulped.

He was upon her.

And without a word, he bent down, picked her up and lifted her over his broad shoulder as if she weighed no more than a sack of twigs.

Oh, my stars and meteors!

She almost quit breathing. She had known he possessed muscles to make a gym devotee jealous, but she was unprepared for the feel of his honed shoulder blades against her soft belly. The stupid life jacket got in the way, preventing her from experiencing the full effect of his spectacular body. But hey, she'd take what she could get.

"This is all your fault," he growled under his

breath. "Just remember that if you happen to catch pneumonia."

"H-h-how is…this…m-my f-fault?" she asked around teeth slamming into each other the way a screen door bangs in a hurricane.

"Standing me up last night. Making me lose my concentration. Giving me that damned 'come hither' look when I was supposed to be focusing on my job."

"So it's my fault you have the attention span of a gnat?"

"Something like that, yeah."

She heard the humor in his tone, realized he wasn't really mad at her. Relieved, she said, "I should be blaming you for causing me to give you a come-hither look."

"How do you figure that?"

"Sitting back there barking orders like some military man. Sending goose bumps down my spine. You should know women are suckers for powerful men."

"I send goose bumps down your spine?"

"Don't pretend you don't know." Her head was bobbing pleasantly against his rib cage as he slogged through the water.

"You think I'm powerful?"

"Ah, now you're angling for a compliment. Ain't gonna happen."

"Too late, you already said I was like a military man."

"Don't let it go to your head."

He dumped her unceremoniously on the shore with the others, winked at her and without another word, walked back out to the overturned raft. He easily righted the craft and towed it to the bank.

"Everyone back in."

"Oh, no," the hysterical sorority sister cried. "I'm not going back out there."

"It's either this or a three-mile hike through the woods. Besides, we're through the worst of it. Just a little ways downriver there's an encampment with a nice fire and plenty of refreshments. Now, all aboard."

Miss Jell-O Shooter and her chubby friend were gazing at him with such longing admiration that Cammie Jo began to think uncharitable thoughts.

Get your eyeballs off my man and put them back in your heads where they belong, ladies.

My man? Where had that come from? Cammie Jo couldn't stop herself from glancing at Mack but he'd assiduously avoided looking at her again.

What was up with that?

Everyone boarded and they rowed downriver. The rapids quickly petered out. In twenty minutes' time, they pulled up to the encampment where the other rafters were already gathered.

Cammie Jo was still shivering to beat the band. She huddled near the bonfire, alternating between warming her hands and hugging herself. Someone gave her a cup of hot apple cider, and she drank it gratefully.

A table was set up with snacks—tidbits of smoked salmon, cheese, wheat crackers, caribou sausage, fried apple fritters—but Cammie Jo was still too cold to nibble. An enterprising T-shirt salesman had set up a booth near the food and was selling sweatshirts that read: I Shot The Mendenhall And Survived.

Mack walked over to purchase something from the vendor. Odd, she wouldn't have figured him buying souvenirs of a river he knew like the back of his hand.

He turned, saw that she was watching him. He crooked a finger. She touched her chest with an open palm and mouthed, "Me?"

He nodded.

Uh-oh. What now?

She left the fire, dropped her paper cup in the trash receptacle provided for that purpose and went to join Mack where he'd moved to the edge of the forest surrounding the little encampment.

He took her by the hand and led her into the trees away from the others.

Hey, wasn't this how Little Red Riding Hood got into trouble with the Big Bad Wolf?

"What is it?" she whispered without knowing why she was whispering. It wasn't as if she had anything to hide. Nothing wrong with lurking in the woods with a wolfishly sexy man.

Right?

"Dry clothes." He handed her the sack he'd

gotten from the T-shirt concessionaire. She peered inside. Saw two sweatshirts, one extra-large, the other a small and sweatpants, also size small and a pair of woolen socks.

"You bought me dry clothes." The clutch in her voice matched the clutch in her tummy. "That was sweet of you."

He shrugged. "Couldn't have you getting my plane all wet."

She grinned.

Then while she watched, Mack casually stripped off his saturated jacket and T-shirt.

Her jaw unhinged and her eyes bugged, she forgot all about being cold and sopping wet.

Glory, glory hallelujah!

She'd seen his bare torso of course. In the pages of *Metropolitan* magazine. But that glossy, one-dimensional shot simply did not do him justice. No siree, Bob.

Nothing could have prepared her for this luscious sight. Although the hair on his head was the same shade as milk chocolate, the hair on his chest was almost coal-black, curly but not overly thick.

In fact, he had just the right amount of chest hair. He possessed a full-fledged six pack rippling beneath his skin, which was divided right down the middle by a slender line of that mesmerizing body hair. The hair circled his navel and disappeared into the waistband of his trousers.

Her fingers literally ached to stroke that male

pelt, and she gulped at the raw intensity of her feelings. It had to be the cool mountain air. High altitude was making her daffy with desire.

Yeah, that's the ticket.

High altitude.

Not masculine magnitude making her knees weak.

Cammie Jo's stomach picked that moment to say howdy-do to her throat.

He was watching her from his peripheral vision, perfectly aware of what he was doing to her. He seemed in no particular hurry to clothe himself.

The heathen.

She fished in the sack, found the extra-large sweatshirt and tossed it at him. ''For heaven's sake, cover up.''

''What for?''

''In case someone sees you.''

''Someone's already seen me.'' He took a step closer.

Her heart tap-danced across her chest.

''Do you have any idea how gorgeous you look all mussed and rumpled?''

''I don't,'' she denied, pushing wet hair from her face.

''Ah, but you do. You look like a wilderness girl.''

''And that turns you on?''

''Oh baby, you have no idea.''

He leaned in and she had no doubt he would

have kissed her if she'd stayed put, but she was worried that in her disheveled state she might look too much like Cammie Jo and he would finally put two and two together.

"Is there a place where I could change?" she asked, desperate to get away from the incredible pull of his bare body.

He pointed into the trees.

"I can't get naked in the bushes."

"Go on. I'll stand guard."

Cammie Jo glanced around. The rest of the group were several yards away in the clearing, and no one seemed to be paying them any attention. "Okay, but no peeking."

"Aw, you're ruining all my fun."

"Promise." She shook a finger in his face.

"I promise." Mack grinned as if he had no intention of keeping his word.

She pushed her way through the trees, trying to find a more secluded spot. She heard a rustling noise and jumped.

"Mack," she called out. "I mean it. No peeking."

"I'm not," he called back. "Stop being paranoid."

Hmph. She trusted him about as far as she could throw him.

She walked a few steps farther. Okay. This looked good. She could barely see Mack from here. That meant he couldn't really see her either.

Perching on a rock, she tugged off her boots and socks, then shimmied out of her wet pants and hung them over a nearby bush. Next came her shirt. She turned and reached for the sack she'd set on the ground.

And found herself nose to snout with a plump black bear.

8

"ER...MACK."

"I swear on the *Edna Marie* I'm not peeking!" Exasperated, Mack shoved his fingers through his hair. You'd think the woman was housing Fort Knox beneath her clothes the way she worried about him seeing her naked body.

"Mack, this isn't about that."

"What then?" He refused to turn around. A promise was a promise and he was not sneaking a peek no matter what the little horned, pitchforked devil on his shoulder was telling him.

"I need your help."

"What's the matter?"

"Well, there's this bear sitting on the sack with my sweats in it."

"What!"

In a flash, Mack was tearing through the bushes to get to her, cursing himself for leaving his pack with the bear spray in it on the plane. He reached her within seconds, his blood muscling through his veins and his heart practically ripping a hole in his chest.

He burst through the undergrowth and found her

standing behind a tree, her wet pants held up in front of her nearly naked body, her bare feet curling into the dirt, that ugly totem necklace dangling around her neck. She didn't look the least bit scared, rather just embarrassed to have been caught in a compromising position.

That surprised him. Most women when faced with a bear would have very understandably screamed or ran. Camryn simply stood her ground and called calmly for him to come help her.

He felt an odd stirring below the belt. Damn if her courage—and of course her near-nakedness—wasn't firing him up like a piston. Mack swallowed hard, fought off his erection and cut his eyes over to view the source of her discomfort.

The black bear rose up on his hind legs, his nose sniffing the air. He pulled back his lips and made a noise of curiosity.

Relief pushed the air from Mack's body and he laughed.

"What's so funny?" Camryn frowned. "There's a bear trying to wear the sweats you bought me."

Mack walked toward the bear, flapping his hands at him. "Go on. Shoo. Get out of here, Leroy."

"Leroy? Don't tell me you're naming him."

"He's already named."

"What?"

The bear dropped down on all fours, pawed the sack. Mack stalked forward and retrieved the bag. "There's no food in there, you dufus. And even if there was, how could you eat it with no teeth? Go on. Get.''

Leroy wagged his head and waddled off into the forest.

''He doesn't have any teeth?'' Camryn tentatively stepped away from the tree.

''Not a one. Everyone around here knows Leroy and they feed him even though they're not supposed to. How's the poor guy to fend for himself with no teeth? He probably was under the impression that you'd brought him a treat.''

Camryn laughed and shook her head.

''I can't believe you weren't a bit scared.''

''Well, I can't say I was totally at peace. But he seemed nonthreatening.''

Despite his best intentions not to ogle her, Mack found his gaze drawn like an arrow to a target. Okay, it was more than ogling. He visually ravished her. It was wrong. He knew it. She was vulnerable and exposed, but heaven help him, he couldn't stop wanting her.

His eyes explored her bare skin, her throat, the soft swell of her full breasts above the plain white bra she wore. He had never seen such a sexy undergarment. His gaze skipped lower, past the narrow tuck of her waist to the gentle curve of her hips. He zeroed in on the vee between her thighs, barely camouflaged by her damp panties.

''Ahem.'' She cleared her throat.

''Oh.'' Damn if his cheeks didn't feel hot. He whirled around. What was going on here? Last night he had scratched her off his list, deciding she wasn't the kind of woman he wanted in his life. But today her behavior had left Mack more confused than ever.

It had been a very long time since a woman stirred him the way she did. Her bravery turned him on more surely than oysters and caviar. But...

Was his desire to get married coloring his perception? Was she really as perfect for him as he thought? Or was he bestowing upon her qualities she didn't really possess? Qualities that eerily happened to match his mate list.

"Okay. You can turn back around," she said breathlessly.

He pivoted to find Camryn appropriately clothed. Thank heavens for that.

"We better get back. The bus will be leaving soon." He jerked his head in the direction of the encampment.

"Before we rejoin the others, may I ask you something?"

"Sugar Plum, you can ask me anything."

She grinned at him. "Have dinner with me tomorrow night. My treat."

"No cold feet like last night?" he asked lightly, but inside he felt hot and weighted and anxious.

"I'll wear three pairs of wool socks," she assured him.

CAMMIE JO was a woman transformed. She was on a date with Mack, and the totem was around her neck. She felt free and sexy and oh, so courageous. She wore a bright red dress with a flirty skirt she'd bought yesterday in a tourist shop in Juneau. And she had borrowed a pair of strappy, red heels from Kay.

She was embarking on her most dangerous adventure of all. Yesterday morning, she had made up her mind. She was seducing Mack McCaulley come hell or high water. She was going to take a risk, roll the dice, spin the wheel.

Unearthing her latent sexuality was one of the ways she planned on discovering herself and she couldn't imagine a better first lover than Mack. He had a droll sense of humor that tickled her funny bone. He was passionate—evidenced by how upset he'd gotten when she'd stood him up. He was loyal and kind and considerate. He was strong and brave and adventuresome. Not to mention that he was one sexy hunk of man.

So here they were, back at his place. They'd had a sumptuous dinner of grilled salmon and Alaskan king crab legs and they'd split a slice of cheesecake for dessert. They'd talked about everything under the sun. From Cammie Jo's job to the spunky grandmother who'd raised Mack and by whom he seemed to measure all women.

They strolled along the shoreline in front of his cabin. She should have been nervous, but she wasn't. Instead she simply marveled over the fact she was with a handsome man on a real date. If her aunts could only see her now. This treasured wish totem stuff was pretty darned awesome.

"It's so beautiful here," she breathed.

Ten o'clock at night and the sun still burned brightly. Clouds hovered around the mountains and the water was a calm icy blue. A pair of bald eagles flitted through the high-topped spruce trees, calling back and forth to each other. She wondered if they were mates.

"I stand in awe on a daily basis."

"Have you lived in Bear Creek all your life?" she asked, and tried not to audibly suck in her breath when he took her hand.

"All my life."

"What's it like, growing up here?"

"It's pretty great. Although everyone knows your business. Sometimes you can just feel the gossip zipping around behind your back. But nobody means any harm."

"Have you ever wanted to live anywhere else?"

"Never." He shook his head. "This has got to be a lot different than where you're from."

She nodded, worrying that if she said too much she would reveal some secret about Cammie Jo's introverted life and give herself away. "It's a million times more beautiful here."

"Do you think you could ever live in Alaska?" he asked.

An invisible hand squeezed her lungs. She would like nothing better than to move here for good and the only thing holding her back was her three dear aunts.

"I don't know," she finally answered.

He nodded and stopped walking. She stopped too, their fingers intertwined. Mack gently drew her into the circle of his arms. The sound of the lapping water filled her ears along with the noise of her own heartbeat.

He lowered his head. She stood on tiptoes.

Their lips came together.

Okay, so their lips smashed together like a car crash. They were that hot for each other and tired of holding out.

She flung her arms around his neck. He buried his fingers in her hair. For a lifetime she'd wanted this and never even realized the magnitude of her need.

They kissed with movie screen frenzy, all lips and tongues and heat. The scent of him mixed with the scent of Alaska. Ocean breeze and soap filled her nose. Sitka spruce and minty toothpaste. It all mingled in her senses, and she knew she could never separate the man from the state. Mack was Alaska. Alaska was Mack.

And then Alaska itself rudely intruded.

At first it was a low-level humming noise, steady and insistent. For a moment Cammie Jo thought the intensity of Mack's kisses was causing her ears to ring.

Then she felt the first stinging bite.

Followed by another.

And another.

And another.

What was happening? Her eyes flew open. Omigosh, what were those huge things surrounding them in a thick black cloud? Insects the size of hummingbirds.

Mack grunted, grabbed her hand at the same time realization dawned. Mosquitoes. Whoever claimed they grew things bigger in Texas had obviously never seen an Alaskan mosquito!

"Run," he said. "The damn things can drain you of a quart of blood in five minutes flat."

"You're exaggerating," she gasped, Mack pulling her headlong toward his cabin. "Right?"

"Only partially."

Ouch! Cammie Jo slapped at her neck.

He wrenched open his front door and they tumbled inside. Mack slammed it closed behind them. Cammie Jo felt like a prairie wife circling the wagon against the Indians.

"That's like something out of a horror movie," she gasped.

"Alaskan mosquitoes are nasty creatures." Mack turned toward her. "Are you all right?"

"Sure. Who's scared of Dracula's second cousins?"

He chuckled. "Let's attend to the those bites. If we get rubbing alcohol and Caladryl lotion on them quick enough they won't swell and itch."

"Really?"

"Come with me."

He led her to a bathroom off the hallway. She was surprised at the whimsical fish decor. A brightly colored shower curtain featuring several local catches of the day. Sand in a jar. Seashell soaps. Dried starfish and sea horses caught in netting draped from the ceiling.

Mack lowered the toilet lid. ``Sit.''

Cammie Jo plunked down while he rummaged through the medicine cabinet.

``Here we go.'' He produced cotton balls, rubbing alcohol and a bottle of pink Caladryl lotion. He crouched in front of her, his knees touching her shins. ``They didn't do too much damage,'' he said, surveying her face. She noticed he had a few welts of his own. ``Ten or twelve bites at most.''

``Ten or twelve!'' Cammie Jo's hand flew to her face. ``Good grief, I don't think I've had ten or twelve mosquito bites in my entire life.''

Of course that was because she hardly ever went outside, but he didn't need to know that.

``Considering the number of the beasts attacking us you should consider yourself lucky.''

``Evidently.''

He took her hand in his to prevent her from clawing the itchy spot on her neck. ``No scratching. Worst thing you can do.''

She met his eyes. ``I'm assuming these words of wisdom come from personal experience.''

``When we were kids, some of us went fishing on Cook Creek one evening and ran into a swarm. By the time we got back home, we were covered in bites. They even got through our clothing. We were pretty sick. Ran fevers. Those things are nothing to mess with. Yes. I'm hoping you'll learn from the pain of my misspent youth.''

"Aren't you the noble one," she teased.

He grinned. "Aren't you going to fall for my heroic gesture?''

I'm falling, she thought. *More than you know.*

"Not for a moment," she lied through her teeth.

He moistened a cotton ball with rubbing alcohol, then gently dabbed it on her skin. She expected it to burn, instead the astringent soothed the sting almost immediately.

"I hate to think of anything marring this beautiful skin," Mack murmured and ran a thumb along her jaw.

His gaze met hers. How he loved the arresting emerald color of her eyes. Green as Alaska in the summertime.

"Now the Caladryl." His voice had grown gruff, and he could hear the rasp in his own ears. He dotted her with pink lotion. Neck, forehead, cheek. When he was finished, he rocked back on his heels.

"My turn," she said and took the supplies from him.

Her slender, delicate fingers handled the cotton ball with deft movements. The easy way she touched him sent a surge of something hot and urgent gushing through him.

Suddenly, his tongue burned with the memory

of her indefinable flavor. He wanted to kiss her again.

``You look like you've got the measles.'' She giggled.

``Me?'' He got to his feet, tugged her after him. ``Look in the mirror.''

They peered into the bathroom mirror, first examining their own faces in the reflective glass and then glancing over at each other.

She looked completely adorable with a cotton ball in one hand, Caladryl in the other, that silly totem around her neck. And Mack didn't miss the fact she was scoping him out as well, her gaze on his lips, which thankfully had been spared from the attack of the bloodthirsty mosquitoes.

Her hair was sexily mussed, her sweet face polka-dotted with pink lotion. The top of her head barely clearing his shoulder. Her delicate petiteness made him feel strong and manly. As if he could protect her from anything.

Except from mosquitoes of course.

``Give me that.'' He plucked the cotton ball and lotion from her hands, set them on the counter, then turned to draw her into his arms.

When the date started he had not intended to bring her up to the cabin. Not because he didn't want her here, but exactly because he did. He wanted her so much, in fact, he couldn't trust himself to be alone with her in his cabin. He wasn't ready to take their relationship to the next level, no matter how much his body might be egging him on.

He didn't want to make a mistake with this one. He wanted to be sure. A whirl through the bedroom would propel them into something neither of them was quite ready to handle and he knew it as surely as he knew his own name.

But despite all his common sense and rational knowledge Mack simply had to taste those lips again knowing full well he was placing himself squarely in harm's way.

Then again, he'd never been one to shy away from danger.

He never felt more alive than when he was testing his mettle. Except in the past those skills had only pertained to physical danger. Like flying his plane in less than perfect conditions or hiking a glacier alone or the summer he spent in the North Sea fishing for Alaskan king crab.

But he'd never really experimented with his emotional resilience.

These thoughts flitted briefly through his head, blotted out almost entirely by Camryn's softness in his arms. His body definitely had a mind of its own.

Camryn sensed his uncertainty and in the end, she took matters into her own hands. Brave, daring Camryn plunged in with a fearlessness that impressed him, rising up on her toes and planting her lips on his.

Man alive, she pushed all his buttons.

Moaning low in his throat, Mack anchored her tight against his chest.

Camryn melted in his arms. It felt as if she'd always belonged there.

He dipped his head and kissed her collarbone.

She moaned and dug her fingers into his shoulders to hold herself steady. The pressure expanding in his groin startled him. Whenever he was around her, his body turned hard as stone.

Her soft sounds incited his lust. He'd better watch out. He was getting in deep and he knew it, yet he was helpless to pull back, set her aside and walk away.

She was pressing her hips against his in an erotic motion that made him ache to take her. She was hot for him, and not the least bit ashamed of her desire. If he wasn't looking for a wife, if he had met her even last year, he would have taken her easily and without this detailed examination of motive and desire.

But he no longer had the freedom to take good sex as he found it. He wanted more from life, he wanted more from Camryn. He wanted a family of his own.

Apparently, though, she was intent on pushing him to the edge of reason and beyond. Her body trembled against his. She ran a tongue along his jaw, brushed fingers through the chest hairs peeping out from the V-neck of his shirt.

Oh to hell with it. She wanted him, he wanted her. He would deal with the consequences later.

For now he was blinded by lust and all he could think about was burying himself deep inside her lush, hot body.

He brought her close to him again and that awful totem managed to wedge itself between them. Every time he kissed her, the stupid thing stabbed him annoyingly in the chest. Why was she so fond of the perverted totem? It wasn't her style.

Irritated, he reached to remove the necklace from around her head and found the button of his shirt had become entangled in the beading.

Gulping in raspy breaths, he struggled to free his button from the bead.

"What are you doing?" She squirmed against him, impossibly causing his rock-hard erection to grow even stiffer. Couldn't he control himself for one second around her?

"We're hung up."

"Let me." She reached for the button. Their fingers clashed.

"I've got it."

"No. I can do it."

"Hang on. It's really stuck."

Oh dear, oh dear, what was she going to do?

Contorting his body, he raised his arms and shimmied out of his shirt while simultaneously lifting the necklace over her head. Cammie Jo gasped, splayed a hand to her throat.

No. No! Oh what now? What to do?

He had taken off her totem!

And his shirt.

The sight was heart-stopping.

She'd seen him bare-chested on the printed page. And she'd seen him bare-chested in the woods. Yet nothing but nothing could compare with being two inches away from his naked torso.

His skin was tan, his muscles hard and firm. His nipples were dark and puckered. Cammie Jo couldn't breathe.

''There.'' He flung the shirt, totem and all across the room.

Frozen in place, she watched the garment sail to the floor, heard the totem clink as it fell. She gulped once, twice, three times.

Mack grinned wickedly and dipped his head to her lips once more. ''Now where were we?''

All her fears rampaged to the forefront of her mind. Without the totem to keep her doubts at bay she was overwhelmed by the reality of the situation. She was alone in a man's house.

Omigosh, what had she been thinking? Making out with a guy she'd only known four days.

Panic wreaked havoc. She felt sick to her stomach, overheated and faint all at the same time. This was awful, horrible. One minute she was Camryn, feeling brave and sassy and very sexy, turning on the man of her dreams with her feminine wiles and then suddenly like Cinderella at the stroke of midnight, she was Cammie Jo again.

But Mack was still kissing her as if midnight had never struck, as if he had no idea she had already turned into a pumpkin.

Run, Cammie Jo, run. Before he finds out the truth.

She couldn't move. Her limbs were liquid. He held her close, doing very inventive things with his awesome tongue.

Be brave, she told herself. But courage was impossible without the totem.

His heartbeat pounded through the material of her shirt. Her own heart was whipping adrenaline through her system like a greyhound on a racetrack, and she felt as if she was melting like a scoop of ice cream on a hot sidewalk.

She dovetailed so precisely into him it was scary. If she hadn't felt so frightened, so out of control, she would have savored how perfectly their bodies fit.

He nuzzled her throat with his chin, stroked the nape of her neck with his fingers. "You're so sexy, Camryn. You drive me wild."

But she wasn't Camryn. Not anymore.

Oh her poor head was scrambled eggs, and panic had her in a vice grip. She couldn't enjoy a moment of what was happening.

Gotta go, gotta run.

His hand was unbuttoning her dress. He was stroking her skin, sending erotic messages screaming to every nerve ending.

Help!

Her stomach churned. She couldn't speak, couldn't even work up the courage to tell him she'd changed her mind.

He pulled her snug against the length of him. His masculine smell invaded her nostrils. His taste filled her mouth. She felt the pressure of his erection through his pants as it throbbed against her thigh.

He was really hard.

And really big.

It was all too much for shy little Cammie Jo Lockhart from Austin, Texas who'd been raised by three maiden aunts.

She took a deep breath, looked up into Mack's brown eyes and keeled over in a dead-away faint.

9

WELL, THAT WAS the first time his kisses had ever caused anyone to faint.

Once again he was struck by the paradox of Camryn Josephine. On the one hand she came across as worldly, sophisticated and very much in control. And yet at times she seemed so innocent, so naive, so utterly lacking in guile. He had a hard time knowing which was the real Camryn and what it was he most longed for her to be.

Puzzled, Mack stared down at the limp woman in his arms. Her eyelashes were shuttered closed, her face relaxed. The magnitude of her beauty and the corresponding tightness in his chest unsettled him.

On so many levels she was exactly what he wanted in a wife. They certainly had chemistry. No denying his body's response to her or hers to him. She was brave and feisty, intelligent and adventuresome, and she had a lighthearted sense of humor that appealed to him.

But he wondered about the other qualities he required in a mate. He had a feeling she was hiding something, but he couldn't imagine what it was.

The notion that she didn't feel comfortable enough to reveal her secrets disturbed him. And as for her loyalty, well, he still didn't know if he could really trust her or not.

Gently, he lifted her up, carried her to the bed and laid her across the quilt. He took off her shoes and her dress. He sat down on the bed beside her and fanned her with his hand, thinking she might have gotten overheated.

"Cam." Mack patted first one of her cheeks and then the other. "Camryn, Sugar Plum, wake up."

She stirred, sighed softly and curled against his thigh.

"Wake up and tell me you're all right." He was starting to get a little worried. If she didn't rouse soon, he would call Quinn's sister, Meggie, who was an emergency room nurse from Seattle. She was living in Bear Creek for the summer, recovering from the recent breakup of her six-year marriage.

"Camryn." He stroked her chin with a finger.

Slowly, her eyes fluttered open and she peered up at him. In that moment she looked like a lost little girl. The tightness in his chest wound into a knot the size of a fist.

She blinked at him, then her gaze fixed on his bare torso. Her cheeks pinked, her eyes widened and she quickly glanced away.

"My totem," she croaked.

"What?"

She held out a hand, palm extended. "Can I have my necklace?"

Mack frowned. The woman had an unnatural obsession with the obscene thing. "Hang on."

"And then maybe you better take me back to the B&B."

"All right.

He got up, retrieved the totem from the floor and handed it to her. She grabbed at the necklace with greedy hands and tugged it over her head.

"Thank you."

"You're welcome."

She sat up against the headboard and this time when she looked at his chest she didn't glance away. In fact, she even wet her upper lip with the tip of her tongue. Here it was again, her strange alteration in personality. One minute reticent, the next moment brazen. She stared at him as if hypnotized.

"Camryn? Are you okay?"

"Yes, yes, I'm fine. Just a little too much excitement."

"Sugar Plum," he said, still a bit disconcerted by the sudden changes in her. "If you faint at the warm-up match, I can't wait to see what happens to you in the main event."

THE NEXT DAY Mack was booked solid flying in more bachelorettes from Anchorage. More than one or two made overt passes at him but Mack deflected their advances with an easy grin. His mind was too occupied with Camryn to bother pursuing anyone else.

By late afternoon, he was chomping at the bit to see her again. They hadn't made plans when he'd left her at the B&B last night—she'd seemed anxious to get up to bed—but he was hoping she would come to Caleb's salmon bake with him that evening. He went through the B&B's lobby and ran into the sorority sisters.

He spent a few minutes listening to their drinking antics before mumbling an excuse and ambling up to the front desk. He asked Gus to ring Camryn's room, but after several rings, Gus shrugged. ''She's not answering.''

Mack turned, saw the sorority sisters eyeballing him like a juicy T-bone. Gulping, he darted out the back way.

And came across Camryn tossing a Frisbee to Lulu in Jake's backyard.

He stared at her a long moment before she realized he was there. Mack admired the graceful way she moved, the way her hair bounced over her shoulders when she lobbed the Frisbee. Her compact tush looked absolutely delectable in a pair of white, snug-fitting denim jeans.

Damn! But he was getting a boner just watching her.

Camryn reached out to take the Frisbee from Lulu and his eyes followed the smooth, clean lines of her bare arms. He trailed his gaze up her shoulder, down to her breasts then past the tuck of her waist.

Mack took a deep breath and tried his best to think unsexy thoughts in an effort to deflate his perky Johnson. He wanted to go over and talk to her, but he didn't want to advertise his flagrant arousal and scare her off again.

Lulu barked. Camryn cocked back her arm and let the Frisbee fly.

The sailing disk came straight toward him.

And it hit with a hard *thunk* against his nose.

``Good God, woman,'' he roared in pain, his hands closing around his nose. ``Watch where you're aiming that thing.''

Oh well, he didn't have to worry about offending her with his overeager boner. It was long gone now.

``Mack!'' She sprang to his side. ``I'm so sorry. I didn't see you standing there.''

``Obviously.'' He winced.

``Let me look.'' She crowded closer. ``Is your nose bleeding?''

Mack took his hands from his face. ``I don't think so.''

She stood up on tiptoes, touched the bridge of his nose with a fingertip. Suddenly, the pain vanished.

She was within kissing distance. He lowered his head, intending to take her lips at the same moment she pulled back, clearly unaware of his plan.

His nose ended up bumping the top of her head. "Ow!"

"Omigosh." She clamped a hand over her mouth. "I hurt you again."

"No kidding."

"Were you trying to kiss me?"

"I made an attempt, yes."

"I'm sorry." She clasped her hands behind her back, lifted her face up to his and puckered her lips. "You can kiss me now."

"Sorry, but the moment's kinda shattered."

Still, there was no way he could resist planting at least a small kiss on those willing lips. He stepped back. She gave a dreamy sigh and smiled at him.

"You're a great kisser."

"You're not half bad yourself," he said gruffly and worried that Mr. Boner might try to put in another appearance. "I see you suffered no ill effects from your mosquito bites. I can barely tell where they were."

"Thanks to you and your quick administration of rubbing alcohol and Caladryl."

Their eyes met and Mack felt weirdly breathless.

"Hey," he said, more to distract himself than to make conversation. "Where's your totem?"

"What?" Camryn's hand flew to her neck. "It's gone!"

Camryn grabbed a fistful of her hair in her hand and tugged. Not again! Frantically she cast her gaze around the yard, saw that Lulu, the consummate thief had disappeared.

Mack was giving her the same funny look he'd given her last night when she'd left his place early. If she didn't stop losing that frickin' totem, he would start believing she was psycho woman.

Still, she couldn't help her reaction to the news that the totem was missing.

It was probably missing when you kissed him and that didn't scare you.

Well, that may be true, but she was scared now. Hyperventilating in fact. Her knees were as shaky as those paint-mixing machines in the hardware store. She felt herself changing right before his eyes, morphing into nerdy Cammie Jo.

Yipes! She had to get away from him. Pronto.

Easy. Take it easy. Don't sprint. You keep running out on the guy and sooner or later he'll write you off as a lost cause.

``What time is it?'' Cammie Jo asked in desperation. She could pretend she had an appointment.

``Five-thirty.''

``Oh, 'scuse me,'' she babbled. ``I gotta go.'' She pointed over her shoulder. ``There's something I've got to do.''

He was standing between her and the back door, blocking her escape into the B&B. Her heart crashed around inside her chest like coins in a change machine.

``Oh yeah? What have you got to do?''

``Uh...'' Darn it. She couldn't even think without the totem.

``Yes?'' He lifted his eyebrows, waited.

``I gotta go somewhere.''

``Where?''

``Um...um...'' She was a rotten liar, and it didn't help that he was staring at her like the Grand Inquisitor. ``I'm going over to Kay's.''

``Kay and Quinn are in Anchorage.''

``They're not!''

``They are. Flew them there myself not three hours ago, and I'm not picking them up until tomorrow morning.''

``Oh.''

``So tell the truth, Camryn. What's going on?''

She couldn't tell him about the totem. It would ruin the magic and with the magic gone, she would no longer be the woman that turned him on. His dark glare quelled her like Godzilla quashing Bambi.

She opened her mouth but no words came out. She couldn't even look him in the eyes.

Get away, go. Flee.

But this might be your last chance to make things right with him, protested her ragged heart.

She darted around him.

He grabbed for her but she was smaller and quicker. All he got was the hem of her shirt.

Cammie Jo heard a loud rip, felt a draft of cool air on her skin, but she didn't look back.

The galloping beat of the *William Tell Overture* pounded in her brain as she ran from him.

Whiz!

She sprinted into the kitchen.

Whoosh!

She barreled through the double doors, hurled her body past the reception desk.

Crash!

He was coming behind her and had obviously knocked something over. But she didn't dare throw a glance over her shoulder to find out what.

"Camryn, you come back here this instant," Mack thundered.

Cammie Jo skidded past a couple of women at the bottom of the staircase. They jumped back in surprise. Hauling in a deep breath, she leaped up the steps two at a time, pounded down the hallway and ran into her bedroom. Without even stopping to turn the lock, she dove into the closet and slammed the door.

Change. She had to change. Get out of her Camryn clothes and into her dull Cammie Jo duds. Pop out those green contacts and slap on her eyeglasses. Pin her hair in a bun and maybe jam on a hat. That way, if he found her, he'd do as he always did when he saw Cammie Jo—ignore her completely.

ENOUGH WAS ENOUGH. Even a patient man had his limits and Mack was not particularly patient. Camryn had just pushed him to the edge of reason. He wanted an explanation and he wanted one now. He deserved to know the real reason she kept running away from him.

``Camryn,'' he shouted, unmindful of the people in the lobby staring and tittering. Look what the woman had reduced him to. He was a man who valued his privacy. A man who hated to be talked about behind his back, and now here he was making a spectacle of himself over a woman.

Shameful.

But his reluctance to put his personal life on display didn't stop him from going after her. His anger was greater than his self-consciousness.

When he reached the top of the stairs, he realized he didn't know what room she was staying in. Dammit.

``Camryn,'' he called again and wasn't surprised when she did not answer.

He trod down the hallway, saw that one of the bedroom doors was standing slightly ajar. He rapped his knuckles against the door and called out, ``Hello.''

From inside the closet, Cammie Jo heard the outer door creak open and she sank back against the wall. Squeezing her eyes tightly shut she realized that in her haste she'd neglected to close and lock the outer door.

``Hello?'' he called again.

She heard his footsteps coming closer as he walked across the floor. Cammie Jo froze. Her pulse pounded like a rabbit hiding from a marauding coyote. She was half-dressed, her torn shirt peeled off and lying on the floor, her white denim jeans unzipped. She was afraid to move. Afraid he would hear her.

Her eyes flew open but she couldn't see much in the pitch blackness of the closet.

More footsteps. Were they receding? Or was he just walking around, checking out the bathroom?

A woolen sweater hanging in the closet brushed against her nose. She shoved the sleeve from her face. Her upper lip itched.

Ach-oo! She sneezed, then held her breath.

Softly there came a tapping, a gentle rapping at her closet door.

Maybe she'd gotten lucky and it was a big fat black raven muttering "Nevermore."

Dream on sister.

"Camryn." Mack's voice had the tonal quality of a parent who was trying to discipline his child without giving in to his anger. "I know you're in there. I can hear you breathing."

Liar! I'm holding my breath.

"Come on out, you're not fooling anyone."

Maybe if she just wished hard enough she'd wake up in her own bed in Austin.

"I think I deserve an explanation. I want to know what's going on."

Cammie Jo exhaled.

"Why do you keep running off every time we start to get close? Do you have some big dark secret you need to tell me about?"

Yes!

"Or," he said, "are you seeing someone else? I need to know. I'm not the kind of guy who likes sharing his woman with other men."

Share his woman? What was this? Mack considered her his woman?

"I need to know."

He was jealous! The realization dawned on her and she felt a strange sense of feminine power. To her knowledge, no man had ever been jealous over her. Oh the poor baby. She longed to cradle him in her arms, whisper reassurances in his ear. All this time he thought she'd been dashing off to keep dates with other men.

But would he be jealous of the real Cammie Jo if he knew the truth?

"Please," he said, "come out and talk to me."

Cautiously, she opened the closet and peeped out to see Mack sitting slump-shouldered on the foot of the bed. He looked hurt, disappointed, dejected.

"I'm not seeing anyone else," she whispered, holding up her bathrobe in front of her nearly naked torso.

He raised his head, pinned her to the spot with his dark-eyed gaze. "Really?"

She nodded.

"'Cause it would hurt me if you were. My mother used to run around on my father. It was a pitiful thing to watch and I swore I'd never have an unfaithful wife. I was engaged once and she dumped me for a richer guy so excuse me if I seem a bit suspicious. If you've got someone else on the string, just tell me. I'll bow out of the picture. No hard feelings. Just please don't lie to me.''

She ached to go to him, to wrap her arms around him, to assure him she was most definitely a one-man woman, but she couldn't. Not without the necklace to give her courage.

''I'm not seeing anyone else.''

''You don't have another date tonight?''

''No.''

He stood up and walked toward her, but she retreated back into the closet. His scent filled her nostrils, his nearness had her shivering.

''I'm not dressed.'' She used the handy excuse to deflect her fear.

''Why don't you and I go to Caleb's salmon bake tonight?'' he proposed. ''Later, we'll have a long talk about a lot of things.''

How could she possibly go without the totem? The idea of walking into a party full of strangers struck terror into her heart.

''I'm sorry,'' she murmured, ''but I can't.''

''Well,'' he said, and clasped his hands together. ''I guess that's it. There might not be another guy in the picture, but obviously there's some reason you don't want to be with me. Either come with me tonight, Camryn, or I'm calling this whole thing off.''

Call off their romance? Before they'd even had a chance to indulge in such fun games as Slap and

Tickle or Red Rover, Red Rover Let The Bare-Chested Hunk Come Over?

No. Not that. Anything but that.

But the serious expression on his face told her if she didn't go to the salmon bake with him tonight it was indeed goodbye, bachelor.

Cammie Jo gulped and her hand went to her throat as if simply by touching the spot where the necklace had lain against her skin she could extract an ounce or two of bravery.

Damn that kleptomaniac Siberian husky.

"Well, Camryn, what's it going to be? I really need an answer because I'm starting to care about you, and I refuse to get serious over a woman who can't commit. So if you don't feel the same way, now's the time to let me know."

Omigosh! Mack was starting to care about her?

Ka-thung, ka-thung, ka-thung, rang her heart.

She dropped her gaze. So this was it. The relationship was over before it ever really began. But what had she expected? How could she and Mack form any kind of meaningful bond based on a myth?

What to do? What to do?

Camryn shook her head, unable to speak.

"Right, then." He dusted his palms, got off the bed. "It's over."

10

"OH, AUNTIES," Cammie Jo sobbed into the phone during the conference call with her three surrogate mothers. "I've made such a mess of things."

She proceeded to tell them what had happened then added, "The thing is, Mack's crazy about Camryn, but he doesn't give *me* the time of day."

"But you are Camryn," Aunt Coco pointed out.

"Not without the totem. Me and my alter ego are as different as night and day. She's beautiful, and I'm not. She loves to flirt, and I don't have a clue. She's brave, and I'm a scaredy-cat."

"That's nonsense," Aunt Kiki said. "You're the same person."

"And when I'm with Mack, I feel like a big old fraud. And a liar."

"You've never told a lie in your life, Cammie Jo." Aunt Hildegard clucked her tongue.

"I have now. Mack thinks I'm this bold, wonderful woman and I'm not. This treasured wish totem is more a curse than a blessing, it really is."

"But without it, you would never have had the

courage to go out with Mack," Aunt Coco pointed out.

"I'm beginning to think that would have been for the best," Cammie Jo replied mournfully. "I've never hurt so badly."

"Oh, honey, I wish you were here so I could give you a hug." Aunt Coco sighed into the phone.

"I'd steep you a cup of chamomile tea," Aunt Kiki chimed in.

"And I'd bake that lemon Bundt cake you love so well," Aunt Hildegard finished up.

How nice to be home and in the comforting protection of her aunties' arms. Cammie Jo sighed deeply. She had an overwhelming urge to book a flight to Texas and leave without a parting word to anyone.

The coward's way out.

She'd used that avenue of escape far too many times in the past, she realized. She'd been hiding behind her aunts too long. Falling back on their TLC when she was too afraid to face the world. She was ashamed of herself.

"Now Mack's under the impression that I'm a cheating, heartbreaking witch."

"Well, sweetie," Aunt Kiki said, "you've just got to prove to him he's wrong."

"I can't!" Cammie Jo wailed. "The totem is missing."

"You could come home," Aunt Coco said. "If it's too much for you."

"Or," Aunt Hildegard put in, "you could stay

there and turn Alaska upside down looking for that totem, the way your mother would have.''

Ooh, what was with the guilt stick? Aunt Hildegard had never spoken to her like this before. Cammie Jo sat up straighter.

''Excuse me?''

''Well dear, you did make the wish, the least you could do is see this through.''

''Please,'' Aunt Hildegard spoke again. ''Take a chance, Cammie Jo.''

''And if he doesn't love me?''

''Then,'' finished Aunt Kiki, ''you'll come home a new woman. A little battered, a little wiser, but free, liberated and as brave as your mother ever was.''

Cammie Jo told her aunts goodbye and hung up the phone. Dejected, she plopped down on the bed. Her aunts' staunch belief in her was touching, but misplaced. They had no idea how lost, lonely and helpless she felt. Without the totem, she was paralyzed.

The jingling sound of dog tags drew Cammie Jo's forlorn attention to the doorway. There sat Lulu, tail wagging, with something dangling from her mouth.

''Lulu!'' Camryn exclaimed and sprang to her feet. ''You've got my totem.''

CAMMIE JO breezed down Main Street in snug-fitting, low-slung denim shorts, high-wedged sandals and a rainbow-hued handkerchief halter top. Heads turned. Men whistled. Horns honked.

She grinned and strutted her stuff, the totem necklace bouncing merrily off her chest. She was on her way to get Mack back.

Humming under her breath, picnic basket swinging from her elbow, she strolled along Inlet Road toward Mack's house. She walked past the pier where the floatplanes were docked, and caught sight of the *Edna Marie*. Mack was untying the plane and it looked as if he was about to take off.

Omigosh, he was leaving.

Cammie Jo took off at a run, waving her hand and hollering for him to stop.

He raised his head.

Their eyes met.

"Wait!" she cried. "Wait for me."

He waited.

She stopped a few feet away from him, panting for breath.

He studied her, unsmiling. "What do you want, Camryn?"

"I came to make peace," she said, and held up the picnic basket. "See, I brought sandwiches."

"I hope you didn't break your other date for this because I'm not interested."

Cammie Jo stamped her foot. "Darn it, Mack. Will you stop being so stubborn. I'm not seeing anyone else."

"So why didn't you agree to go to Caleb's party with me?"

"Because, I don't like being given ultimatums."

"I see."

"Where are you going?" She inclined her head in the direction of the floatplane.

"I need some time alone to think."

"Want some company?" Her heart was pounding a thousand miles an hour. She was afraid he would turn her down, tell her to get lost.

A slight smile raised the corner of his lips. He opened the passenger side of the plane. "Get in."

Woo-hoo! Cammie Jo hopped inside.

Mack flew them up out of the mountains and she wasn't a bit afraid. "Where are we headed?" she asked.

"My favorite hideaway."

"Hmm, sounds intriguing."

Several minutes later, he landed the *Edna Marie* in a lake near a lush grassy meadow. It seemed they were a million miles from nowhere. He helped her from the plane, took a blanket out of the cargo hold and spread it across the grass. He lay down on the blanket, and patted the spot beside him.

Cammie Jo eased to her knees. The big wide Alaskan landscape seemed suddenly small and very intimate, with Mack's brawny body taking up most of the space. She'd never been so vitally aware of another human being in her life.

They ate their picnic in silence, enjoying the quiet meadow, savoring the food. But once the meal was over, they had no more distractions.

Mack lay stretched out on his back, palms cradled under his head, staring up at the wide expanse of sky. Cammie Jo sat next to him, admiring his hard, masculine body.

"I'm sorry," he said. "For acting like a caveman back there at the B&B. I had no right to issue you an ultimatum."

"That's true."

"I was being selfish. You're such an incredible woman. I didn't want to share you with anyone." Mack snaked an arm around her waist, tugged her against his body. "Will you forgive me, Sugar Plum?"

"But of course."

Sugar Plum. She adored the way he said those words. Loved the look in his eyes when he spoke them. His soft, sexy growl made her feel very special.

All her life, she'd been too shy to get this close to a man, had no real notion of how to act around the opposite sex. She had suppressed her sexual needs, sublimated them through her academic achievements. Created her own safe little cell. A jail from which to view the world.

The totem had freed her from that cozy prison of her own making. Freed her to make fantastic choices. Freed her to explore the depths of her uninvestigated desires.

She wanted Mack to make love to her. Wanted it very, very much.

But how could she make love to him under false pretenses? And how could she tell him about the totem, knowing that once she did, the very qualities he loved most about her would disappear?

Mack traced a finger along her bare arm at the same time he dropped kisses on her neck. Her world narrowed in the eternal flow of passion. What was reality anyway? She was Camryn and Camryn was she. Did it really matter that she had to wear a totem in order to be what he wanted her to be?

When Mack rolled her over onto her back and ran his lava-hot tongue down the hollow of her throat, Cammie Jo chucked caution to the breezy wind. She'd come here for an adventure, and she was having it.

Tomorrow loomed far in the hazy distance. All that mattered was this moment. She was living her fantasy. Indulging in the most far-fetched dream imaginable. A handsome, eligible, marriage-minded Alaskan bachelor was kissing her.

And doing a lot more than kissing, it seemed.

His fingers had undone her skimpy halter top and he was running his work-roughened fingers over her smooth, satiny skin.

Mack seemed to know exactly where to touch to elicit the most sensations from her receptive body. He stroked and nibbled. Kissed and caressed. He licked and sucked. Kneaded and massaged.

The meadow flowed into a montage of sensation. The tall grasses rustled and rippled like party streamers. The fresh smell of sunshine and mountain air roused her libido.

Here she was, acting like the brave, wild woman he thought her to be. Something, either Mack's kisses, the untamed environment or the totem necklace released the spirit of the Alaskan woman buried underneath a lifetime of shyness.

She wasn't born here, but her mother had been. It seemed that bond reached through space and time. She felt grounded, settled, content in a way she'd never felt before coming to this beautiful, primitive land.

Her halter top fell away from her shoulders. Mack's teeth nipped lightly at her exposed skin. He buried his face in her hair and inhaled deeply.

''You smell so good,'' he murmured with a tenderness that touched her soul. ''Like summer itself.''

His hands were undoing her halter bra. He flicked the material away then bent his head to draw one nipple into his mouth.

Cammie Jo gasped at the sensation. ''Oh,'' she whispered, ''oh.''

He lifted his head. His gaze met hers and held it for a long, long time. She saw in those delicious brown depths exactly how much he wanted her.

His desire was a powerful thing.

This man wanted her. Her! The girl who, until this week, had never even been on a real date.

Not you, stupid. He wants Camryn Josephine.

His mouth seized hers, numbing her to any and all thoughts except his passion. Shivering, Cammie

Jo forgot about everything else and simply surrendered.

Mack gazed upon Camryn with awe. Her nipples perched like hard little buttons atop her gorgeous breasts. Her bare skin glowed ethereal in the evening sunlight.

He ached just looking at her. He wanted to make love to her so badly he'd almost forgotten his own name. It felt so right.

And yet the risk of getting involved with the wrong woman at the wrong time in his life held him back.

But what if she was the right woman at the right time? He wanted to trust her with his heart, but did he dare? He propped himself up on one elbow, and stared into her vivid green eyes.

``Camryn,'' he murmured her name, intending then to tell her about his ``wife'' list and whisper to her that he thought she was the perfect woman for him.

``Yes, Mack?''

``There's something I've being meaning to ask you.''

``Oh?'' She sat up, tucking her legs beneath her. Her hair was a soft, disheveled cloud of caramel. Her scent filled his lungs.

Something, he couldn't say what, although he suspected it might well be fear, held him back. Instead of speaking the words that would bare his soul and place his heart firmly in her hands, he asked, ``Would you like to go glacier hiking with me next week?''

``WHAT DO YOU THINK?'' Mack asked, raising his voice in order to be heard over the helicopter noises. He'd flown them in the *Edna Marie* to Haines, where he'd borrowed a buddy's helicopter. He'd learned to fly both planes and choppers during his stint in the Air Force.

For the past few days, they'd been dating nonstop.

This was his final test. Camryn would be leaving Bear Creek in two days, and he had to know for sure whether their relationship stood a chance of working or not. On the glacier, he would find out if they really could trust each other. If things went well, then he would tell her exactly how he felt about her before she left for Texas.

Mack had spent all his free time with her, neglecting his friends, neglecting his chores, neglecting everything but Camryn. They'd fished and kayaked. They'd ridden horseback and trekked into the woods to photograph wildlife. And with each passing day he'd come to admire her more.

She grinned and hollered back, ``It's fantastic.''

Ahead of them the glacier loomed cold and imposing in its frigid beauty. Mack had seen it a thousand times but the sight never failed to strike awe inside him. Much in the same way gazing at Camryn did.

They flew low to the water. Camryn laughed out

loud when she spotted harbor seals lounging on ice floes. And when he pointed out a humpback whale, she literally choked up at the sight.

"It's so beautiful."

"You okay?" he asked and patted her leg.

Camryn nodded. "I'm just going to hate leaving all of this."

He set the helicopter down on an icy plateau nestled in a cradle of mountain peaks. They put on their climbing gear and collected the supplies they would need for a morning of glacier navigation.

Cammie Jo was so excited she could barely stand herself. Mack helped her down from the chopper. Even though she had on four layers of clothing, the bite of cold air was unexpected. She gasped in surprise and delight. Now this was how she'd imagined Alaska.

The ice was slippery beneath her feet and if Mack hadn't been there to catch her, she would have fallen. But because he was at her side, because the totem lay around her neck buried under the layers of her clothing, she had nothing to fear. His strong, vibrant arms spanned her waist, holding her steady, anchoring her in place.

In that moment, Cammie Jo realized there was nowhere else on earth she'd rather be than in Alaska with this man. She'd spent a lifetime dreaming of this, while at the same time fearing that her heart's desire would never come true.

And now she had it all.

But for how long?

As if sensing her mood he reached out a gloved hand and tenderly caressed her cheek.

She looked into his eyes. She was leaving Bear Creek in two days time. Was there any hope for a long-distance relationship? Was there any chance he could love the real Cammie Jo?

She smiled with false brightness. ``Let's start hiking.''

``That's what I love most about you—your gung ho attitude.''

Love.

There was that word that warmed her to her toes at the same time it worried her.

To hide her confusion, Cammie Jo took action. She tossed her head and marched bravely out across the mountain of ice.

It was like walking on the inside of a freezer, cold and crunchy. Her crampons bit into the ice, holding her secure. She felt invincible.

She could scarcely believe she was the same Cammie Jo who used to hide behind the couch as a child when visitors came over, too shy to even come out despite promises of sweets and treats.

The heady reality of finally living her dream was a powerful enticement. She'd never felt so free, so fully alive as she did at this moment.

``Careful,'' Mack warned. ``A glacier is a dangerous place.''

Ha! She wasn't scared. Bring on the glaciers and the polar bears.

Mack hurried to catch up with her, a strange

clutch in his guts. Camryn was scurrying over the ice like a crazed woman, laughing and joking. He had wished for a brave woman, an adventuresome wife. A lady wild enough to handle Alaska without blinking twice. And he thought he'd found that woman in Camryn.

Now, he was beginning to wonder if maybe she was too much of a good thing. He thought of his list. When he'd recorded his desirable qualities in a mate, he'd neglected to consider the negative side of those traits. Bravery could translate into fool-hardiness. An adventure could easily become tire-some. He wondered for the first time if maybe he needed different qualities in a wife. Did she really need to be his best buddy?

But then his eyes trained on Camryn's fanny, bundled so enticingly in tight ski pants. He had to admit he was helpless when it came to chemistry. Briefly, he closed his eyes, and fought off his arousal.

"Wait up for me, Camryn. You could easily fall into a crevasse."

"Catch me if you can!" she called out, and damned if she didn't take off running.

Real fear for her safety kicked him into high gear and moving as fast as caution would allow, Mack took off after her.

"Camryn, Sugar Plum, no kidding, slow down." His voice echoed eerily off the surrounding mountains. The crisp cold air he normally loved suddenly seemed far too frigid.

She was twenty yards ahead of him, blithely gawking at the majesty around her. "Don't be a fuddy-dud, Mack, let's have some fun. Tag, you're it."

Was the woman bonkers? Didn't she realize they were treading on the face of an ice field?

"Camryn Josephine," he scolded. "Stop in your tracks right this minute."

"Or what?" She turned and saucily stuck her tongue out at him.

He wanted to whip her off the ice, toss her over his shoulder, cart her back to the helicopter and make love to her right then and there.

"Or I'll turn you over my knee and spank your fanny."

She didn't look the least bit intimidated. In fact, she was walking backward, still moving away but facing him. "And what if I like it?" she dared.

He could just see her falling into a crevasse, breaking that pretty neck before he had a chance to wring it. "You probably would, you ornery critter."

Her grin widened. "Why don't you try it?" she teased.

"Stay right where you are and I will." He took several long-legged strides. The ice cracked ominously beneath him.

She didn't look the least bit concerned. Not about falling into a crevasse or the risk of him paddling her backside. "Like I'll make it that easy for you."

"Seriously, Camryn, I'm not joking. Please wait for me."

"Nah, nah, you can't catch me."

"I'm not trying to catch you."

"I'm not falling for your ploy." She zipped ahead of him, out of reach.

When he got hold of her, he would kiss her until she promised never to do anything this foolish again. Determined to snag her before she hurt herself, Mack stalked after her.

He was so busy watching to make sure she didn't slip and fall that he neglected to watch his own step. One minute he was standing upright on the glacier. The next minute, he was sliding sideways down a sheet of ice.

"Oh, Mack," Cammie Jo teased in a singsong voice.

This was so much fun! She was playing the way she'd never been able to play as a kid. Her aunts had never let her ride a bicycle. She might fall off and skin her knees. They'd refused to let her have skates or play sports or even run. It was as if Mack had shown her how to reconnect with the little girl who'd lost out on so much fun.

She stopped and peeked over her shoulder. Hmm. No Mack. Where had he gone?

"Mack? Where are you?"

She sobered immediately and began to retrace her steps. There was nowhere to hide except in the helicopter, and it was a good quarter-mile away.

He couldn't have gotten back to it that fast. There was only one place he could be.

Numerous crevasses cut their way through the ice. Deep fissures that went down into the belly of the glacier. They hadn't scared her at all. She'd watched and dodged them. But if you were to fall into one...

"Mack!" she shrieked. "Where are you?"

"I'm here, Camryn." He sounded supremely calm and his composure soothed her.

But all she could see was a white-blue expanse of ice stretching out endlessly before her and the gathering of clouds rolling in through the mountain pass.

"Where is here?"

"Step carefully to your left."

She eased over, head down, eyes searching the fissures and cracks running under the ice. Surely none of these were large enough to swallow a man's body.

"Mack?"

"Keep coming, Sugar Plum."

"I'm so sorry. I didn't mean for this to happen."

"No recriminations. It wasn't your fault. It's simply a risk of walking on the glacier."

"But if I hadn't been acting so silly, if only I'd listened to you."

"Hush," he commanded sharply. "No more of that."

Her throat tightened. If anything happened to him she would never forgive herself.

Up ahead, she spotted a big crevasse. Why hadn't she seen it before? Cammie Jo crabbed forward, angling her head sideways to peer over the icy ledge.

Her breath caught in her throat when she glimpsed Mack's dark head.

He was three feet from the surface, his body wedged into a narrowing by his backpack, his pickax buried into a shelf of ice. He was holding on with both hands to prevent himself from slipping deeper.

Gingerly, Cammie Jo sank to her knees and leaned out over the crevasse.

He smiled up at her.

Her heart somersaulted.

"You okay?"

"I'm okay. But we're in something of a pickle. When I fell, I dropped my cell phone. I need for you to go back to the helicopter and radio for help. Can you do that?"

Could she do that? Well of course. She had the totem. She could do anything.

Cammie Jo reached up to caress her necklace but she didn't feel the reassuring bulge. She patted her thick coat.

Panic welled inside her. No! Not again. Not now.

Frantically, she sat up and stripped off her coat. It had to be here. Even if the clasp broke.

She stripped off her sweater, her shirt, right down to her bare skin. She had to face facts.

The totem was gone, and Mack needed her.

"Camryn? What's the matter? What's wrong?"

Mack's urgent voice yanked her back to reality. Shivering with fear and cold, she buttoned up her shirt, slipped back into her sweater and coat. Her breathing came in short, shallow jerks. She couldn't answer him. She couldn't even think, her fear was so great.

She was on a glacier in the wilds of Alaska and the man she cared about most was trapped in an icy tomb.

"What's going on?" he asked. "Talk to me, Camryn."

She whimpered, hugged herself and rocked to and fro.

"Come back to the ledge," he demanded. "Where I can see your face."

Tremulously, she shook her head.

The clouds rolling in grew thicker, became a dark fog that blotted out the sun. Her chest squeezed, and she found it hard to breathe.

"Camryn! Answer me."

"I'm not Camryn," she whimpered, inching toward the edge of the crevasse once more. She looked down to find him staring at her with a mixture of concern and confusion on his face.

11

"WHAT ARE YOU TALKING ABOUT?"

"I'm not really Camryn Josephine. I mean I am. That's my real name, but I'm not who you think I am. I'm not brave and carefree and adventuresome."

"Then who are you?"

"Cammie Jo Lockhart."

"Cammie Jo?" He frowned.

"You know. You flew me into Bear Creek and when I thought we were crashing I stuck my head in your lap."

"Oh, you mean Tammie Jo."

"No, Cammie Jo."

"I don't understand any of this."

"I'm petrified. I can't make it all the way back to the helicopter."

"Why not?"

And she told him then about the totem. What did it matter now if she ruined the magic? Everything was ruined anyway. She told him why she wore it. Why she had run away from him, why she'd fainted in his arms. Because she was too scared of life without the magic power of the neck-lace.

"But your eyes are green. Cammie Jo's are blue."

"Contact lenses," she said.

"And you're...more well-endowed."

"Push-up bra."

"Don't tell me you've got a wooden leg, too."

"Please, don't try to make me laugh. I'm deadly serious."

Mack stared at her, incredulous. This was crazy, illogical and yet he knew she believed every word she was saying. Because as he watched, she changed before his eyes and the transformation was stunning.

Gone was brave, confident Camryn. Instead, at the edge of the crevasse trembled timid Cammie Jo. Her shoulders slumped. Her eyes lost their lus-ter. This was not the same woman he had fallen in love with.

Love?

He felt betrayed by his own heart. He'd been so busy trying to find the perfect woman he'd over-looked the obvious.

"I never lied to you on purpose," Cammie Jo murmured. "Remember when we met at the *Metropolitan* party? You didn't recognize me. And then you kept seeing Cammie Jo at the B&B and you never even looked at her, at me. I was a noth-ing to you. A nobody."

She was right. Guilty as charged. This situation

wasn't her fault. He had no grounds to feel hurt or hoodwinked.

"None of that matters now, Cammie Jo," he said. "Look at me."

Briefly, she swung her gaze his way. The anguish on her sweet little face cut him deep.

"You did all those brave things, not some magic totem. You hiked the Tongass. You shot the Mendenhall rapids. You faced down a bear."

"Who turned out to be toothless."

"But you didn't know that, and you were just now scampering fearlessly over this glacier like a professional mountain climber."

"Yeah, and look what happened."

"The totem was just a symbol of bravery. You believed in it and therefore you believed in yourself."

She shook her head. "I wish that were true."

"It is true. Listen to me. We're in deep trouble here, Cammie Jo, and only you can save us. You've got to get to the helicopter and radio for help or we're both going to die out here on this glacier. And as much as I like the wilds of Alaska, we're too young to die. I haven't even kept my promise to my father."

"What promise is that?"

"To have a son, to pass down the McCaulley name. I'm the last surviving male. It was so important to me I even made out a wife list." He told her about his list, how he'd tried to find the perfect wife. How she'd matched every aspect on his list.

"But you see, Mack, I'm not that woman."

"Yes you are. Cammie Jo, I believe in you."

She bit down on her bottom lip. "I'm just so scared."

"Do it for your mother. She was an Alaskan, right? And a bush pilot. That means she was one courageous woman and you're her daughter. Her genes are in your blood. Come on, Sugar Plum, you can do this!"

You can do this.

Mack's encouraging words rang in her ears. Cammie Jo took a deep breath and got to her feet. She had to do this. For Mack's sake. She didn't need the totem.

She thought of all the times in her life when she'd been afraid. All the times she'd been too scared to go after her dreams. All the compromises she'd made because she was too chicken to face her fears head-on.

Then she thought of all the fun she'd had as Camryn. How free she'd felt. How liberated to be out from under the tyranny of shyness.

She inched her way through the thick mist in the direction she prayed the helicopter lay. She kept her eyes trained to the ground, on constant alert for treacherous crevasses.

After she'd traveled only a few feet, she heard a crashing bang like the sound of a rifle being fired off in her ear.

She screamed in terror and clutched her hands over her head.

``Cammie Jo,'' Mack called out to her when the echoes had subsided. ``Don't be afraid. That was just the glacier calving.''

``You mean like breaking off into the sea?''

``Yeah, but we're far enough back from the bay that the glacier won't give way beneath you.''

``Nice to know.''

``Keep going, Sugar Plum. You're doing great.''

Easy for him to say. He couldn't see her. She was a ragged mess.

After what seemed an eternity of trudging over ice in a thick fog, she finally made out the hulking black shape of the helicopter and Cammie Jo broke into tears of triumph and exhaustion. She'd made it.

``I'm here, Mack,'' she called out, not certain any longer in which direction he lay.

``You did good, sweetheart.'' He sounded so far away, but she could hear him. ``Now get on the radio and get us out of here.''

THE RESCUERS, who included Quinn, Jake, Caleb and Quinn's sister, Meggie, arrived to pry Mack from the crevasse. It had been tricky work but eventually, they pulled him free unharmed.

Cammie Jo's instincts had been to run to him and throw her arms around him, but she was too afraid. Worried what he might think of her now. Afraid that their romance was over.

The rescue squad bundled them into blankets and gave them hot chocolate from a thermos. Another bush pilot flew the chopper back. Meggie rode with them. She took Mack's vital signs and examined him.

Mack made light of the situation and never once let on that Camryn's foolhardiness had been the cause of his fall. Every Alaskan who undertook to traverse a glacier understood the inherent risk and he wasn't blaming her, even though Cammie Jo blamed herself.

But as Meggie told Cammie Jo, "Living is worth the risk, because what kind of life do you have when you stay on the sidelines cowering in fear?"

Meggie didn't even know Cammie Jo, but it seemed as if she'd spoken straight to her central conflict. Cammie Jo turned her head and found Mack studying her intently.

Gulping, she looked away.

When they reached Bear Creek, Mack assured Meggie he was perfectly fine and didn't need to be checked out by Doc Henderson over in Haines.

Cammie Jo stood on the dock not knowing what to do. Mack took her elbow and guided her toward his truck. "Come on," he said gruffly. "I'll take you to the B&B."

Once they were in the truck, he turned to her. "I'm very proud of you."

Her heart fluttered, but still, she could not meet his gaze.

"It took a lot of guts to walk over those crevasses in a deep fog. Especially when you were so scared."

``Th-thank you.''

``But I'm really confused about a lot of things. I need some time to think.''

She nodded. ``When will I see you again?''

``Honestly, Cammie Jo, I don't know.''

He left her at the B&B and drove away without a look back.

IT WAS OVER. The totem was gone for good, lost somewhere on the ice tundra of the Margerie glacier. Her grand adventure had come to an end. She'd be leaving for Texas the day after tomorrow.

And she had no idea how Mack felt about her.

She wanted to stay in Bear Creek, but how could she? Now that Mack knew she wasn't brave Camryn, that she could not live up to his fantasy woman, he wouldn't want her anymore. And without the totem she could never be that recklessly carefree woman again.

Be careful what you wish for, Aunt Coco had warned her. *Because you will get it.*

And her most treasured wish had come true.

Only to be snatched away before she ever got a chance to find out who she really was.

Despondent, Cammie Jo flopped on the bed in her room at the B&B, picked up the telephone and called the only three people in the world she knew would understand.

Aunt Hildegard answered on the second ring.

Cammie Jo started crying at the sound of her dear aunt's voice.

``Honey, what's wrong?''

Sobbing, Cammie Jo told her about losing the totem for good. About losing Mack.

``Are you sure it's over between the two of you?'' Aunt Hildegard asked. ``Maybe he just needs time to think.''

``It's over,'' she said mournfully.

``Well, I'm so sorry to hear about that. And it's a shame the totem's gone. Your mother put another note inside it for you to read in case you got into trouble.''

``What? I didn't even know the totem was hollow.''

``There's a little stopper in the bottom of it.''

``What did the letter say?''

``I don't know. The message was for you. We didn't read it.''

Fresh misery washed over her. She would never read her mother's final words of comfort.

``Oh, Aunt Hildegard what'll I do?''

``Come home, sweetheart. We love you.''

Coddled. Pampered. Protected. Kept safe from the world. Hidden away.

She'd failed miserably at being an adventuress. She might was well go back to her secure world in that quiet little house and let her days in Alaska fade into a favorite memory. It was for the best.

MACK VIGOROUSLY BUFFED *Edna Marie* with a butter-soft chamois and tried not to think about

Cammie Jo, but he wasn't having much luck. He'd spent a fitful night recalling everything that had happened on the glacier.

It was six-thirty in the morning, and his first fare wasn't until eight.

He yanked opened the passenger door of the plane to clean out any litter lurking there. He picked up an empty foam cup and a bubble-gum wrapper. His eyes settled on something wedged between the seats. Was that Cammie Jo's totem? He reached for it, picked up the unsightly necklace and held it in his hands.

"I wish," he said, "Cammie Jo could have her happy ending."

In that instant, Mack had a moment of crystal clarity. For most of his life he'd been content with beautiful but shallow women. As long as he went out with them, he didn't have to worry about losing his heart or breaking theirs. He'd been seriously afraid of marriage, of having his union turn out the way his father's had, so he'd avoided the issue entirely by choosing gals who weren't the marrying kind.

But when his father lay dying and made him promise to wed and have children to perpetuate the McCaulley name, Mack had made up his "wife" list. He'd picked qualities that were the opposite of his flighty mother or his fickle girlfriends. With the future mother of his children in mind, he'd constructed the list.

And then, he'd met Camryn. She seemed to embody the best of both worlds. Brave and loyal but at the same time beautiful and fun-loving.

Until yesterday, when he discovered Camryn wasn't who he thought she was.

She was more.

So much more.

She was also Cammie Jo. A woman with heart and spirit and verve to spare. She'd wanted so badly to overcome her shyness, to vanquish her fears that she'd placed all her belief in a totem. So strong was her belief, she'd transformed herself to become the very best person she could be.

A full, well-rounded woman. Smart, brave, loyal, beautiful. Fun-loving and adventuresome.

She simply didn't realize the power had come from her own heart, and not the necklace.

CAMMIE JO was packing her bags. With a heavy heart, she'd decided to leave Bear Creek a day early. What was the point in hanging around? The totem was gone, her adventure over. Mack hadn't asked her to stay in Alaska.

Her tummy gave a lonely squeeze.

There was a knock at the door. Maybe it was Kay coming to see her off.

Pushing her heavy black-frame glasses up on her nose, she moved to open the door.

And found herself face-to-face with Mack.

She sucked in her breath.

``Hi,'' he said softly.

Cammie Jo said nothing. Her whole body was alive with sensation at just being near him, but her tongue wouldn't move to form words.

"You doing okay?" His eyes were dark with concern.

Tentatively, she nodded. "Would you like to come in?"

She stepped to one side, waited for his response with a sense of suspense that would have thrilled Alfred Hitchcock.

He moved into the room, closed the door behind him and pulled something from his jacket. "I found it in the plane."

She stuck out her palm and he slowly lowered the necklace into it. She felt the familiar warmth spread up her arm and she stared, incredulous. "I lost the totem before we ever went on the glacier?"

"Looks like you were leaping and jumping over crevasses all under your own steam."

"Oh." She remembered then, what Aunt Hildegard had told her about the totem being hollow and the second letter from her mother hidden inside. She turned it over and saw the black rubber stopper.

Anxiously, she removed the stopper then shook the totem against her palm. A small scroll of rolled paper fell out.

She unfurled it with care. The paper was crisp with age, the ink faded. She held it to the light and read:

By now my darling, I hope you've achieved your heart's desire. Whatever you dream of, you can do it. The power to fulfill your destiny and the magic of the totem was in your heart and mind all along. The strength of your belief is what made the magic real. So now you know the truth. You are the creator of your own future. I have no doubt you'll make the right choices.

Love,

Mom

Stunned, Cammie Jo read the note again and again. There was no magic in the totem. No ancient spell. Camryn, her shadow self, had been buried inside her all along. Her potential was there, it only took faith to release it.

She'd acted bravely because she believed she was brave. Acting brave had led to facing her fears. And facing her fears had given her a sense of peace and freedom, if not every detail of her heart's desire.

She looked over at Mack and her heart tugged.

"What's that?" Mack asked.

"A letter from my mother." She passed it over to him to read. Their hands brushed and he smiled at her.

"Well," he said after a long moment. "Well."

"Looks like I wasn't lying to you."

"I never thought you were."

"But last night…"

"Shh." He placed a finger over her lips. "I came over here for more than one reason."

Her eyes widened. "Yes?"

"I've been doing a lot of thinking."

"Uh-huh."

"And I realized something."

"What's that?"

"This wife list is a load of hooey." He pulled the list from his pocket and slowly began to shred it as he walked toward her. "You can't write down the ingredients for a good wife like a recipe."

"No?" Cammie Jo took a step back.

"Nope." Mack took a step forward.

"Then how will you find the perfect woman?" She took another step back.

His eyes met hers and he took another step forward. "I believe I've already found her."

"Miss Jell-O Shooter?" she guessed and took a step back.

"Wrong." He took a step forward.

"The chubby sorority sister?" Two more steps back. Uh-oh, there's the wall.

Three steps forward. And there was Mack looming over her. "No, not her."

"Who then?" she whispered.

"As if you didn't know."

"Camryn?"

He shook his head. "Cammie Jo."

Skip-a-dee-do-dah, her blood sang through her veins.

"I love you, Cammie Jo. You. All of you. The

daring Camryn side of you and the side of you that sips hot chocolate in Bugs Bunny slippers. I love you with your glasses on and I love you with them off. I love you with makeup and without.''

''Are you sure?''

He took her hand. ''More sure than I've ever been sure of anything in my life. But if you're not ready I understand. If you need more time to think about things that's okay. No pressure. We've only known each other two weeks.''

''I feel like I've known you my entire life.''

''I feel like I've just been waiting for you to show up in mine.''

''You're something else, Mack McCaulley. A true Alaskan hero.''

''Move to Bear Creek. Rent a room in Jake's B&B. They have a job opening for an information specialist at the public library in Juneau. And you can finish your Ph.D. via the Internet.''

''How do you know?''

''I made a call before I came over here.''

She sucked in her breath. ''Really?''

''I could fly you to work every day.''

''Or better yet,'' she said. ''You could teach me to fly.''

In that moment, Mack realized he had been holding his breath, waiting for her reaction to his declaration of love. ''Does this mean you'll consider the idea of moving to Bear Creek?''

''Oh, Mack.'' She sighed. ''I've never wanted anything more in my entire life.''

He tossed the shredded list over his shoulder, then gently took off her glasses and kissed her.

Cammie Jo's heart beat wildly against her rib cage but the erratic thumping sprang from excitement, not fear. Her nostrils flared at his scent, his taste, his urgency.

More. She had to have more.

There was no reason to hold back. She wanted him. This magnificent man who'd just declared his love for her. She moaned low in her throat, amazed by her passion and the steadily increasing pressure burning low in her abdomen.

She wasn't going to regret a single thing that happened. With a growl of sexual pleasure, she grabbed him by the collar and dragged him toward the bed.

Mack's eyes widened. "Whoa, what's this? What's going on?"

"What do you think?"

The corners of his mouth turned up and his dimples deepened. "You're not going to faint on me again, are you?"

"That's the old Cammie Jo. No fainting. I promise."

He inhaled deeply when she sank into the plush mattress and pulled him down on top of her.

"Are you sure about this? I want the moment to be just right."

"You got a condom on you?"

"Yes."

"No kidding?"

"No kidding."

"Then darling, it's just the right moment."

She was ready, willing and able to make love to the man of her dreams. She'd waited so long for this moment and now that it was finally here, she wasn't the least bit afraid. With Mack, there was nothing to fear. He made her feel safe and loved and oh, so ready to indulge in her most wicked midnight fantasies.

Mack groaned and kissed her with all the passion he possessed. Many minutes later they broke apart, panting for air.

"There's something I must tell you first," she confessed.

More secrets? He froze, preparing himself for whatever she might say. Because no matter what words tripped off her tongue, he wasn't leaving this room. He loved this woman. Loved her with a depth of emotion that shook him to the core of his previously held beliefs. Whatever she had to say, whatever challenges she presented, they would solve them together.

"What is it, Sugar Plum?" He peered down into her dear face and held his breath. His stomach turned to pudding and a thousand scary scenarios flipped through his head.

"I've…er…never done this before."

He blinked and a thickness of joyful tenderness wrapped around his heart.

"You're a virgin?" he whispered in awe.

"Uh-huh. Is that going to be a problem?"

He laughed, and damned if a tear didn't bead up at the corner of his eye. "No problem at all. We'll just take things nice and easy."

Her beautiful blue eyes, unchanged by contact lenses, unhidden by thick glasses, stared up at him.

She made him feel as if *he* could leap tall buildings in a single bound. For Cammie Jo he would do anything to keep that enduring smile on her face, that trusting light shining in her eyes.

Slowly, he unbuttoned her blouse, exposing her creamy skin and then he unhooked her bra.

Lord, she was incredible, soft and willing, her chest rising and falling with each quavering breath. A myriad of emotions washed over him, all of them good.

He brushed his lips along her bare belly and she giggled. He was light-headed, dizzy on Cammie Jo's sweet, sweet taste and the knowledge that he was to be her first and only lover.

Her nipples beaded in response to his mouth on her skin and he gleefully heeded their call. Mack suckled first one straining nipple and then the other, giving them equal attention. He kissed the fine sheen of perspiration that sprang up in the hollow between her breasts, his tongue eagerly laving the salty flavor.

While his lips were sinking into heaven, his fingers weren't lazy. He unsnapped her jeans, tugged down the zipper and slowly slid his hand beneath the waistband and past her satiny panties. He stroked her lovingly in the warm, moist spot between her thighs.

Cammie Jo groaned and arched her pelvis against his palm. Her eagerness sent his body into overdrive. He was literally consumed with the fire of desire. So much for nice and easy.

"Mack, oh Mack. I'm so hot for you. I don't think I can stand much more of this."

"Me either, Sugar Plum."

"Make love to me now. Hurry. Hurry."

Spurred on by her urgings, he stripped off his clothes in nothing flat and slipped on a condom. He tugged off her jeans and sent them sailing across the room and then made short work of her panties. In a matter of seconds, they lay stretched out, bodies entwined on top of the downy comforter.

He rolled over onto his back and lifted Cammie Jo up to straddle his waist. His erection throbbed eagerly against the sumptuous curve of her bottom.

"If it hurts, you tell me and we'll stop."

"I'm not afraid," she whispered. "I trust you."

Her words made his heart hitch. She trusted him and never, ever would he consciously violate that trust. Slowly, his eyes fixed on her face, alert for any signs of her discomfort. He eased her gently down on his burgeoning shaft.

What a snug fit! She was so tight and slick he almost lost it right then and there.

Cammie Jo gasped and he instantly froze, his hands spanning her tiny waist.

"No," she said, "don't stop."

"But I'm hurting you."

"No." Her breathing was raspy, her eyes wide with surprised pleasure. "I just feel exceedingly full. Go on."

After a few minutes of meeting with resistance, then slightly pulling back, he finally slid deep into her sweetness. He heard himself groan aloud with the wonderment of entering her body.

She was his. He was hers. Together, they became one person. One so much more than two alone.

She rocked forward in a maneuver so bold he had to close his eyes and bite down on his bottom lip to keep from crying out.

When he opened his eyes again, he saw tears tracking down her cheeks. Instantly, fear shot through him. "Oh, Cammie Jo. You're in pain. I'm sorry. So sorry."

She shook her head and smiled at him through her tears. "I'm crying because it feels so wonderful, because I'm so happy to be here with you, because I never thought this day would happen."

"Ah, Sugar Plum." His voice was gruff with unshed tears of his own. He cupped the back of her head in his palm and inched her face down to his so he could kiss those sweet lips.

She broke off the kiss after a few moments and then began to move over his shaft in a slow, seductive rhythm that sent goose bumps charging up his spine.

In beautiful slow motion, they made perfect love. She climaxed before he did. He felt her muscles tense around his erection, heard her cries of pure surprise and delight, smelled the scent of her womanhood. A few seconds later, his own release followed hers.

Cammie Jo lay spent, her body still wrapped around his, her head resting on his chest. Her hair lay damp against her scalp and her heart was filled with a rapture so great she scarcely dared breathe for fear that it was all a dream.

So this was what she'd been missing all these years. Incredible.

"I love you, Cammie Jo Lockhart," Mack whispered in her ear and combed his fingers through her hair. "Now and for always. Don't you ever forget it."

"And I love you, Mack McCaulley. To the very end of my days."

Epilogue

WILD WOMAN FOUND. Cammie Jo Lockhart Has What It Takes To Become A Wilderness Wife.

Cammie Jo stared down at Kay's latest article for *Metropolitan* magazine, then glanced at her friend, who looked resplendent in her wedding gown. The two women were in the church rectory waiting for the wedding march to begin. Shortly, Kay Freemont would become Mrs. Quinn Scofield.

``Thought you'd like to see the final draft.'' Kay grinned.

``Why are you thinking about me? It's your special day.''

``Because you're my best friend, silly. I'm always thinking about you. The story will run in the October issue, along with your engagement announcement. And the history of the totem, of course. I can't believe you actually wanted me to give away your secret to our readers.''

``If my story provokes just one shy woman to overcome her fears and follow her heart's desire,'' Cammie Jo said, ``then the power of the totem is strengthened by sharing, not weakened. The real magic is about believing in yourself.''

"I'm so glad you moved to Bear Creek." Kay's eyes twinkled. "And that you conceded to be my maid of honor."

"Two months ago I would never have imagined I would have such a wonderful friend, or that I would even possess the courage to walk down the aisle as her maid of honor."

"I'm so proud of you."

"I'm proud of you, too!"

They hugged each other, and tears of joy welled in their eyes.

"No crying," Cammie Jo said, passing Kay a tissue. "It'll ruin your gorgeous makeup."

Kay pressed the tissue delicately to her eyes. "You'll be walking down the aisle yourself, soon enough. Mack's a great guy. I'm so glad you found each other."

"Me too. He's opened up a whole new world for me and put me in contact with my past. You know he took me to Fairbanks last week, and we looked up my mother's relatives. I have aunts and uncles and cousins I never knew anything about. And I learned a lot of new things about my mother, as well."

"That's just great, Cammie Jo."

"And now that my aunts Hildegard, Coco and Kiki have decided to move to Bear Creek, too, I couldn't be happier."

"You deserve all the happiness in the world."

"So do you."

The swell of the music interrupted their second embrace.

Cammie Jo patted Kay's shoulder. ``Time to go.''

With her bouquet of lupines clutched in her hand, Cammie Jo opened the door and started down the aisle ahead of the bride.

The church was rustic, the organ was old and many of the guests were dressed in flannel and jeans. But to Cammie Jo, this was the most romantic wedding she'd ever attended, and she was honored to be part of it.

She moved to her place at the front of the church. Across from her stood Mack, Quinn's best man. Cammie Jo's heart almost burst at the sight of her handsome Alaskan bush pilot. Her man.

He smiled at her, his brown eyes full of love.

Soon, he silently mouthed. Soon it will be our turn. Then he surreptitiously lifted something out of his pocket for her to see.

The totem. As naughtily suggestive as always.

For good luck, his glance told her.

She shook her head. They didn't need luck. They had belief in their love to see them through. She couldn't wait for all the wonderful adventures that lay ahead of them. It was going to be one hell of a ride.

EAGER, ELIGIBLE & ALASKAN

Lori Wilde

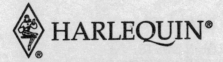

HARLEQUIN®

TORONTO • NEW YORK • LONDON
AMSTERDAM • PARIS • SYDNEY • HAMBURG
STOCKHOLM • ATHENS • TOKYO • MILAN • MADRID
PRAGUE • WARSAW • BUDAPEST • AUCKLAND

Dear Reader,

Take one prim-and-proper heiress who's reluctantly agreed to go on a cruise to Alaska. Put her in a stripper costume. Have someone hypnotize her at a costume party and tell her she's a vampish seductress by the name of Sexy Sadie. Drop her off in Bear Creek, Alaska, to meet the state's most eligible bachelor, who just happens to be laid-back, fun-loving Jake Gerard. A man who's finally decided he's had enough of wild women and wants to settle down.

I was writing this book during the tragedy of September 11, 2001. At first, it was very difficult for me to put my grief aside and get back to work. But the more I explored Jake and Sadie's relationship, the more they pulled me into their world. At last, I'd found a funny, happy place I could run to when reality got too dark.

If Jake and Sadie can provide you with just a few hours of escape, then I feel I have done my job. We read romance fiction not to forget our problems, but as a respite from our burdens. I hope you enjoy my story.

Best wishes,

Lori Wilde

Books by Lori Wilde

HARLEQUIN DUETS
63—BYE, BYE BACHELORHOOD
63—COAXING CUPID

HARLEQUIN BLAZE
30—A TOUCH OF SILK *Bachelors of Bear Creek, Bk. 1

To all the Duetters, you know who you are. Thanks for the virtual tea and sympathy, the great advice and late-night pep talks. You guys are the greatest.

1

"YOU ARE GETTING very sleepy."

Sarah Stanhope shifted her scantily clad fanny across the hard wooden chair. The blasted seat felt like a torture device direct from the Marquis de Sade collection. The way her luck was going, she'd probably pick up a splinter. She kept her knees primly pressed together, her back razor-straight and pretended she wasn't utterly humiliated as she sat on the stage in the *Alaskan Queen*'s grand ballroom.

"Please, try to concentrate," the hypnotist scolded. "Keep your eyes on the watch."

Hypnosis. What a load of hooey.

Sarah ignored the man standing in front of her and instead stared out at the audience garbed in a wide variety of costumes. She fixed her glare on Cleopatra and Marilyn Monroe, AKA her two best friends, Lizzy Magnason and Kim Bishop, respectively.

She flashed them a tight-lipped, I'll-get-even-with-you-for-this smile. Because of Cleo and Marilyn, she was stranded up here in front of a hundred people, dressed in this ridiculous stripper costume, while some silly man with a goofy-looking Gomez Adams mustache attempted to mesmerize her. If

Lizzy and Kim hadn't double-dared her, if they hadn't accused her of being a serious stick-in-the-mud without the slightest sense of humor, she wouldn't be in this predicament.

In the guise of celebrating Lizzy's birthday, they had lured Sarah on this ten-day Alaskan cruise. Once aboard, her friends admitted it was a ploy to get her to let her hair down and live a little. They were concerned because she spent too much time running the Stanhope vinegar empire and playing nursemaid to her ailing father (their words, not hers). Sarah herself resented neither working hard nor taking care of Papa. What she did resent was Lizzy and Kim force-feeding her their idea of a good time.

And the outrageous costume and cheesy, second-rate hypnotist weren't the worst of the surprises they'd sprung on her. There was also the rather disagreeable matter of Harvey Donovan.

Oh, Harvey was good-looking and he ran in their social circle. Actually, it was her own fault for not speaking up when Lizzy and Kim had oohed and aahed over what a "catch" he was.

She'd mumbled, "uh-huh," instead of saying what she really thought of him. Now the fact that Lizzy and Kim invited him along on the cruise in hopes of kindling a shipboard affair between the two of them went far beyond matchmaking and veered headlong into meddlesome busybody territory.

She had been polite about the fix-up so far, knowing her friends meant well. But she couldn't keep pretending she was the least bit interested in a man who never missed the opportunity to smirk at his reflection in mirrors.

And plate-glass windows and water puddles and the shiny chrome of his vintage Bentley.

Sarah flicked a quick glance to where Harvey—dressed rather aptly as Pepe Le Pew—sat in the front row next to the stage. He winked, pursed his lips and blew her a kiss.

Yuck. The mere idea of kissing him made her lust to scrub her mouth with a scouring pad.

She jerked her attention back to the hypnotist. Okay, this sideshow attraction was as corny as a grain silo, but it was better than watching Harvey make fish lips at her.

And to think she had nine more days of this.

"Concentrate," the hypnotist commanded.

Sighing deeply, Sarah complied and focused her attention on the pocket watch he dangled before her face.

"You are now falling into a deep, relaxing sleep."

Uh-huh. Sure.

"Sleep."

Her eyelids grew heavy.

"Deeper and deeper."

All right. Sarah closed her eyes. She would be a good sport and play along, but no way was this guy hypnotizing her. She did not have a suggestive mind.

"When I say the words *hot sex*, you will become a seductive striptease artist by the name of Sexy Sadie."

Yeah, that's happening. Not.

He kept talking, telling her all about this Sadie person, but his voice became a soft drone and Sarah couldn't really make out what he was saying. She decided to enjoy the delicious weightiness settling over her body and not worry what he was blabbing about.

"Married!" The hypnotist shouted and snapped his fingers.

Sarah opened her eyes. The audience applauded wildly.

She glanced at her watch and realized a good fifteen minutes had passed. She must have fallen asleep, and the hypnotist was convinced he'd actually put her under. Shaking her head at the gullibility of some people, she got up and marched offstage.

"Wait," the hypnotist said. "Miss, come back. I haven't deprogrammed you yet."

Sarah waved a hand. Deprogrammed, de-shmoe-grammed. As if that stuff really worked. Besides, she wasn't about to endure one more minute in the spotlight. She hated being on display.

Lizzy and Kim surrounded her. "You better go back up there and let the hypnotist do his thing."

"For heaven's sake, why? It's all a sham. Like late-night television dial-a-psychics."

"Because you're one hot stripper when you're Sexy Sadie," Lizzy teased. "Apparently, the apple doesn't fall far from the tree. No matter how much you'd like to pretend otherwise."

"What are you yammering on about?"

"We always suspected your mother's passionate nature was lurking beneath your prim-and-proper reserve, and boy, were we right. You knocked the crowd's socks off," Kim said.

Sarah felt as if an invisible hand had encircled her throat and was squeezing hard. They were wrong. She was nothing like her mother. Nothing.

"You can certainly shake your bon-bon." Lizzy nodded.

"You guys are nuttier than a Baby Ruth. I did not do anything untoward."

"You danced for the hypnotist."

"I did not."

"You did so, and we've got the pictures to prove it." Lizzy shoved a Polaroid photograph into her hand.

Sarah's jaw dropped. In the photograph, her head was thrown back, her boobs were thrust out and she was twirling away like some...some... dance-hall floozy.

It was suddenly hard to breathe. She couldn't believe she had performed such an indecent act in front of all these people.

"Sarah?" Kim asked. "Are you all right?"

"I need some air," she said, reluctant to let her friends know how upset she was. Cheeks aflame with shame, she turned on her heels—the stupid three-inch hooker heels Lizzy and Kim had conned her into wearing—and sprinted for the nearest exit.

"Sarah, wait for me!" Harvey called after her.

That only made her flee faster. She had to get back to her cabin and change out of these clothes— if you could call four scraps of lacy material cloth-ing—ASAP.

She skipped the elevators and plunged down the

stairwell. She zigged. She zagged. And she thought she had given Harvey the slip, until she rounded the corner that led to her stateroom and spotted him waiting patiently at her cabin door.

"Sarah! There you are, you naughty girl."

The length of the corridor stretched between them, but he was coming toward her at a fast clip.

Egads! She turned and took off again. Fine. Great. Call her a coward if you wished, but she wasn't going to stay here fending off a giant sex-starved skunk.

Although she hated strutting around in this ridiculous costume, there were worse things. Like spending the next nine days on a cruise with two well-meaning but misguided friends and one overly amorous polecat. She would just go ashore in the sleepy hamlet where they were currently docked, find a telephone since her cell phone was in her room, call Papa and have him send his private plane to pick her up.

She took the elevator to the disembarkation level and rushed down the gangplank, fearful Pepe Le Pew was not far behind. She felt like that beleaguered little black cartoon kitty with the stripe of white paint down her back.

"Sarah!" Harvey alias Pepe called again at the same time her heels hit the dock.

Clackety, clackety, clack. Her shoes clattered as she scurried faster.

Not fast enough. She heard him breathing behind her.

"Wait up."

Couldn't the guy take a hint? She welcomed his

attentions about as enthusiastically as a case of scurvy.

"Hot sex."

Sarah stopped short. She blinked, turned around and stared at Pepe, who stood only a few feet away, a wide grin on his face.

"What? What did you say?"

"Hot sex."

JAKE GERARD LOUNGED in a canvas deck chair with the August afternoon sun warm on his face. He'd put in many long hours for the past month and even though it was Saturday, his busiest day of the week, he'd granted himself a few much-needed hours of R and R before returning to the restaurant in time for the dinner rush. Since the sun stayed out until midnight, most tourists didn't show up for dinner until 10:00 p.m.

He was surrounded by beautiful women. Candy, a shapely blonde from Memphis, had just popped the top on a can of beer for him. Lola, a green-eyed brunette from Kansas City, was feeding him slices of cantaloupe. Amber of the coal-black hair, from Tucson, baited his hook and dropped his fishing line into placid waters.

Letting gorgeous babes cater to his every whim probably wasn't such a smart idea. He certainly didn't wish to lead them on—he was into having a good time, not breaking hearts—and he'd made it clear from the moment he'd met them that his new business venture came before pleasure. But what was the point in advertising for a wife if you couldn't enjoy the search?

Keep things light. That was his motto. Or rather, it had been until in an impulsive move last winter, he had decided to go in with his three friends on their Alaskan-bachelors-looking-to-get-hitched ad in *Metropolitan* magazine. At the time, he hadn't been quite certain he was ready for marriage, but he could now clearly see the benefits of the national exposure.

Bear Creek, Alaska, which had once lamented the lopsided ratio of ten men to every woman, had been inundated with females since the ad appeared in the June issue. His search for the right wife could take a long time. Might even stretch out over years. Especially since he'd just bought the Paradise Diner and was working hard to turn it into a first-class dining establishment.

Jake grinned. Yep. No sense in making a premature commitment simply because his buddies were falling in love right and left.

You can't hurry love, so the saying goes.

"Another slice of cantaloupe, Jake?" Lola asked.

"No thanks, darlin'. But you can go back to massagin' my neck if you wish."

"Hey," Candy whined. "It's my turn to rub your neck."

"You got to slather him down with sunscreen, you don't get to massage him, too," Amber chimed in.

"Ladies, ladies. There's plenty of me to go around."

"Hey," Lola interrupted. "What's going on over there?"

Jake shaded his eyes and squinted in the direction Lola pointed. "Well, I'll be damned," he said.

Jake pushed his sunglasses up on his forehead, picked up the binoculars resting on the dock beside him and focused in for a closer look.

A giant skunk was stalking after a determined young red-haired woman striding away from the ship. She was dressed in a very provocative outfit. Black bustier, black fishnet stockings, red garter, red-and-black feather boa and three-inch heels that showed off a heart-stopping pair of legs. *Whoaaaa, baby.*

"Are they putting on some kind of skit or something?" asked Candy, who although extremely lovely, wasn't exactly the brightest bulb in the box.

"I think they're having a fight," Amber said.

The skunk, who upon closer examination looked rather like Pepe Le Pew, grabbed hold of the inadequately clad woman's elbow. In the next moment, he was pulling her into his arms and planting a big kiss on her lips.

"If they were fightin', I think they're making up now." Jake put the binoculars down and shook his head. Crazy tourists.

"No, wait. Look. She's really trouncing him. Apparently he's not a very good kisser." Candy laid a hand on Jake's arm.

Sure enough, the red-haired woman was whapping the skunk over the head with his own tail. Vicious.

He grinned to himself. He liked skimpily dressed, feisty, redheaded women.

Face facts, Gerard, you like women, period.

"Don't you think you should intervene?" Lola nibbled her bottom lip in distress.

"Oh, it looks like she can hold her own."

"Not for her sake, for the skunk's."

"You got a point."

He would hate to see law-enforcement authorities haul the redhead's sassy little patooty off to jail for first-degree skunkslaughter. Plus, he'd be lying if he said he wasn't dying for an up-close-and-personal gander at that dynamite body. He rose to his feet and started down the dock to where Miss Oops-I-Forgot-to-Wear-Pants had Pepe on his knees groveling for mercy.

Jake stuck his sunglasses in his shirt pocket and strolled at his normal leisurely pace over to where the ship was docked. Some of the ship's crew members were also watching the altercation, and it appeared they were passing cash back and forth, betting on the outcome. Jake's money was on the redhead, all the way.

By the time he reached them, the skunk was blubbering like a baby. "You got tail fuzz in my eye."

"That Pepe Le Pew costume has obviously gone to your head," she said. "Do you think you can just manhandle a woman, kiss her against her will and get away with it?"

"No." Pepe sniffed. "I was wrong, okay? I shouldn't have kissed you without your permission."

"Need any help, folks?" Jake drawled.

Pepe scrambled to his feet. "This is a private matter between my lady and me."

"Baloney." She glared at Pepe. To Jake she said, "I've never seen this skunk before in my life."

"You're just saying that because of what happened onstage," Pepe said.

"I am not," she protested.

"So does he know you?" Jake cocked his head.

"Yes," declared Pepe.

"No," denied the woman.

"You don't understand," Pepe said to Jake. "She's not in her right mind."

"Are you saying I'm crazy? Don't make me take that tail to you again," she threatened.

Pepe raised his arms to block his face in a defensive gesture. "No, you're not crazy. It's just that…"

"Yes?" Her hands were on her hips, jaw thrust out, her forehead furrowed in a frown. She was clearly waiting for him to say the wrong thing so she'd have an excuse to light into him again.

Jake felt downright sorry for old Pepe. "Maybe you better move along."

"I'm not leaving without her," Pepe stubbornly insisted.

He couldn't blame the skunk on that account. Jake slanted the woman a sidelong glance. Her waist-length red hair hung down her back in a shower of curls and soft little wisps framed her heart-shaped face. Ultra-long lashes accentuated brilliant blue eyes, and a sprinkling of freckles dotted her cute little nose. Her peaches-and-cream complexion looked good enough to eat.

And what about those lips. Yowza! Ripe and full and crimson. Any man's dream.

She laid a hand on Jake's shoulder and his pulse beat faster. "Could you do me a favor?"

"For you, Blue Eyes, anything."

"Make him go away."

Jake looked at Pepe and lifted his shoulders. "Sorry bud, but the lady doesn't want to have anything to do with you."

Pepe glowered at him.

"Shoo." She flapped her hands at Pepe. "Buzz off."

"You're making a huge mistake," Pepe said to Jake. "You don't know what you're getting into."

"Just leave us alone," she said.

Jake stepped toward Pepe. He was a lover not a fighter, but the woman had made her desires clear. "I suggest you head on back to the ship."

"Okay. Fine. She's your problem now, but don't say I didn't warn you. She's not what she seems." With that strange warning, Pepe picked up his bedraggled tail, tossed it over his arm and marched up the gangplank.

"Thank God, he's gone." She sighed and slipped her arm through Jake's as if he were a longtime friend. For some reason the gesture caused an odd, but very agreeable squeezing sensation in the pit of his stomach. "I thought he'd never leave."

"Quite the stinker. Eh?"

"You've got a pretty face, honey. Don't stretch for funny, too."

"Ouch. The lady's been sharpening her tongue."

"Don't you forget it." She smiled and stuck the tip of that wicked pink tongue out at him. Yipes!

She fanned a hand at her neck. "Whew. With all that exertion, I worked up a sweat. Can we find a shady spot? Five minutes in the sun and I freckle like nobody's business."

He'd been incredibly polite so far, sneaking surreptitious glances at that incredible body of hers rather than full-out ogling. But her comment drew his eyes to that sensational cleavage on prominent display. Sure enough, tiny beads of perspiration had collected at the hollow of her throat and started to trickle south in a languid trail to Never Never Land.

He escorted her down the dock, a sense of pride swelling his chest. He felt oddly possessive and the feeling startled him. She smelled absolutely terrific. A pleasing combination of roses and soap and healthy woman.

"By the way," she said. "I'm Sadie. What's your name?"

"Jake, Jake Gerard."

Or at least that's what Jake thought he said. He was so bowled over by Sadie's sexy strut, the feel of her arm tucked against his side and the silky sound of her voice filling his ears that he might have recited the Pledge of Allegiance for all he knew.

"Nice to meet you, Jake. Appreciate your help with Pepe."

"Don't mention it."

She shaded her eyes against the sun with her free hand and sized up Amber, Lola and Candy, who were heading toward them with the fishing gear in tow. Compared to worldly Sadie, they looked like innocent schoolgirls out to build sand castles.

"Your posse?" Sadie lifted an eyebrow at him.

She was quick on the uptake. He had to give her credit.

"Nah. Just some fans to while away the hours with."

"Fans?" She leveled him with an amused expression. "My, you do think a lot of yourself, don'tcha?"

He loved the way she teased. Loved the ways she used her body as an instrument of seduction. She was boldly flirtatious, but not the least bit simpering. Nothing hesitant or covert about her. This was a woman who knew exactly the sexual impact she had on a man. An impact with the force of say…oh…a head-on collision between two supersonic jets.

"I'm not as egotistical as I sound. They really are fans."

"Fans of what? Cock-and-bull stories?"

He had to laugh. "You're a tough one to impress."

Sadie scrutinized him with a long, lingering glance. "Just because I'm dressed like this doesn't mean I'm easy. As Pepe found out, the hard way."

Right there on the spot, Jake got an honest-to-Pete shiver that began at the base of his spine and worked its way straight to the pleasure center of his brain. Unbidden, he glanced down at her shapely figure. He couldn't help noticing that the ribbon closures on her bustier had loosened while they were walking. Her navel peeped coyly out at him between the gaps in the lace. His eyes epoxied themselves to that heavenly spot that swayed gently with each step she took.

If I was struck by a meteor at this very moment, I'd die a happy man.

Jake tripped on a raised plank and stumbled into her.

"You okay?" She placed a hand on his shoulder to steady him.

Way more than okay, doll-face.

She pursed her lips in concern and for a moment there Jake thought he wouldn't be able to stop himself from kissing her. But he didn't want to make the same mistake as that erstwhile skunk. Damn. He understood with complete clarity why Pepe had been so besotted with her.

Watch it, Gerard, remember you've sworn off the kind of women who parade around in public wearing racy undies.

Ah, but there was no harm in a little flirtation. Right? Wasn't that what he'd been doing with Lola and Amber and Candy?

Yeah, but this was different and he knew it from the moment he gazed into the depths of those baby blues.

Unlike Lola and Candy and Amber, Sadie was dangerous.

She was exactly the kind of woman he fell head over heels for and always ended up getting hurt over. Everyone told him he was attracted to the wrong kind of women and he had to admit it was true. What he *needed* was someone nice and steady. A sensible woman with strong nurturing instincts. He needed an anchor.

And yet the thought of marrying an anchor gave him the heebie-jeebies. He loved his freedom and wasn't so sure he was ready to surrender it to a lady.

But he was also something of a fraud, cruising along on his Lothario reputation. He liked to flirt— and with Bear Creek being a tourist town there was plenty of opportunity for that—but he wasn't a playboy, no matter what people might think. He simply enjoyed having a good time. His childhood had been a traumatic one. As a consequence, he spent most of his adulthood trying to forget the past by living every moment to the fullest.

Was it his fault that women responded to his fun-loving nature and wanted to be around him? He'd dated a lot, to be sure, but even his closest friends would be surprised to discover how few of those dates he actually took to bed.

"Hey, Jake." Lola's voice snapped him from his musings. She and Amber and Candy were staring at him expectantly. "Who's your new friend?"

He blinked, cleared his throat and made the introductions. The women sized each other up like heavyweight prizefighters before the opening bell.

"Nice to meet you all." Sadie smiled.

"We saw you having it out with that skunk," Candy said. "Is he your boyfriend?"

"Heavens, no." Sadie rolled her eyes. "Just some creepy guy who was coming on to me."

Lola scrutinized Sadie's skimpy outfit. "I can see where he might have gotten the wrong impression about you."

Meow. Jake darted his gaze back to Sadie and wondered if the fur was about to fly.

Instead of taking affront at Lola's catty comment, however, Sadie shrugged nonchalantly. "I was performing in a vaudeville revue on board the cruise ship."

"You mean like a stripper?" Candy asked.

"Yes. Before the gig on the *Alaskan Queen,* I worked for Strippers-Are-Us. You know, people order a stripper for bachelor parties, things like that."

"Did you ever pop out of a cake?" Candy asked. "I always wanted to pop out of a cake."

"A time or two," Sadie admitted. "But I hated getting frosting in my hair. My specialty was the Naughty Nurse. Nobody could twirl a stethoscope like me. Not even the girls who were stripping in order to put themselves through nursing school."

He shouldn't be having impure thoughts, but damned if he couldn't easily visualize Sadie doing some very creative things with medical supplies. Ulp.

"But," Sadie continued. "I've come to realize I bring the Pepe Le Pews of the world upon myself. That's why I've decided to give up exotic dancing." She glanced over at Jake. "And this town certainly looks like a promising place for a fresh start."

Wow. She'd just walked off that cruise ship and decided to begin a new life?

He gazed at her with deepening admiration. He understood impulsiveness, had alternately followed it and fought it his whole life, with varying degrees of success. What she had done took a lot of courage, even if it wasn't particularly prudent.

Jake grinned. He'd never been overly fond of prudent women.

"Well, then if you've decided to come here to start over you must have heard about the Bear Creek bachelors," Amber said, possessively slipping her arm through Jake's on his right side, while Sadie still clung to his left.

"Nope." Sadie shook her head.

"Come on, you're saying you didn't know that Quinn Scofield, Mack McCaulley, Caleb Greenleaf and Jake here advertised in *Metropolitan*." Lola frowned hard at first Amber and then Sadie. Clearly she was distressed at not having an arm to latch on to. Jake felt like the last Rolaid at a chili cook-off.

"Sorry, never heard of the publication," Sadie said.

Jake could tell the other three women didn't believe her, but he did. Sadie hadn't come to their seaside community trolling for a husband. She just wanted a new adventure.

Boy, could he relate. He'd been chasing adventures his whole life. From scaling Mount McKinley with his pal Quinn, to skydiving with Mack, to sailing with Caleb in a hurricane. He was always up for testing the limits of fun.

"Come on. You mean to tell us that you just

happened to come ashore—'' Candy waved a hand at Sadie's outfit ''—dressed in that skimpy stripper get-up and yet you claim to have no idea that Jake's looking to get married?''

2

"Married."

Sarah blinked and then stared at the people surrounding her. Three very pretty women and...what was this! She had her arm linked with a man so ruggedly handsome he took her breath away.

Bewildered, she jerked away from him and stepped back, pulse pumping at a furious pace. Where was she? What was going on? Who were these people? And omigosh, was that the *Alaskan Queen* pulling away from the dock?

All her belongings were on board that cruise ship. Her identification, her money, her cell phone...her clothes. Plus Lizzy and Kim were bound to be frantic when they found her gone.

The realization that she had not only suffered a slight memory lapse but that she was standing nearly naked on a dock in some teeny town in Alaska with a group of total strangers sucker-punched her in the gut.

Sarah raised her hands to cover her bare cleavage and struggled to remain calm. She would call Papa. Just as she'd been intent on doing when she'd run away from Harvey. Nothing had changed. She was in control.

"Could I..." She looked to the man who was

studying her with a quizzical expression on his face and a sudden shyness swept over her. "Could you...er...show me to a phone? And if it's not too much trouble, perhaps you might find me some clothes to wear?"

"Sure."

He seemed really nice and helpful. If only she could remember his name.

"Thank you so much."

Sarah smiled her gratitude and fought to calm the panic clawing through her. What had happened and why couldn't she remember?

Darn this strange mental fogginess. She felt as if she'd awakened from a long slumber. *Just call me Sarah Van Winkle.*

Jake turned to his three female companions. "You ladies go ahead and enjoy the rest of your afternoon."

"But, Jake," whined the blonde, "we're leaving town tomorrow morning."

"And you never did take any of us out on a date like you promised," the brunette said.

"I'll come see you off tomorrow," he told them.

None of the women looked very happy. In fact, not only were they pouting, but they were shooting daggers with their eyes at Sarah. What was their deal? Did they think she wanted to steal away their man? Ha! Not hardly.

Lordy, they could have him. The last thing she wanted was to get involved with Mr.-Quirky-Grin-Wilderness-Man from some back country Alaskan town.

Not that he wasn't cute, she quickly amended,

because he was definitely a hunk. But she was a city girl through and through, and she wanted to go home. Now.

Jake turned to Sarah. "This way. I own a bed-and-breakfast called the Red Lantern just down the road. You can use the phone and wait there while I find you something to wear."

He took her hand and led her up the rustic wooden walkway toward the town. The tenderness of his gesture surprised her and made Sarah wonder if he sensed her apprehension.

She wasn't accustomed to being on her own, and she felt a little lost. She was almost always with her father, since she worked as his executive assistant, and she still lived at home with him. In fact, if Papa hadn't insisted she accept Lizzy and Kim's invitation to take the cruise, she would never have gone.

They strolled past quaint, picturesque shops, a radio station with the call letters KCRK and a bar named the Happy Puffin. Passersby eyed them, openly staring at Sarah and her skimpy outfit. This was like one of those humiliating dreams where you were nude in public and couldn't find a place to hide.

Except, unfortunately, she wasn't dreaming.

"What was your name again?" she asked, drawing upon years of good breeding to distract herself from her shameful situation. When in doubt, fall back on the good old Stanhope motto: Decorum in the face of disaster.

"Jake."

"Oh, yes. I'd forgotten."

She averted her eyes from his frankly inquisitive gaze. He was probably wondering if she had the shortest short-term memory on record. Actually, she was kind of wondering that herself. What was wrong with her? She shivered.

"Goodness, woman, you've got goose bumps on top of goose bumps."

Sarah glanced down at her arms and realized he was quite correct. Between the barely-there stripper costume, the cool summer breeze wafting off the mountains and the shadows from the store awnings, she was freezing.

Jake had stopped walking. He dropped her hand and unbuttoned his shirt.

"Wh…what are you doing?"

"You're cold."

"I'll be fine."

He didn't bother arguing with her, he just stripped off his shirt, exposing his chest to the world at large without the slightest hint of awkwardness. Stepping close, he wrapped the shirt around her shoulders.

"There. All better?"

She nodded, a lump the size of a cruise ship anchor in her throat. But it wasn't better. Not at all.

Now, not only was she still dressed in this flimsy floozy outfit, but her escort was as bare-chested as the day he was born.

And what a chest he possessed.

Sarah's mouth went dry. She didn't mean to stare, but she simply couldn't help herself. It was like ignoring the statue of David, like stuffing one's fingers in one's ears at a Van Cliburn competition, like ordering a diet shake at a gourmet restaurant.

Not gonna happen.

She breached every rule of good taste and proper comportment. Sarah Jane Stanhope, heiress to the one-hundred-year-old, four-generation San Francisco Stanhope vinegar empire, ogled.

He was extraordinarily, unmistakably male, no ifs, ands or buts about it. He stood before her in nothing but faded cutoffs that hung entirely too low on his lean hips. His chest was hard, solid and rippled with more muscles than those buff guys strutting their stuff in infomercials for work-out equipment.

A patch of hair the color of glazed caramel spread from his breastbone outward then swirled downward past his navel to where it disappeared beneath the waistband of his jeans. His legs were long and strong, his skin tanned, his big feet encased in a pair of scuffed deck shoes.

He was more naked than not. Just like her.

Suddenly, Sarah was no longer cold in the balmy seventy-degree weather but hot, hot, hot.

A grin quirked the corner of his mouth. "Do you see anything you like?"

I will not blush, and I will not rise to the bait and give him a response.

"Thank you for the use of your shirt," she said stiffly and drew the garment more tightly around her shoulders as if the ridiculously thin material could protect her from his overt sexuality.

Her ploy didn't work. Not at all. The shirt

smelled of his warm, heady masculinity. His spicy, tantalizing guy scent assailed her nostrils, and teased her brain with a enticing blend of male pheromones.

She noticed he was studying her with serious intent. As if he saw so much more than her outward appearance—which at this moment was appallingly blatant.

He wanted her. Raw desire lurked in his hazel eyes. But not in the same needy, creepy way that Harvey had wanted her. She felt at once both pleased and flustered.

His gaze rocketed to hers. His eyes narrowed and he stared. Hard. For a good long minute.

Her breath fled from her body and a silly, girlish dizziness washed over her. Getting flustered over a good-looking man was *so* not like her.

"The telephone?" she croaked and forced herself to wrench her gaze from his.

"Ah, yes. The phone." He extended his arm and she thought he was going to offer her his hand again, but he seemed to think better of it and instead threaded his fingers through his sexily disheveled hair. He inclined his head northward. "This way."

She followed him to the entrance of a three-story country inn painted a deep, vibrant green with white accent trim. The house appeared to have been constructed sometime in the nineteen-twenties. It had a bucolic, cozy feel and from the minute they stepped through the front door, Sarah felt as if she'd come home.

The sensation disturbed her. As a woman born

and bred in the heart of San Francisco, she'd never felt an affinity for small towns or the countryside. She loved a fast-paced lifestyle. She could not adequately explain her attraction to this place.

Or for that matter, to this man beside her.

She went in for polished, courtly men, not rugged, outdoorsy types who thought nothing of stripping to their naked skin.

They were greeted at the door by an enthusiastic Siberian husky who Jake introduced as Lulu, the consummate kleptomaniac. He warned her not to leave her belongings unattended around Lulu.

What belongings? She could hardly get any less encumbered than she was at the present moment.

Nervously, she petted the inquisitive dog, who kept sniffing her feather boa. She was a bit afraid of large creatures, but Lulu seemed friendly enough.

Jake shooed the husky away and led Sarah to the front desk. He pointed out the phone.

"Um...I was wondering if you had somewhere a bit more private." She nodded toward the guests in the lobby, then swept a hand at her outfit.

"Oh, yeah. Sure. You can use the phone in my bedroom."

His bedroom.

Yikes. Which was worse? Standing in the lobby enduring everyone's stares and getting sniffed by a dog who looked big enough to take her arm off at the elbow or being invited into the inner sanctum of a strange man's bedroom?

But he didn't leave her any choice, he'd already

rounded the desk and started down the hallway. "Come on."

She scurried after him, wondering what on earth she'd gotten herself into when she'd abandoned the *Alaskan Queen*.

"Here you go." He opened the door to his bedroom, and ushered her over the threshold.

His bed looked as if it had been ordered straight from the Mountain Man's Dream Cottage catalog. It was king-size—but of course, she couldn't imagine this large man crammed into anything smaller—and hand-carved from sturdy cedar. The headboard was covered in elk hide, while the bed itself was made up with a bold red-and-black checkered quilt and lots of red-and-black throw pillows.

The bed mesmerized her. She couldn't seem to stop staring at it. To think he slept here every night.

She caught her breath. She would bet her bottom dollar that he rarely slept here alone.

"Phone's on the bedside table."

She remained acutely aware of his bare chest. Whew, there was no denying this was one genetically blessed specimen of the male sex. Ducking her head, she slipped his shirt from around her shoulders and handed it over to him.

"You might want this."

"Oh yeah. I almost forgot about it." He took the shirt from her but didn't put it back on.

He probably was one of those egotistical guys who loved parading around naked to the waist, inviting feminine eyes to enjoy the honed contours of his body.

Well, if that was his game, he was barking up the wrong girl. She wasn't the sort of woman who willy-nilly followed her physical desires. Come to think of it, she'd never followed her physical desires, willy-nilly or otherwise.

"I'll just let you make your call while I see if I can find something for you to wear." He sized her up with a sidelong glance. "Size six." He said it as a statement, not a question.

"Uh-huh," Sarah said, amazed at his ability to guess a woman's dress size. No doubt he'd had lots of practice dressing and undressing women.

"And you'd probably like a more comfortable pair of shoes." He eyed her three-inch-heels with a speculative gleam. "Seven? Seven and a half?"

"Eight," she admitted.

"Gotcha covered." To her utter relief, he put his shirt back on, and then shut the door behind him.

Sarah collapsed on the bed—which smelled distractingly of him—exhaled deeply and realized to her chagrin, she was trembling.

"Calm down, everything is going to be all right," she soothed herself. "Just as soon as you get hold of Papa."

She picked up the phone and dialed her father's private number.

"Hello," said a cool, feminine voice that did not belong to Margaret, their housekeeper.

"Oh," Sarah said. "Please excuse me. I must have the wrong number."

She hung up, certain that she had misdialed and punched in the numbers a second time.

The same woman answered.

"Oops," Sarah apologized. "Silly me. Looks like I goofed again."

"Who are you trying to reach?"

"Charles Stanhope."

"He's in the shower right now. May I take a message?"

It took a second for her words to sink in. A strange woman was answering her father's private phone line while he was in the shower? Sarah gripped the phone tighter, telling herself the woman must have misunderstood her.

And then she heard it.

The sound of her father's voice. Singing an off-key rendition of "Love Is In the Air."

"Hang on a minute," the woman said. "I think he just stepped out of the tub."

But Sarah had no intention of hanging on. Heart pounding, she slammed down the receiver and stared at the phone as if it had morphed into a poisonous snake.

Could her father actually have a girlfriend? But how and when and why?

Okay, scratch the why. That was self-evident. No wonder he'd been adamant that she go on the cruise. In her absence, he'd been planning a romantic tête-à-tête.

Sarah twisted a lock of hair around her forefinger. She normally wore it up in a chignon but had taken it down for the costume party. Now her hairstyle felt messy and out of control. Just like her current situation.

Had she been standing in the way of her father's love life all these years? Spending so much time with him, fussing over him after he suffered that mild heart attack five years earlier that she'd cramped his style?

She was reluctant to admit she'd never thought of Papa marrying again. They'd always been so close, she'd just assumed he hadn't wanted or needed anything more than a loving daughter. How could she have been so thoughtless and so naive?

Sarah buried her face in her hands.

Maybe the woman wasn't a girlfriend. Maybe this was a one-time fling. She couldn't really call her father again and run the risk of embarrassing him. If he had wanted her to know about this woman, wouldn't he have just come right out and told her?

Well then, if he didn't want her to know about his romantic escapade, she couldn't let on that she'd discovered his secret. Sarah tried to call her friends on board the ship but couldn't get through. How in the world was she going to get home?

CLEOPATRA AND MARILYN Monroe were knocking on his cabin door. Harvey Donovan, who had changed out of the Pepe Le Pew costume after he had come back from Bear Creek, peered out through the peephole.

He was still plenty steamed at Sarah for taking up with that Alaskan wild man, and he couldn't wait to get back at her for rejecting her.

Marilyn and Cleo knocked again.

He opened the door a crack. "Hey, what's going on?"

"Harvey," Cleopatra, otherwise known as Lizzy Magnason said. "Have you seen Sarah? We've been searching for her ever since the ship left port."

He smiled smugly and put a suggestive tone in his voice. "Have I seen Sarah."

"She's with you?" Kim asked.

Harvey wriggled his eyebrows. "Yep."

"Can we talk to her?"

He glanced over his shoulder, pretending to look at Sarah stretched out on his bed. He lowered his voice. "She's sleeping right now. 'Fraid she's a little done in."

"So you two got together?" Lizzy grinned. "That's just great. But be gentle with her. She's led a sheltered life."

"Don't you worry about Sarah. I'll treat her right. And just so you know, we've decided to spend the rest of the cruise in my cabin ordering room service. If you know what I mean."

"Oh, okay. We'll see you guys later."

Harvey shut the door and leaned against it. There. As long as Lizzy and Kim thought Sarah was holed up with him, no one would know she was missing. Let her be stranded as Sexy Sadie in Bear Creek without any money or clothes. That ought to show snotty Miss Priss Stanhope a thing or two.

HIS BEDROOM DOOR stood slightly ajar. Jake peered in to find Sadie sitting on the edge of his bed staring off into space, a pensive expression on her face. His pulse bounded erratically at the sight of her.

He was carrying a stack of clothing borrowed from his surrogate sister, Meggie Scofield. Meggie was a hell of a gal who could be counted on to come through for him any time, any place.

He loved Meggie and her older brother Quinn as much as if they were his biological siblings. After Jake's father had been killed in an accident fishing for Alaskan King crab and his mother had died of cancer brought on by a broken heart, the Scofields had taken him in and raised him as their son. He owed them a debt of gratitude he could never repay. Without the Scofields, Jake knew he would have ended up in a great deal of trouble.

"Knock, knock." He moved over the threshold, and crossed the room to deposit the clothes on the bed beside Sadie. She seemed distant, distracted, and quite different from the bold, self-confident woman who had brought Pepe Le Pew to his knees.

He recognized what was behind the changes in her. The consequences of impulsive ship-jumping had come back to haunt her.

Remorse. He understood that feeling far too well. How many times had he done something on a whim and lived to regret it? A million. A billion? Hell, did numbers even go that high?

"Sadie?"

"Huh?" She looked up, clearly startled by his appearance.

"Brought you some clothes."

She was watching him with a hefty dose of uncertainty. "What did you call me?"

"Er...Sadie."

"How did you know my nickname? That was my mother's pet name for me, and no one else ever uses it."

"But you told me that was your name."

"Did I?" She looked seriously confused. "That's so weird."

"What do most people call you?"

"Sarah."

"Okay. If that's what you want, I can call you Sarah."

She hesitated a moment. "No, call me Sadie. It's nice to hear it again after all these years."

"Your mother doesn't call you that anymore?"

"My mother took off when I was three, and she died not long after that."

"That's tough. I lost my father when I was ten, my mom when I was twelve."

"I'm so sorry."

They looked at each other and for a moment shared something in their common loss, but Jake quickly shrugged off the feeling. Talking about unpleasant things made him uncomfortable.

"It was a long time ago."

He stuck his hands into the pocket of his jeans and fingered the gold nugget on his key chain. The nugget his father had given him before making that last fatal fishing trip.

"This is a reminder, son," his father had said, while his mother stood to one side, begging him not to go. Fishing for Alaskan King crab was one of the most dangerous jobs in the world, but it paid phenomenally and his father loved it. "Remember, you come from Gerard stock. We're a long line of adventurers and we don't let anything stand in our way."

"Not even love," his mother had said, sobbing.

His father laid a gentle hand on her shoulder. "A man's gotta do what a man's gotta do, Gretchen. Jake's no different. Listen to me, son. Your grandfather was a gambler who wrestled grizzly bears, your great-grandfather worked on the Whitehorse railroad in awful conditions. And your great-great grandfather came to Alaska looking for gold. He found this nugget, and I'm giving it to you as a reminder that you have to be true to yourself, no matter what. You're a Gerard, boy, stand proud."

Then his father had tousled Jake's hair, kissed his mother goodbye and that was the last time he had ever seen him.

And from then on, Jake had striven to live up to his family's illustrious reputation.

Sadie sighed, thankfully breaking into his memory. Jake had a desperate urge to make a joke; anything to lighten the mood.

"I don't remember much about my mother," Sadie said, still hung up on her trip down memory lane. "She smelled like strawberries, and she loved to dance. She was crazy about the Beatles. "Sexy Sadie" was her favorite song. Guess that's where the nickname came from. What do you remember about your mother?"

Other than the fact his mother had constantly told him never to get married? That he would end up breaking some poor girl's heart simply because he was a Gerard. He remembered Gretchen being irrevocably sad at the loss of her husband and bitter that an adventuresome life had always meant more to him than she did.

Jake nodded at the telephone, anxious to get Sadie off the gloomy subject of dead parents. "Did you get hold of the person you were trying to call?"

"No." She shook her head. "Sort of leaves me up Bear Creek without a paddle."

He grinned at her attempt at humor. "Indeed. Is there anything I can do to help?"

"Well, I need a job and a place to stay for a while. Do you know if anybody in town is hiring temporary help?"

"It's kinda late in the year. Tourist season will be over in a couple of weeks."

"Oh." She looked dejected.

He needed help at the diner. Especially since he had started renovating the place from a short-order grill into a real restaurant with linen tablecloths and expensive silverware and a gourmet menu. He'd even changed the name from the Paradise Diner to the Paradise Inn. But was offering her a job such a smart thing to do when he was so attracted to her?

Don't do it. She'll get you into trouble. She's a stripper.

A stripper who was trying to turn over a new leaf. He'd made more than his share of mistakes in his life and he was a big believer in second chances. Who was he to judge anyone?

Remember your ill-fated affair with Renny? Remember why you went in with the guys on that Metropolitan *ad in the first place?*

Yeah. He remembered. All too well. After being deceived by Renny, he'd finally gotten weary of fast, fun-loving women.

Let's see, there'd been Jenna, Miss-I've-Got-a-Death-Wish bush pilot from Juneau, who called him a wussy when he refused to crawl out on the wing of her plane and fix a loose flap—*in flight*. He'd about had a heart attack when she'd made him take the controls while she repaired it.

Following Jenna, he'd dated Cara, Miss If-I-Insult-That-Guy-at-the-End-of-the-Bar-You'll-Beat-Him-Up-For-Me-Right? After her came, Miss I-Can-Open-Anything-With-My-Teeth, Miss Keep-the-Engine-Running-While-I-Go-Get-the-Beer and last but not least, Mrs. Oh-Did-I-Forget-to-Tell-You-I'm-Married, Renny.

He'd felt like a clichéd chump escaping out her bedroom window with his pants around his ankles while her husband came barreling through the front door demanding to know whose car was in the driveway. Never again.

That's when he'd agreed to go in with Quinn and Mack and Caleb on the *Metropolitan* ad.

"I'll take any kind of job," Sarah pleaded, pulling him from his litany of reasons why he shouldn't get involved with another irresponsible woman. "Sweeping up, washing dishes. I really need the money. I'd appreciate any help you can give me."

When she turned those wide blue eyes on him, Jake knew he was a goner. She worried her bottom lip between her teeth, tugging his gaze helplessly to her full, rich mouth.

So what if she had gorgeous lips? Pink and pretty and pouty. And so what if she was a damsel in distress and he had the potential to be her knight in shining armor. He didn't need the aggravation. He wasn't going to do it. He wasn't.

"Anything at all," she echoed.

"Are you married?"

She shook her head. "No."

"You're sure?"

"Pretty sure." She laughed and crinkled up her cute little nose. "In fact, you can quote me on that."

He was supposed to be cleaning up his act. He was supposed to be looking for a wife. He was supposed to be...ah, hell, he'd never been any good at doing what he was supposed to.

In spite of everything, he heard himself asking her, "Ever wait tables?"

"No, but I'm a quick learner."

"Would you like to come work for me at my restaurant?"

Her dazzling white smile did fizzy-type things to his heart.

"That's so generous of you. Thank you, thank you very much."

The next thing he knew she had sprung off the bed and thrown her arms around his neck. Her bustier pressed erotically against his chest, her silk stockings rubbed against his leg, her wild red hair tickled his nose. She hugged him. Tight.

Ack! He was in serious jeopardy.

She pulled back and looked up at him. "Now all I need is a place to stay. Any suggestions?"

He knew what she was angling for. *Just say no!*

His nostrils were filled with the scent of her. His eyes overflowed with the sight of her. His hands tingled with the feel of her soft skin. He knew this was not a good idea but he couldn't stop his mouth from dropping open, his lips from flapping dangerously and his tongue forming the words.

"You could bunk here at the B&B."

Wrong answer. His conscience clicked its tongue.

Mark my words, Gerard, you're going to live to regret this hasty decision.

3

HOW HARD COULD waiting on tables be? Sarah asked herself the next day. After all, she helped run a vinegar empire, schlepping food from the kitchen to the dining room shouldn't be any big deal.

Right? Right, Sarah assured herself and tightened her apron strings. Except she had never held a position outside the family business. Sure, she'd studied at the Institute of Culinary Arts in San Francisco for three years and she could make a wicked chocolate soufflé, but a good cook did not a good waitress make.

You can do this. You're a Stanhope.

She squared her shoulders, lifted her chin and stared at her reflection in the mirror of the diner's ladies room. Her hair was pulled back in her signature chignon, her white uniform blouse was buttoned up tight and her face was completely devoid of makeup. Not by choice, but out of necessity. She had no money to buy lipstick and mascara and her cosmetic kit was on the cruise ship bobbing contentedly on its journey through the Inside Passage.

Perhaps that was just as well. Last night, Jake Gerard had seemed far too attracted to her. Without benefit of the tarty makeup she'd worn for the shipboard costume party he would no doubt be less impressed with her.

That was good. Things were complicated enough now without having to acknowledge the flicker of something potent that tickled her tummy whenever she glanced his way.

The man gives you a bellyache for crying out loud. Stop mooning over him.

But the bellyache felt kind of good.

It's just because he called you Sadie. Don't go transferring your childhood longings onto him.

Still, she couldn't stop thinking about him. The man was—for lack of a better word—delicious. He possessed thick, longish brown-sugar hair that just begged for feminine fingers to thread through it. And those eyes!

Warm, intelligent, charming green eyes dappled with interesting brown flecks. And please, don't forget the shape of his face—rugged, angular and yet appealingly symmetrical.

Oh and his hands…

Okay, Sarah, okay. We get the picture. He's a hottie. So what? It's not like anything can come of this attraction. Forget about it.

Ah, easy to say, but not so easy to erase the epitome of manhood from one's mind. Especially when one happened to be working beside such a paragon during the day and sleeping in the very next bedroom at night.

Sarah shook her head. She'd been listening to Lizzy and Kim for too long. Enough. She had work to do.

Taking a deep breath, she washed her hands, left the bathroom and marched into the diner, ready, willing and able for her first day on the job.

Jake was behind the bar stocking up on Bloody Mary and Mimosa fixings for the Sunday brunch tourist crowd. The rest of his staff hurried to and fro, getting ready for business. He barely noticed the hustle and bustle, but when Sarah entered the dining area, his attention was immediately drawn to her. For one crazy moment, his heart actually stuttered to a stop.

Then started up again with a restless, pounding rhythm. He had already introduced her to her co-workers and shown her around the place but every time he laid eyes on her, he got this strange jolt of awareness.

She looked especially formal this morning—the picture of propriety. Quite a difference from the bustier-clad goddess he'd sheltered the night before.

And she wasn't wearing a speck of makeup, but that only added to her allure, not detracted from it. Without gobs of mascara, her big blue eyes seemed even larger.

And those lips!

She came over. "What do I do now?"

Stop staring, dimwit.

Desperately, Jake swung his gaze away and searched the dining room, looking for a chore to get her out of his vicinity. "Uh…you fill the salt and pepper shakers." He waved toward a table lined with the leaded crystal shakers that he'd blown a bundle on. Nothing too good for the Paradise.

"Got it." She nodded with the seriousness of a Marine marching into battle.

Jake breathed a sigh of relief when she moved off. He was going to have to stop getting so worked up around her. Now, what had he been doing before she intruded upon his senses?

Oh, yes, stocking the bar.

He'd managed to focus his concentration back on the task at hand when Quinn slipped in through the employees' side door.

"Hey, buddy," Quinn said. This was the first time they'd seen each other since Quinn and Kay had returned from their honeymoon on Friday.

Jake came around the corner of the bar, slapped Quinn on the back. "How's Kay? How was Hawaii? How's married life?"

Quinn's eyes lit up at the mention of his new bride. "Kay's an incredible woman. I thank the northern lights every day that I found her."

"You two are great together," Jake admitted and felt a kick of jealousy. Would he ever have that kind of relationship with a woman? Or was he, as his mother had contended, too cursed with his father's restless genes to ever make anyone a good husband?

"Hawaii was unbelievable. You gotta go there sometime. As for married life..." Quinn's grin turned downright sinful. "I know you're the hot sex expert, but believe me, buddy, you haven't had hot sex until you've made love with your soul mate."

The sound of shattering glass interrupted their discussion. Jake jerked his gaze over to Sadie. A busted salt shaker lay at her feet, a startled expression on her face.

Their eyes met.

"Oops," she exclaimed and tossed a pinch of salt over her left shoulder.

"New waitress?" Quinn sized up Sadie and then arched an eyebrow at him. "Looks like you've been a busy boy."

"Don't go jumping to any ridiculous conclusions. I'll tell you about it later."

"Later then." Quinn raised his palm and scooted back out the side door.

Jake went to retrieve a broom and dustpan from the supply closet and hurried over to bend down beside Sadie.

She was picking gingerly through the glass shards. "I'm so sorry," she apologized. "I don't really know what happened. I sort of blanked out there for a moment."

"Watch out," he said, adrenaline pumping through his blood like water through a fire hose. "Let me do that. I don't want you to cut those pretty fingers."

"Oh, futz. This is crystal, isn't it?"

"Yes, but don't worry about it."

"I'm working here, aren't I? As a waitress."

"Er…yes." What was this all about?

"Oh. Okay. That's what I thought. I want you to deduct the cost of this shaker from my paycheck."

Jake stared at her, confused by what she'd just

said. Had he heard her correctly? Had she forgotten he had hired her? Nah. He must have misunderstood. Nobody was that ditzy. Not even a runaway cruise ship stripper.

She reached for another shard of glass at the same time he went for it with the whisk broom. Their hands brushed.

And he forgot about everything else except the touch of her velvet soft skin. They crouched side by side, their mouths inches apart. She blinked at him. Tendrils of hair had fallen from the bun atop her head. Her voice was different. Deeper, more provocative. Like yesterday on the dock. Her cheeks were flushed. She looked aroused. Excited.

And sexy as hell.

Back off, Gerard. Pronto.

He rose to his feet, salt shaker guts littered in his dustpan. With a thumb, he pointed in the direction of the kitchen. "I'm just gonna go dispose of this. You carry on."

"With filling the salt shakers?"

"Uh-huh."

What was happening to him? Why did he feel dazed and kind of foggy-headed? Why was his heart leap-frogging around in his chest? Jake shook his head.

This had to stop. Delectable as Sadie was, he simply would not let himself pursue the attraction. He really was looking to get married. Just as soon as he put the Paradise Diner, recently renamed the Paradise Inn, on the map. That was his first priority and he wasn't going to let a pretty face trip him up.

He sauntered into the kitchen on the pretext of dumping the broken glass. He stayed to try and soothe his Cordon Bleu trained chef, Henri Renault, who was put out because Jake had neglected to order fresh dill for the salmon.

When he suggested the chef use the dried spice, he thought the round little man might take a butcher knife to him. The guy might cook like the Galloping Gourmet but he was as temperamental as a pop music diva.

"Out! Out of my kitchen," Henri thundered and pointed toward the dining room.

"Sheesh, okay. I'm going." Jake raised his palms in surrender and found himself back through the swinging doors in dangerous Sadie territory.

Damn. When had his own restaurant morphed into a virtual land mine?

The hostess had opened up for business, and Jake was heartened to see a string of customers lining up for the brunch buffet. He glanced around, looking for Sadie.

He spotted his best friend, Mack, with his fiancée, Cammie Jo, queuing up at the omelette station but there was no sign of his erstwhile employee.

"Hey, guys." Jake went over to greet Mack and Cammie Jo. "How are things?"

"Great." Cammie Jo grinned at him. "We met your new waitress. Sadie's adorable."

Adorable? Humph. The woman was a real nuisance. Breaking salt shakers, distracting his attention from his work, sneaking off when she should be waiting tables.

"And she's cute, too," Mack said, nudging him in the ribs. "Ask her out."

Cute? Well, he couldn't argue with that. But he wasn't about to ask her out. Who cared if she was cute? Nuisance trumped cute and adorable every time out of the gate.

"Do you happen to know where she went?" Jake asked.

"Sure. She was completely panicked because she didn't have any makeup. I loaned her mine and she went to put it on."

"Oh."

"Look." Cammie Jo inclined her head. "Here she comes now."

Jake turned and watched Sadie sashay toward them. He snagged in a ragged breath. She was just about the hottest thing he had ever seen.

Gone was the librarian's bun riding atop her head. Instead, the dismaying mass of auburn corkscrews tumbled over her shoulders and down her back like liquid fire. It was the same kind of incredible, sexy hair that every woman in every one of his fantasies possessed. His hands twitched to dive into that wild tangle of play-with-me curls. The notion shifted his testosterone level to maximum dosage.

She had undone the top three buttons of her white uniform blouse and tucked the collar under to expose an enticing expanse of creamy skin. She had also rolled up the waistband of her black skirt, shortening the hemline to reveal far more leg than good taste allowed, and she'd troweled her face with a heavy-duty application of cosmetics.

He felt a definite stirring below the belt. Mr. Friendly was making his presence known.

And Mr. Friendly was clearly impressed by the changes in Sadie's appearance. What a freakin' embarrassment.

Down, boy, he admonished his wayward body part, to absolutely no avail.

Sadie strutted across the room with the swagger of a woman who knew men were staring at her. Jake swallowed. Hard.

Oh, Sexy Sadie. What had she done to herself? He couldn't figure her out. One minute she was poised and demure, the next outlandishly kooky.

He knew that he should favor the demure Sadie and in his head, he did, but he couldn't deny the facts. Mr. Friendly much preferred Miss Kook.

She waltzed over and handed Cammie Jo a small makeup bag. "You're a lifesaver."

"Don't mention it." Cammie Jo grinned. "Anytime you need to borrow something just let me know."

"Thanks." Sadie boldly winked at Jake and then said to Cammie Jo, "I better get back to work before my boss chews my fanny."

Boy, would he love to chew her soft fanny.

That was his main problem.

She pranced off, the fanny in question beckoning to him provocatively.

"You got a live one on your hands, buddy," Mack teased. "Better watch your step."

"Tell me," Jake mumbled under his breath.

After wishing his friends a good brunch, Jake went over to help out behind the bar. Unfortunately, his attention kept wandering to wherever Sadie happened to be.

The woman was outrageous. She flirted with the men, but then just as easily won over the female customers. She even got gripey old Gus, his desk clerk at the B&B, to crack a smile. Jake decided the woman could persuade the salmon to stop spawning if she so desired.

Good thing she was so captivating, because within the first twenty minutes it was painfully obvious she was a horrible waitress. She couldn't keep decaf beverages straight from the caffeinated variety. She mixed up customers' orders and lost their tickets. But she laughed so sweetly and cajoled so nicely, no one got upset with her.

No one, that is, except Jake.

The woman was a hazard, a menace, a distraction. Every time she leaned over a table to refill a coffee cup, he got an eyeful of generous cleavage and Mr. Friendly sat up to take notice. Jake forced his gaze from her chest, but then his eyes got hung up on a long, lean length of leg. From supple thigh to perfectly shaped ankle, he couldn't stop staring.

He was burning up from the inside out. His skin sizzled as if he'd been lying in the full heat of a tropical sun. His scalp tingled. His stomach burned. His brain was scorched.

And as for his other body parts...well...enough was enough. There was only so much a fella could take.

You got it bad, buddy and that ain't good.

He needed a cold shower and a heaping dose of

common sense before he did something really stupid like follow his natural instincts and ask her out.

Sadie bellied up to the bar and gave an undershorts-melting grin. "I need two Bloody Harrys."

"Bloody Harrys?"

She crinkled her nose. "That's not right, is it?"

"Don't think so."

"Wait." She nibbled her bottom lip, taking his gaze prisoner once more. "Don't tell me. That'll be two Dirty Marys."

"Dirty Marys?"

"Darn. That's not right, either."

"I think you're mixing up your references. Alcoholic beverages, vs. Clint Eastwood movies."

"I've got it," she crowed and proudly placed her hand on his. Jake's heart thumped like a tomtom. Her scent invaded his nose, scrambled his mind. "That'll be two Dirty Harrys."

"Two Dirty Harrys it is," he croaked.

He made two Bloody Marys and hoped like heck that that was what the customers had ordered. Strange though, that a woman who had worked as an entertainer on a cruise ship didn't know her cocktails.

Okay, so she's a lousy waitress with a bad memory, Mr. Friendly argued. *But get a load of that body.*

The skin on the back of his hand still blazed where she'd touched him, and if he thought he'd been hot before, well, he'd just hopped from the proverbial frying pan into the depths of Dante's inferno.

Huffing in a breath, he dragged a palm down his

face. What in the hell was wrong with him? Maybe he was reacting so strongly to Sadie because it had been, let's see…eight months since Renny. Eight long months without sex. For Jake, that was an eternity.

"I'll be back in a minute," he told his bartender, Linc Crenshaw.

He tugged off his apron and dropped it onto the bar. He told himself he was going into the kitchen to check on the food preparation but the truth was he had to get away from Sadie.

The kitchen was steamy hot and filled with sizzling noises that nudged his core body temperature even higher. The radio perched in the window over the sink was blasting some song about sexual starvation that seemed very apropos to the situation at hand. He needed relief and he needed it now.

What about the walk-in freezer installed in the connecting hallway between the diner and the B&B?

Perfect. That ought to cool off his incendiary libido. He hurried through the back door of the kitchen, and down the corridor to the freezer.

He stepped inside. Ah. Frigid air swirled around him. Yes. Cold was what settled an Alaskan man's soul.

Jake plunked down on a box of frozen chicken parts, took a deep breath and savored the frosty sensation filling his lungs.

He was in control now. No more Sadie meltdown. What had come over him anyway? She was just a woman—albeit an incredibly sexy one—but just a woman all the same. He could resist her. He would. Yes, all right, so they were going to be working together by day and her bedroom was adjacent to his at night, but she wouldn't be in town long. Women like Sadie never stayed put.

Just when he thought he'd regrouped enough to return to the dining room, the freezer door opened and in bopped Sadie.

Oh, for crying out loud.

"Eek!" she cried, spun around and grabbed for the door.

Jake heard a solid "click" but he didn't think anything about it, he was that overwhelmed by her presence. He stood.

"What's wrong?"

"Oh." She laughed shakily. "I didn't see you sitting there. You scared me half to death."

"What are you doing in here?"

"Linc sent me after vanilla ice cream. Somebody ordered a milkshake."

"Sadie," he said. "Your job is to wait tables, not fetch and carry for Linc."

"I know, but he was really swamped. Everyone was complaining about their drink orders. Apparently he doesn't make Dirty Harrys the way you do."

"Imagine that," Jake said.

"I better fetch the ice cream and get back."

"It's heavy. I'll carry it for you."

"Oh, okay." She moved to open the freezer door but it didn't budge. She pushed harder. "I think it's stuck."

"Hang on. Let me try."

He came over to the door and gave it a solid shove. His wrist flexed against the exertion. Ouch.

He used his body as a battering ram, but the door still wouldn't give. Then he remembered the solid clicking sound the lock had made when Sadie grabbed for the door in her panic. The errant lock that slipped too easily. The lock he had planned on repairing but hadn't gotten around to. Uh-oh.

Apparently, she reached the same conclusion at the same time he did. Their eyes met.

They were locked in a freezer. Trapped. Alone. Together.

FIVE MINUTES OF POUNDING on the door and calling for help later, Jake had to admit defeat. He turned his head, searching for the source of his frustrations and found her perched on the box of frozen chicken parts he'd vacated earlier, rhythmically swinging her legs.

"You're wasting a lot of lung power," she observed.

"How so?"

"They can't hear us from the kitchen. Not with the radio blasting and dishes clattering and the sounds of food cooking."

"You got any bright ideas how we'll get out of here? I mean, you were the one who locked us in."

"Ah," she said. "I was wondering how long it'd take you to get around to blaming me."

"I'm not blaming you."

Jake sighed in exasperation and stabbed chilly fingers through his hair. He'd known the freezer lock was faulty when he bought the diner. The blame rested clearly on his shoulders.

"That snide remark you made suggests otherwise," she said.

"I did not make a snide remark."

"Did."

"Did not."

"You said I was the one who locked us in here."

"Maybe you're just feeling guilty for trapping us."

She angled him a saucy smile. "Maybe I did it on purpose."

"What!"

"Not so loud." Sadie winced and scrunched her shoulders up around her ears.

Okay, he shouldn't have shouted. That wasn't cool. But he was feeling so...so...what?

Backed into a corner?

"I was just joking," she said. "Jeeze Louise."

Jake smiled back at her in lieu of an apology. When had he gotten so uptight? It most certainly wasn't like him. Jake Gerard rolled with the punches. Just like his father and his father's father and his father's father's father. Just ask anyone. He was a laid-back guy. Not much bugged him.

So big deal if they were locked in here together. Not the end of the world by any stretch of the imagination.

"You know," she pointed out rather sensibly, "It shouldn't be long before Linc comes looking for the ice cream."

"You're right." He nodded.

Silence fell. One minute passed. Then two. Then three.

They avoided looking at one another. Jake paced the four-by-four-foot space. Sadie hummed under her breath.

Pace, pace, turn. Pace, pace, turn.

He dropped a quick glance in her direction and his gaze snagged on her spectacular display of cleavage. The pearl buttons were undone to the top of her bra. If he tilted his head just a little bit he could see frilly lace peeking at him. The soft rise and fall of her breathing held him prisoner. How had the woman managed to turn a simple white cotton blouse into a instrument of sexual torture?

Then, through his fog of physical arousal, he realized Sadie was shivering.

"You're cold."

"Let me guess, you were the star of your class."

"There you go with that wicked tongue again."

"Honey," she drawled. "You ain't seen nothing yet."

She might be cold but Jake's insides blazed hotter than a butane torch.

Where in the hell was Linc?

Her teeth chattered. She hugged herself and hunched her shoulders forward.

"Come here," he said, fighting every sensible bone in his body—which granted wasn't many—urging him not to do this.

"Wh-what?"

"Come here." He opened his arms. "Let's share body heat."

"I thought you'd never ask." She leaped off the box and hurled herself straight into his embrace.

He tensed at their body contact. Mr. Friendly jumped for joy. She certainly couldn't mistake his arousal for anything other than what it was. She wrapped her arms around his upper torso and he pulled her flush against his chest.

"How's that?" he asked huskily.

"Nice."

"Warmer?"

"Oh, yeah."

She was incredibly soft, incredibly curvaceous. Her mass of copper-colored hair, as tantalizing as silk, brushed his cheek. He took a deep breath and the sweet, womanly scent of her filled his head, adding another layer to the chaotic haze clouding his thoughts.

It was as if he'd downed a dozen of her Dirty Harrys. He felt inebriated, intoxicated, crocked right out of his gourd and the strongest thing he'd had to drink all morning was orange juice. This sensation had to be an aberration. Some sort of weird vitamin C high.

Jake looked into her eyes. Oooh, damn. Mistake.

Those eyes deep and blue as the ocean invited him to come right in and swim a spell.

Somebody throw me a life preserver. Now.

Too late.

Her pouty, lipstick-moistened mouth beckoned him, urging him to forget that he was supposed to be seriously searching for a wife. She made him want to forget everything.

He looked into her eyes again and he could not

deny the electrical surge of something powerful that sparked between them. He lowered his head.

She made a soft, startled-yet-pleased sound.

Every muscle fiber in his body tensed.

She lifted her chin and blinked those baby blues.

There was only so much a red-blooded man could take.

4

OH...MY...GOSH.

His arms banded her like steel cables. His lips plumbed hers. His hands cradled her buttocks. She reveled in his strength, his warmth, his unique scent.

He ate her up and she allowed herself to be consumed.

She absorbed his flavor, extended her tongue to meet his. They explored each other like kids let loose in a toy store. Part of the way through the kiss, she peeped at him. His eyes were closed. Aw, Jake was a romantic. Her heart thumped faster.

Kissing him was sooo much better than she imagined, and she'd been vividly picturing this all morning. His mouth was hot, his tongue accomplished. Had she ever in her life received such a toe-curling smooch?

Sadie searched her memory banks, but between the cold of the freezer and the contrasting heat of Jake's body and the warm moistness of his lips, she couldn't seem to think straight.

In fact, she couldn't think at all.

She'd been having these little memory blips she couldn't quite explain. Was her attraction to him causing the gaps in her recall? Had sexual chemistry short-circuited her brain?

Interesting theory. Was Jake so potent, so virile, so decidedly male, he could make any woman forget her own name?

I'd vote for that. Heck, she would vote for anything just as long as Jake was involved.

She threaded her arms around his neck, arched her back and dragged his head downward in a desperate attempt to draw him closer into her. This guy was a pistol and a half and with those deadly lips of his it wouldn't take much to have her cocked, loaded and ready for...*bare.*

Not that a walk-in freezer was exactly conducive for lovemaking, but hey, Sexy Sadie was the kind of girl who would try anything once. No shrinking violet she. When she saw something she wanted she went after it. No regrets, no remorse, no second-guessing. And she wanted Jake Gerard.

She pulled his shirt tail from the waistband of his pants and slid her hands upward. He hissed in his breath as her icy palms touched his hot torso.

"What are you doing?" he croaked.

"Warming my hands." She was lying and they both knew it.

"Sadie..."

"Yes?"

"Maybe it's not such a good idea for you to have your hands up my shirt."

"No?"

He shook his head.

"Why not?"

"'Cause you're turning me on."

"I am?"

"Don't play coy. You know exactly what you're doing to me."

"And that's a bad thing?"

"Yes."

"How come?"

"Because I can't do this."

"Why not?"

"Well, for one thing we're locked in the freezer in my place of business."

"But that's not your main objection."

"No."

"Then why did you offer to share body heat?"

"You were shivering so hard I thought you were going to rattle the teeth right out of your head."

"And you kissed me because…?"

"A mistake in judgment."

"Oh." She blinked. "I get it."

"Get what?"

"You don't think a cruise ship stripper is good enough for a successful restaurateur."

"Come on, Sadie, I never said that."

"You didn't have to."

"You're wrong."

"Am I?"

"Yes. Believe me, much as I would love to, I can't let myself get sexually involved with you. I'm looking to settle down, Sadie. I want a wife."

"And I'm not wife material."

"It's not that…honestly, it's just I need certain things from a woman."

"Things I can't supply?"

She looked into his face and her tummy swooped.

Passion blazed in his eyes, but so did confusion. He was conflicted between his physical needs and his emotional desires. She couldn't give him what he needed. She'd walked off the cruise ship without a cent to her name. She didn't know where she was going or what she wanted out of life. She certainly was not prepared to become anyone's wife.

"Come on. This doesn't have to lead anywhere. Can't we just enjoy each other?"

His gaze was on hers. Her hands were inside his shirt. She wished he would kiss her again, blot out the uncertainty swimming around in both their heads.

She moistened her mouth with her tongue. He bit down hard on his bottom lip, fighting his impulses. She knew he would have kissed her again. She felt him wavering.

Except, auspiciously or inauspiciously, depending on your point of view, Linc chose that moment to open the freezer door.

"Oh! I'm sorry. I didn't know I was interrupting something." Linc said and backed out.

"No, don't go!" Jake cried and lunged for the door.

JAKE STARED at the stack of invoices in front of him and tried to concentrate on the work at hand. After that freezer fiasco, he'd hurried over to the B&B on the pretext of going over the books, but that had been nothing but a dodge. He had an accountant. No reason for him to be sorting through the bills, but he needed something to do far, far away from Sadie.

If he wasn't careful, that killer-diller body of hers was going to be his undoing. Not to mention that smile and her laugh and the way she batted those ultra-long eyelashes at him.

Oh man, oh man, oh man. He was in a serious pickle. This…this…*thing* he felt for Sadie was counterproductive.

Counterproductive? That was like saying winter in the Arctic Circle was a little chilly.

Face it, Gerard, you screwed up big-time.

Despite all his assertions to the contrary, he'd gone and done it again. He'd acted on impulse, allowed Mr. Friendly to run the show. Just the way he'd been doing since he hit puberty.

Hadn't he learned anything in his thirty years?

Ack! Cease and desist. No more thinking about her.

But no matter how he chided himself, Jake couldn't stop waxing about those heart-stopping moments in the freezer.

Why had he kissed her?

She's not the one. She can't be the one. She's too much like the women you've dated before. She's too much like you.

Clearly, from the way she'd responded—running her soft, delicate hands up inside his shirt, returning his kiss with abandon—he'd opened up a Pandora's box of illicit passion.

The woman was a bomb and he'd lit her fuse. Now everything was threatening to blow up in his face. Hi-yi-yi.

Realizing what he had inadvertently started, Jake chuffed out a deep breath. He wanted her and that's all there was to it and he wasn't accustomed to denying himself. Before eight months ago, before he'd taken out the ad with his friends, before he'd made the decision to try to settle down for good, he would have made love to her in the freezer and done his masculine Gerard family background proud.

Sadie had been willing. Oh, yes. And so had he, but he was no longer free to act on his desires and that was driving him around the bend.

Keeping relationships light and superficial had worked for him in his youth, but no more. He wanted a partnership, a real love match, like Quinn had found with Kay and Mack with Cammie Jo.

His friends had convinced him that his mother was wrong. That he could find the right woman and live happily ever after.

But could he?

Maybe Sadie is that woman, a tiny voice in the back of his head whispered.

Jake snorted. Who was he kidding? Sadie was fickle, impulsive, mercurial. One day she was a dancer on a cruise ship. The next day she'd gone AWOL and was waiting tables in Bear Creek. Who knew where she'd end up next week?

No. If he was going to do this holy matrimony thing, then he was going to do it right. No instant replay of his parents' tragic marriage. No more following Mr. Friendly.

And he was making his plans for the future by transforming the Paradise into a four-star establishment. When his restaurant and B&B became as legendary as he envisioned—appearing in guidebooks, being featured on the travel channel, hosting celebrities and dignitaries alike—then he would make the kind of money to support his wife and kids in style.

Then, he would meet and fall in love with a sweet, prudent, practical woman.

It was a tall order and he knew it, but he could not give in to Mr. Friendly's desperate urgings. He would not accomplish his goals if he allowed himself to be sidetracked by Sexy Sadie.

A knock sounded the door.

"Come in," he said and for one moment, he found himself wishing Sadie was on the other side of that barrier.

The door swung open and Caleb Greenleaf, the town's resident poet and naturalist, sauntered across the room and dropped into the chair opposite Jake's desk.

Caleb wasn't any closer to finding a wife than he was. Since Quinn and Mack had found their ladyloves, he and Caleb had taken to hanging out together more, even though they were quite different. Caleb was quiet, somber and studious whereas Jake was boisterous, fun-loving and action-oriented. Still, the two of them forged a deeper friendship over the course of the summer, sharing their laments at being left out of the matrimonial loop.

"Hey," Caleb said.

"What's up?" Jake greeted his buddy.

"Brought you the latest batch of letters from the

lovelorn responding to the *Metropolitan* ad. They're all yours. I've decided to give up the search.''

"What? You're kidding.''

Caleb shrugged. "I haven't met a single woman who's really interested me.''

"Not one?" Jake asked, immediately thinking of Sadie. "But hundreds of women have come to town, and we've gotten almost a thousand letters.''

"Can't help it.''

"You're still hung up on her, aren't you?''

"Her who?''

"Don't play dumb. The woman who broke your heart when you were a teenager. What I can't figure out is why you've never told any of us her name.''

Caleb waved a hand. "She's not the reason.''

"Go ahead, lie to yourself.''

"So do you want the letters or not?" Caleb snapped, clearly anxious for Jake to leave the subject of his anonymous lost love.

Jake eyed the stack. Receiving letters from women eager to marry an Alaskan bachelor had been exciting at first, but now, he didn't feel the slightest urge to read them. Only one woman had hooked his attention, and she was the wrong woman for him.

So look through them. Maybe someone else will pique your interest.

Listlessly, he leafed through the stack of correspondence Caleb had tossed on his desk. When he saw the envelope with the return address of *Yodor's Guidebook,* his hopes leaped. He had forgotten he'd given them the same post-office box address they had used for the *Metropolitan* ad.

All right. This was what he'd been waiting for. Three weeks ago he'd written the managing editor asking them to review his restaurant in their prestigious publication.

He reached for the letter opener and sliced into the envelope. His heart thumped as he read the contents.

"What are you grinning about?" Caleb asked.

"They're sending a food critic to review the Paradise Inn. She'll be arriving on Friday."

"A woman?" Caleb grinned. "You're a shoe-in for that four-fork review."

Friday! That left him three days to prepare for the most important moment in his life.

As he mentally ran through his to-do list, one thing stuck out painfully clear. He couldn't have Sadie waiting on the critic, mixing up drinks, dropping salt shakers and the like.

He couldn't even risk having her in the same vicinity as the reviewer. Between her ineptitude as a waitress and the incredible distraction she caused in his head, he only had one choice.

Like it or not, in order to put his restaurant on the map and achieve his lifelong goals, he was going to have to fire her.

"THE FIRST MEETING of the Wild Women City Girls Club is now officially in session," announced the sleek-haired Charlize Theron look-alike seated in a booth at the back of the Paradise.

Sadie hurried over with the tea and finger sandwiches the blonde and her friends had ordered. At three-thirty in the afternoon, they were the only customers in the restaurant, and Sadie was the only waitress. Everyone else had gone on break.

The three women, one of whom was Jake's friend Cammie Jo, looked ready for fun. Sadie felt a twist of wistful longing. She wished she could slip into the booth beside them and absorb their enthusiastic energy.

"Here's your order." Sadie set their food on the table in front of them.

The blonde gave Sadie a curious once-over. "You're new to Bear Creek, aren't you?" She extended a hand and smiled warmly. "I'm Kay Scofield. A newcomer myself."

"And a newlywed," Cammie Jo added. "Plus, she's a super-duper journalist. She's the one who wrote the articles about the bachelors in *Metropolitan* magazine."

Kay blushed prettily. "Thanks, Cammie Jo."

"Not to mention that she's from New York and she's the president of our newly formed Wild Women City Girls Club," the third woman, a statuesque brunette said. "I'm Meggie Scofield, Kay's new sister-in-law. I loaned you the clothes."

"Oh yeah, thanks."

"You're more than welcome. Why don't you join us?" Meggie asked, indicating the empty space next to Cammie Jo. "We were just going discuss ways to bring Bear Creek into the new millennium, now that we've got so many young women moving to town."

Sadie glanced over her shoulder at the empty

restaurant. "I probably shouldn't. I'm sort of in dutch with Jake."

In dutch? That was the understatement of the year. At last count, she had broken six plates, four saucers, three cups and that leaded crystal salt shaker. Plus, she had sent that testy French chef into a tailspin when she'd asked him to fry a corny dog for a customer's toddler. She couldn't blame him if he decided to fire her, although she had no idea where she would go if he did.

"Jake is ready to skin me alive," she admitted to her new friends, as she slid into the seat beside Cammie Jo.

"Jake? As in Jake Gerard?" Meggie looked puzzled.

"Uh-huh."

"But he's the most laid-back man on the face of the earth. He never gets bent out of shape."

"Ha! He gets bent out of shape with me so much he could qualify as a pretzel," Sadie said.

"I noticed Jake's been acting really different lately," Kay said. "Ever since he bought the Paradise. Not like himself."

"That's true," Cammie Jo agreed. "He keeps telling Mack that he can't get hitched unless the Paradise is a success. Mack thinks he's using the restaurant as a stall because now that it's come down to the nitty gritty, he's too chicken."

"Oh?" Sadie asked, suddenly feeling breathless.

"Jake's always gone in for adventuresome women," Meggie supplied. "You know, fun-loving, no-strings-attached types. It goes back to his childhood. He's afraid he won't be able to commit to just one woman. He's afraid settling down will be dull and boring.''

"Boy, is he off-base.'' Kay grinned enthusiastically.

"Ditto,'' echoed Cammie Jo. "Although Mack and I are just engaged, I've gotta say nothing beats true love.''

"Well,'' Sadie ventured, not really understanding this whole thing. "If Jake's so scared, then why did he advertise in that magazine? Why put himself through this if monogamy goes against his nature?''

"Peer pressure for one. Jake hates to be left out.'' Meggie leaned in close and dropped her voice. "But secretly, Jake's a big old softy. I grew up with him, I should know.''

"Really?'' Sadie tilted her head.

"He likes to pretend he's a playboy, something to do with all the men in his family being rapscallions, but mostly it's an act.''

"No kidding?''

"Absolutely. More than anything he wants a home and family of his own, but he's afraid of messing up a good relationship if he gets one—he never got over losing his parents—so the poor guy dances all around the issue of marriage. He'll make someone a really good husband, if he would just get out of his own way and realize how much he really wants to be loved.''

Sadie's heart pinched when she remembered the way he'd hugged her to his chest, sharing his body heat. He *was* a generous guy.

With very generous lips.

Yo, baby.

One simple kiss from him, and they'd created enough steam to melt that box of chicken parts. What would happen, she dared to consider, if they ever made love?

Hell's bells, she'd probably evaporate in a cloud of very satisfied smoke. She sighed dreamily.

There will be no lovemaking with your boss, Sadie Stanhope. Absolutely none at all. You're looking for a new career, not a husband. Jake's looking for a wife and he certainly doesn't need you messing up his plans.

Unless he wanted her for his wife.

Just the idea made her sweat. She wasn't ready to get married. Not to Jake, not to anybody. For reasons she couldn't explain to herself, she felt like she'd just grabbed hold of life with both hands and had started living. She wanted to taste everything, try it all, inhale the world. Being a wife sounded a bit too stodgy. Even if she was married to a man like Jake.

Still, she couldn't help wondering what would have happened in the freezer if Linc hadn't shown up when he did. But Linc *had* interrupted and things hadn't gone beyond a few sizzling kisses.

Thank heavens.

So what if Jake was a dynamite kisser? So what if they seemed to have this explosive chemistry? That's all it was. A chemical reaction. No sense coming unglued over him. Especially since he'd made it clear he wasn't disrupting his plans for her.

Her resolve sounded sensible and right and practical and...boring.

Good, Sadie. That's exactly how it should be. You've spent too much of your time shaking your bon-bon onstage for people like Pepe Le Pew.

Well, no more. She was a woman of the world. And she would prove it to herself by not giving in to the temptation that urged her to go find Jake and kiss him silly.

"Sadie?"

She blinked to find all three members of the Wild Women City Girls Club were staring at her. "Uh-huh?"

"You don't happen to have a thing for Jake, do you?"

5

"HERE'S THE DEAL," Jake told his assembled crew that evening after they'd closed the restaurant. Busboys, wait staff, bartenders, cooks, his prize-winning chef and Sadie sat around a large dining-room table, all eyes trained on him. "A food critic from *Yodor's* is arriving on Friday to review the Paradise Inn."

The group cheered and applauded. Linc whistled.

Surreptitiously, Jake glanced Sadie's way, but he wasn't fooling her. She caught his gaze and winked boldly as if they shared some secret.

Lord but the woman was audacious.

And relentlessly flirtatious.

He had waited all day to make this announcement, mainly to put off telling Sadie she was fired. It was going to be damned hard looking into her smiling face and telling her he was canning her for incompetence.

That's not really why you're dumping her, Gerard. Admit the truth. You could just give her Friday off if this were only about the food critic's review. Face facts. You're scared to death that if she keeps working here you won't be able to resist temptation.

"This is a celebration." He ripped his gaze from Sadie's and indicated the iced champagne buckets at the end of the table with a nod. "But it's also a planning meeting. It's imperative that Friday night's dinner go off without a hitch and each and every one of you are integral to our success."

"Of course, I am zee most important part of your success," Henri said. "I am zee reason the critic would come to such a place as zis." He waved a disdainful hand at the restaurant.

Now that's who you should be firing.

Except he couldn't fire Henri. The arrogant chef—who was costing Jake a not-so-small fortune—was right about one thing. His reputation for culinary excellence was the sole reason the reviewer had agreed to come to Bear Creek.

Jake stroked the chef's ego, praising his talents to high heaven, then he spent the next half hour outlining his strategy for perfect service and a perfect meal.

Sadie's hand shot in the air.

He tried to ignore her, but she kept wriggling in her seat. Finally he had to acknowledge her question.

"Yes, Sadie, did you have a comment?"

"I know I haven't been in the restaurant business for very long…"

"One day to be exact," Henri sniffed contemptuously.

"That's right." She flashed the chef a brilliant smile that quelled him for a moment. "But I think you're making a mistake kowtowing to a VIP."

"Excuse me?" Jake blinked at her.

Enthusiasm fairly oozed from her pores. "You should treat all the customers as if they were VIPs."

"Ha!" Henri exclaimed. "As if zeeze crazy Alaskans could tell chateaubriand from Limburger cheese."

Everyone at the table turned to glare at the chef, who suddenly realized he'd let fly with too much opinion. He was, after all, surrounded by Alaskans.

"Sadie's right," Jake said. "Our standards should be the same for all our customers. Excellent food at an excellent price with excellent service."

"Hmph," grunted the chef. "I am warning you. If one more person orders zee corny dog with zee tater tots, I am walking out zee door and then we will see if your local citizens are really zee VIPs."

"Thank you for sharing your feelings, Henri. I promise no one will be ordering corny dogs and tater tots." Jake said.

Of course, he had a gaping hole the size of Wisconsin in the center of his tongue from biting down on it to keep from saying what he was really thinking, but it was worth the effort to keep Henri happy. Without the chef, he was sunk and they both knew it.

Jake inhaled sharply. If he managed to survive the making of this restaurant, then he would most definitely be ready for the give-and-take of marriage.

"Let's drink to the success of the Paradise Inn."

Corks were popped. Toasts were made. Champagne was drunk. Lively conversation filled the air and even Henri settled down after a couple of swigs of bubbly. Jake sent his staff home with promises of a big raise if Friday night came off without a hitch.

He'd had his meeting. He'd motivated his employees, and he'd soothed Henri's ruffled feathers.

Only one task remained, but it was a grim one.

Firing Sadie.

"Could you hang back a moment." He rested a hand on her shoulder as the others got up to leave. "I need to speak to you in private."

"Private, huh?"

A flicker of excitement lit her eyes like a blue flame and a corresponding stab of guilt arrowed through him. "Yes."

"Why, sure." She beamed at him. "I've got some great ideas on how to improve the restaurant."

"Um…that's nice."

"I was thinking you might want to replace the lighting with candles for the dinner hour and…"

"Have a seat."

He pulled out a chair for her. She plunked down. He waited until the last employee had driven out of the parking lot, before grabbing a chair of his own, and turning it around so he sat with the back of the chair against his chest.

"This is so thrilling." Sadie rubbed her palms together. "Just think, a food critic for *Yodor's* coming here. A good review will put your restaurant and Bear Creek on the map."

"One can only hope."

"I can't tell you how honored I am to be part of the process."

"Sadie..." He looked into her eyes. He wasn't a coward. He'd done more daredevil stunts by the age of thirteen than most men did in a lifetime, but facing Sadie and telling her she was fired was even more difficult than he'd imagined.

"Uh-huh."

"I've...er...noticed you've been having some trouble keeping your orders straight."

"But I did better this evening."

"I know."

"There's something else on your mind, isn't there?"

Did his face give him away, or was she just that perceptive in reading him? It was an unsettling thought.

"Listen," he said at the same time she said, "If this is about what happened this morning in the freezer..."

"Go ahead." He inclined his head.

"No, you."

"Ladies first, I insist."

She grinned. "Then you take the floor. I'm rarely confused for a lady."

There she was again with that suggestive innuendo that he loved but shouldn't.

"Please, say what's on your mind."

"I just wanted to thank you for taking a chance on me. I really, really appreciate it."

"Uh...you're welcome."

Why was he saying this? Why didn't he just come out with it and tell her this arrangement wasn't working and that he was going to have to let her go?

"I know I made some mistakes this morning but I'm really trying harder."

"Sadie…"

"No seriously, Jake, I won't let you down. I don't know what I would have done if you hadn't offered me this job. I was in desperate straits." She looked at him with honest gratitude.

"You're welcome," he murmured.

Oh, brother. How could he dump her now? Then again, how could he not?

"I love the people in this town and believe it or not I love waiting on tables even though it's obviously not my forte. I'm sorry about what happened between us in the freezer, and I swear nothing unprofessional like that will occur again."

Come on. Give her the heave-ho. She's bad for business and even worse for you.

"What did you want to say to me?"

What indeed?

"Um, did you happen to find a place to cash the advance check I gave you?"

"Yes," she beamed. "Thanks so much."

"No problem."

"I went shopping and picked up a few items. Underwear was on sale, so I stocked up on thongs in a variety of colors," she chattered blithely.

He imagined that tight little fanny of hers barely covered with thong panties and felt a pinging sensation deep within the most male part of him. He mentally saw his hand glide over her flat smooth abdomen. He fantasized that she'd had her navel pierced and she wore a gold belly ring.

Stop it, stop it, stop it.

"I got a bra too and one of those baby-doll nighties. You know, they're really short." She measured off an area just below her hip with the side of her hand.

"Uh, Sadie."

"Yes?" She smiled brilliantly.

"Please don't tell me about your lingerie purchases."

"Oh, right. Completely unprofessional."

He forced a tight smile. "Yeah."

"Guess I'm just used to vaudeville revues where lingerie was our costume."

"Well, you're not on the ship anymore."

"Sorry." Her apologetic smile was genuinely sincere. She had absolutely no clue what effect she was having on him.

"That's okay. Just be careful."

"Was there anything else?" She looked straight into his eyes and he felt something dangerous slip in his heart. He could really fall for her if he let himself.

But he wasn't going to let himself, even if he was too buffaloed to fire her. "No. Nothing else."

"Maybe we could have a private toast of our own," she said, indicating the champagne flutes. "And then I'll help you wash up these dirty glasses."

He should say no. Not only no, but hell no.

Instead, he found himself saying, "Sounds like a great idea."

Sucker!

She poured the champagne, and handed him a glass, then lifted her own flute in a salute. "To the

Paradise Inn. May it succeed beyond your wildest dreams.''

"To the Paradise Inn."

The lips of their glasses clinked.

Sadie raised the flute to her mouth.

Her rich, robust red mouth.

Jake couldn't seem to stop watching her. His gaze hung on lips moist with champagne. A surge of desire tore through him.

She giggled and lifted her glass a second time. "To the best boss ever."

"I can't drink to that. I'm not the best boss ever."

"Oh, yes you are."

She clinked her glass against his but a bit of champagne sloshed over the side and landed on the back of his hand at the juncture of his thumb and index finger.

"Oops."

Then before he knew what was happening, she lowered her head and licked the liquid from his skin.

"Sadie, what are you doing?" He hissed through clenched teeth when all he wanted was to lick her right back.

"Why, I'm cleaning up my mess." Her grin was wicked and a little lopsided.

That's when he realized she was tipsy.

Strange, she hadn't had more than half a glass of champagne in total. He would have supposed a stripper in a vaudeville revue could hold her liquor a bit better than that, but some people were really sensitive to the effects of champagne.

"Sweetheart..." he started, but that's as far as he got.

She was running her tongue up his wrist to his forearm to his elbow. A shiver of delight sprinted up his spine.

There was just so much he could take. He was trying his best to be good and responsible. He'd vowed to his friends he'd be sensible when it came to women, but he was a weak, weak man.

Especially since Sadie had leaned forward in her chair and was now brushing her lips across his with a featherlight touch. She tasted of champagne and magic and mischief.

He shut his mind against the alarm bells going off in every part of him, except of course where Mr. Friendly resided. His baser self chortled with unabashed glee.

Yesssssssss. I thought I'd lost you forever to that Metropolitan *ad, Jake the rake.*

She playfully nipped his bottom lip between her teeth and sucked lightly.

He moaned low in his throat, cupped her head tenderly in one palm, felt his fingers slip through the warm silk of her hair. His hand had itched to touch that mass of fire-red curls all day. Such glossy, satiny curls the color of fox pelt.

Her taste, that sweet, now slightly tart flavor from the champagne filled his mouth. How long had it been since he'd kissed her? Hours? Days? Forever? It seemed forever.

More. He wanted more. Even as he knew he shouldn't be doing it, he crushed her lips against his and teased her with his tongue. Her cry of delight arrowed through him. He loved pleasing her, but he felt helpless and little out of his league.

"You taste yummy," she murmured.

Pulling back a little, he gazed into her eyes feeling dazed and bedazzled and downright bewildered. What was this mysterious hold she had over him? Her eyes shimmered full of passion, brimming with the dizzy effects of champagne.

He shouldn't be doing this but he simply could not stop. He was like a junkie helplessly drawn to the source of his addiction. He kissed her eyelids and eyelashes. His mouth roved over her cheekbone and the smooth, clean line of her jaw.

She was so soft, and her pampered skin was perfect, except for that cute little dusting of freckles across her nose, which just seemed to enhance her beauty. Jake knew without asking she used special creams and expensive unguents and gobs of sunscreen. Her diligence had paid off. Her complexion was exquisite.

He had the irresistible urge to explore every inch of her body, but he wasn't the only one with urges. Sadie was not sitting idle while he catalogued her virtues. One of her hands was slowly stroking his arm while the other was tugging gently at his neck, drawing his head down to meet her lips…asking, searching, seeking.

The urgency pounding through him clawed his tenuous control to tattered shreds. Jake groaned and surrendered, kissing her long and hard until they were both breathless with need.

The back of his damned chair separated them.

He wanted to press his flesh to hers, enjoy her fully, without any hindrances.

With his hands, he urged her to her feet and as he guided her around his chair, he turned in his seat until he was facing forward. He drew her onto his lap.

She must have felt the proof of his desire for her because her eyes widened and she grinned like she'd discovered the key to Fort Knox. She growled low and lusty, startling him with the extent of her passion, and kissed him roughly.

He loved wanton women who weren't afraid to let themselves go but Sadie blew him away. She writhed in his lap, causing his errant body part to go ape wild. She tore his shirt from his body. Buttons popped and scattered across the floor with a series of soft plunking sounds.

Jack sucked in air. First time a woman had ever ripped his shirt off his chest.

She nuzzled against his oh-so-sensitive skin, ran her fingernails over his chest, rubbing and stroking and pushing her body flush against his as if trying to burrow inside him.

And damned if he didn't welcome her with open arms. He wanted to be joined with her. Blood pounded through his ears. If Mr. Friendly got any friendlier, it would take an exorcist to relieve the poor fellow of his demons.

Jake rearranged her in his lap until she was straddling him and they were face to face with Mr. Friendly wedged between both their bellies. Her breasts swayed against his chest. He realized the room was filled with the noise of their harsh intake of air.

Her skirt had ridden up to her thighs, revealing a delicious expanse of soft skin and honed muscles. No mistaking those dancer legs. This woman worked out.

With a thumb and forefinger, he slowly began to undo the buttons of her blouse, just as he'd secretly been wanting to do all day. He eased the blouse from her shoulders, exposing the lacy white bra beneath. That bra had been driving him crazy, invading his fantasies, taunting and torturing him.

Using both his hands and his mouth, he stroked her pale creamy skin, so velvety smooth beneath the rough texture of his callused, work-roughened palms.

She purred like the engine of the classic, chick-magnet Camaro he'd souped up when he was in high school. That car had been his pride and joy. But no vehicle, no matter how fine, could compare with his Sadie.

The woman was as unstoppable as lightning. She leaned her head down and flicked that devilish tongue over his nipples, then gently nipped his skin.

He arched against her as ragged, famished need powered through his body like a riptide. When he arched his body, the chair they were sitting in tipped on its two back legs. Jake's feet left the ground. He knew they were in trouble, but Sadie was oblivious—she was so into what she was doing—her mouth still latched on to his.

Frantically, he windmilled his arms in a futile attempt to keep them from toppling over.

They teetered.

And tottered.

Jake grabbed for the table, but it was too far away.

Ka-wham. The chair hit the ground with an ear-grinding thud. Luckily, he had braced for the fall and hadn't struck his head on the floor. But he found himself flat on his back, Sadie above him, one knee planted on either side of him.

"Wow," she whispered, grinning. "That was some kiss."

"Are you okay?" he asked. Concern for her was his number one priority. At the first sign of trouble, Mr. Friendly had skeedaddled. Coward.

She looked down into his eyes, her long curls draping over his face, and giggled. "Nothing could be finer."

"You're tipsy," he said.

"I'm certainly not," she slurred indignantly. "I only had one glass of champagne."

"Apparently one is all it takes."

She hiccupped. "Perhaps you're right. Now, where were we?" She leaned down to kiss him again.

"No, Sadie. No more. Let's get up."

"Why? Aren't you comfy?"

"Not particularly, no."

He wished she'd stop wriggling around. Mr. Friendly was working on getting his second wind.

"Oh, okay." She rolled off him.

Feeling as graceful as an ox stuck in a mud hole,

Jake got to his feet. Immediately, his eyes went to her torso covered only by that thin, lacy bra. He glanced down and saw he wasn't in much better shape than she, the buttons ripped from his shirt, his bare chest exposed for her perusal.

And she was perusing him like the Yellow Pages. "Nice pecs."

He jerked the edges of his ravaged shirt together. "Listen, Sadie. I'm not blaming you for what just happened, but it shouldn't have happened. I stepped over the line."

"I wanted you to step over the line." She grinned at him.

"It doesn't matter. I shouldn't have been here alone with you. We shouldn't have drunk champagne."

"Shouldn't, shouldn't, shouldn't." She pouted. "I'm beginning to think those rumors I've heard about you aren't a bit true."

"What rumors?"

"That you're a fun-loving party animal."

"I am. I mean I was, but I'm trying to put that part of my life behind me."

"But why?" She walked her fingers over his shoulders.

He grabbed her fingers with a hand. "I refuse to take advantage of you, Sadie."

"Not even if I want you to?" She batted her eyelashes.

"That's just the champagne talking. You'll feel differently tomorrow."

"I don't know about that."

"Look, you're a terrific woman and I like you

a lot. But the truth is, I'm ready to settle down and get married. You're obviously looking for something a lot more casual.''

''What?'' Sadie blinked at him. She seemed confused. ''Did you say married?''

He repeated himself.

''Oh, my.'' With an expression of pure horror on her face she glanced down at her near-nakedness and slapped a palm over her mouth. ''What did we do?''

''Now don't overreact. It's not that big of a deal.''

''Maybe not to you,'' she said, scrambling to retrieve her top, which he had draped over the champagne bucket while they were in the throes of passion. ''But I don't go around stripping off my blouse in front of just anyone.''

That made no sense. She was a stripper. She took her clothes off for everyone. He stared at her quizzically.

''And what about you? Where are your buttons?'' She jammed her hands through the armholes of her blouse, not realizing at first she had it on inside out.

''You tore them off.'' He gestured toward the buttons strewn across the floor. A virtual button graveyard.

''I did that?'' she gasped.

''You don't remember?''

''I…I…I…''

He thought for a moment there she was going to burst into tears. Jake frowned. What was going on here? In a matter of seconds she seemed totally different. Going from wildly seductive to primly mortified. One minute she was tipsy, the next minute stone-cold sober, but nobody sobered up that fast.

She blushed, clearly shocked by her own behavior. Drinker's remorse?

Maybe she had some kind of weirdo allergy to alcohol. He had heard of such things but knew next to nothing about the symptoms. Maybe she had an allergy that made her get drunk quick, sober up even quicker and block out everything that happened while she was under the influence.

"I gotta go." Flustered, she fumbled with her top, trying to do up the closures.

"Your blouse is on wrong side out."

"I know that," she snapped.

"So why don't you switch it?"

"Because I don't want you to see me naked again."

"I didn't see you naked."

"Well, almost and that's close enough."

"There's no reason to be ashamed. You didn't do anything wrong."

"I didn't?"

"No."

She blew out her breath. "Are you sure?"

"Positive."

"Whew, that's a relief. I was afraid I'd made a fool of myself."

"Never," he said. But he found himself wondering if sly Sadie was really as confused as she seemed or if she was instead making a fool out of him.

6

THE NEXT MORNING, Sarah awoke with a throbbing in her head and a heavy ache in her heart. Something was very, very wrong, and she had no idea how to fix it.

Why was she having these strange memory lapses? What did it mean? Was she buying a one-way ticket to the funny farm?

And in the grip of these—for want of a better term—blackouts, apparently she exhibited rather uncharacteristic behavior. Like stripping off her blouse and getting down and dirty with her boss.

Sarah cringed. How could she ever face him again after last night? He probably thought she was a shameless hussy to end all shameless hussies.

What was going on with her subconscious? Why was she blanking out large chunks of time? How could she tell Jake what was happening without him thinking her mental choo-choo had jumped the track?

Just go to work, do your job and fly low under the radar, she coached herself. *Get through the day. By the end of the week you'll have enough money to book a flight home.*

That is if her scandalous alter ego didn't keep spending her money on vulgar undergarments.

She squared her shoulders and walked over to the restaurant, mentally rehearsing what she was going to say to Jake. She was both relieved and disappointed when she discovered he'd flown to Juneau on business.

All morning long, her co-workers had commented on how quiet she seemed. Where's that infamous Sadie grin? they asked. Their questions disturbed her. Obviously, they liked this wilder side of her. The side she couldn't remember.

By the time Jake returned late that afternoon, Sadie had worked herself up into a state of agitation.

"Can I speak with you alone?" she asked, desperate to question him about the night before but dreading to hear his answers.

"I'll meet you out back in ten minutes," he said.

Sarah went on break and paced the parking lot, muttering under her breath as she practiced her speech. She didn't hear him approach.

When he touched her shoulder and asked, "What's up?" she gave a little shriek and jumped a good foot off the ground.

"Sorry. Didn't mean to startle you."

"No. It's not your fault. It's me."

"You've got your hair up." He reached to touch her hair but she backed up fast.

"Yes."

"And your shirt's buttoned up to the last button."

"I thought it looked more professional."

"Professional." He nodded. "Right. It looks professional."

"And dignified." She patted a hand to her chignon, making sure no tendrils had escaped.

"Dignified it is." He stuck his hands in his pockets and stared off at the beautiful blue mountains rising up in the distance.

She realized then that he was as nervous about this meeting as she. At the mere thought of what she might have done last night, Sarah felt the color blanch from her face. No doubt she'd behaved in a manner completely unbecoming to a Stanhope.

"You wanted to ask me something?" he prompted after a long moment of silence.

"Um...yes."

Out with it, Sarah. You've been running the vinegar business long enough to know it's better to just go ahead and say what's on your mind rather than pussyfoot around the issue.

"I'm listening." He crossed his arms over his chest and waited.

"This is rather embarrassing."

"You don't have to be ashamed of anything with me, Sadie."

There it was again. That name her mother used to call her. The name her father never used because it reminded him of his feckless wife. The name everyone in Bear Creek seemed to know her by. The name, that when it tripped off Jake's lips, sounded comforting and melodious. The name that made her feel wild and sexy and just the tiniest bit naughty.

She both loved and hated that name. She inhaled sharply. "Right. About last night..."

"Yes?"

"I'm having a little trouble remembering what happened."

"You didn't have that much to drink."

"Still, I'm a bit foggy on the details. Did we...did you...how far did we go?"

"Nothing happened."

"Nothing?" She poked her tongue against the inside of her cheek. "Nothing at all?"

"Well, something, but it's not important."

"What? I need to know."

"Let's not make a big deal of it."

"What!"

"Okay. All right. We came close to making love but it was strictly my fault. You were tipsy on champagne. I was tipsy on the news my restaurant is going to be reviewed in *Yodor's*. We both lost our heads but thankfully common sense prevailed."

"Thankfully," she echoed.

He raised his palms. "You don't have to worry. It won't happen again."

"No." She said it as a statement but it sounded oddly like a question. She didn't want a repeat of last night's performance.

Did she?

Jake frowned. "Sadie, you're not acting controlled and subdued because of what I said last night, are you?"

What had he said last night? She didn't remember.

"I'm not following you."

He frowned. "Don't play mind games."

She didn't know what he was talking about, and

she didn't know how to confess without revealing that she was Miss No-Short-Term-Memory.

"What do you mean?"

"The bun, the buttoned-up shirt, the stiff posture. It's not going to work. If you're using this prim-and-proper routine in order to lure me into bed for hot sex, then you're barking up the wrong tree."

"Hot sex?"

"Yeah. There's no sense in pretending to be something you're not just to seduce me into the sack."

Jake touched two fingertips to his temple and stared at Sadie with a mixture of disbelief and desire. He couldn't believe what she was up to. Even with her skirt back to its proper place just above her knee and that mound of red hair anchored securely to her head and a light application of makeup rather than her usual super-shellacking of cosmetics, she was impossibly sexy.

"Oh, is that what you think?"

"It is."

She made a derisive noise, then winked the saucy wink that never failed to bring him to his knees. "Sugar Bear," she drawled. "If I was trying to seduce you, you'd certainly know about it."

And with that, she spun on her heels and strolled away.

Was it his imagination, or did she put an extra roll into those hips? Jake angled his head for a sideways view and watched her go.

The woman drove him crazy. He wanted her so badly, he couldn't think straight. She wasn't what he was looking for in a wife, not in the least. They would make a terrible married couple. Both of them too impulsive and spontaneous. But man, he just knew they would burn up the sheets.

You've done enough sheet burning in your life, Gerard. Time to extinguish those deadly flames.

Aw, but that was so hard to do with Sadie around. If he didn't stay away from her, Jake knew he was gonna cave.

JAKE MANAGED to keep his distance from Sadie for the remainder of the week by concentrating on preparations for the food critic's visit.

The reviewer, who turned out to be a pipe-cleaner thin, forty-something woman by the name of Ms. Penelope Snidely, arrived early Friday morning at the B&B. Jake wasted no time in turning on the charm. But he quickly discovered she thought he was sucking up in order to get a good rating—which granted, he was—so he prudently backed off.

Ms. Snidely was, however, quite demanding in her lodging requirements, and he found himself scrambling to meet her every request.

"I want flowers in my room," she said. "And I'll need extra towels and an electric blanket on my bed. I'll require a CD player and classical music CDs."

"Your wish is my command." Jake bowed slightly.

She looked down her nose at him and sniffed audibly. She carried a yappy little Yorkshire terrier on her arm. The dog's name, she told him, was

Brigadier BonBon. A champion sire who garnered three-thousand-dollar stud fees.

Jake filed this information in the part of his brain marked—More Information Than I Ever Needed To Know About A Total Stranger, subtitled—Rubbish Bin.

She proceeded to tell him BonBon's dietary restrictions and his intolerance to lactose. Jake barely listened, his eyes glazing over. She'd just about lulled him into a complete coma, when she let out a sudden, terrified shriek.

Huh? What was up? Had she spotted a mouse? Had she spied a ghost? Jake spun around and saw nothing but Lulu slinking up the staircase behind him.

"What is it? What's wrong?"

"The horrid mutt." Ms. Snidely pointed with a trembling finger. "What's she doing running loose?"

"Lulu? She wouldn't harm a fly."

"You don't understand, young man. Brigadier BonBon is a world-class stud."

Meaning he'd hump anything with fur?

BonBon's yaps grew louder, deeper and more frequent. The little guy was working himself up into a quite a state.

Lulu's ears stood up and she boldly approached. Ms. Snidely backed against the door of the bedroom next to hers, which just happened to be where Sadie was staying. She clutched BonBon so tightly her knuckles turned white.

"Shoo! Leave. Get out of here. Make her go

away, young man. This very instant, if you prize
a good rating in *Yodor's*.''

"Lulu," Jake commanded and pointed sternly.
"Out."

Lulu ignored him completely, her full attention
focused on BonBon.

BonBon looked at Lulu.

The husky stared deeply into the Yorkie's eyes.

Their amorous gaze reminded Jake of the spa-
ghetti-eating scene from *Lady and the Tramp*.

Uh-oh, he realized with a start. Lulu just might
be in heat. He'd been planning on letting her raise
one set of puppies before having her spayed, particularly since Mack and Cammie Jo had expressed
an interest in having one of Lulu's offspring. He
wondered how they'd feel about a Yorkie/husky
cross.

Better question, how would Ms. Snidely feel
about it?

Clearly, she wasn't too keen on the idea, but the
brigadier was obviously smitten and his taste ran
to bigger girls.

The next moment was pure chaos. Sadie's door
opened and she managed to say, "What's going
on?" at the same time Ms. Snidely lost her balance
and tumbled backward into Sadie's bedroom.

Sadie put out her arms to catch the woman.
"Who are you?" she asked.

"She's Ms. Penelope Snidely. The food reviewer from *Yodor's*," Jake said.

BonBon yelped, leaped free of his owner's embrace and landed on the ground in front of his
would-be lover.

Ms. Snidely screamed.

Lulu sprang forward and grasped the little Yorkie by the scruff of the neck.

Snidely screamed a second time. Shrieked bloody murder to be exact.

Sadie looked startled to be holding a hysterical woman in her arms. But not half as startled as Jake was to see Sadie clad only in skimpy pink baby-doll pajamas and feathered mules. What legs, what breasts, what a woman.

His mouth dropped open.

Their eyes met.

"What happened?" she asked.

"Lulu's in heat, and Ms. Snidely's BonBon happens to be a prize-winning stud."

"Oh, my."

"Stop them, you imbeciles," Ms. Snidely hollered and gestured toward the stairs. "Before something terrible happens. If you don't stop them, you owe me a three-thousand-dollar stud servicing fee."

Jake turned to see Lulu, with BonBon still grasped firmly in her clutches, sprinting through the lobby.

Laughter gripped him. Grabbed him by the gut and tickled. The sensible side of his brain urged him to get going, a disaster was about to befall his business if he didn't rescue BonBon. He tried to move. Really he did. Tried to put his legs in gear, but the scene was so damned funny, he couldn't stop laughing.

Someone whizzed by him in a blur of pink.

Someone in high-heeled mules and sexy baby-doll pj's.

Sadie. In hot pursuit of the lovesick Lulu, who'd just eloped with her star-crossed boyfriend.

"Do something," Ms. Snidely exclaimed. "Do something right now, save my BonBon from that hideous hulking beast or I won't rest until your restaurant is a parking lot."

That put an end to his laughing spell. Jake launched himself down the stairs after Sadie.

SADIE CORNERED LULU in her doghouse in the backyard of the B&B, intent on rescuing the high-powered stud. A single thought dominated her mind.

Save Jake's hide.

The food reviewer was bound to be furious that her purebred Yorkie had been kidnapped by the enamored husky. Sadie also felt guilty when it dawned on her that she'd had a hand in the abduction. If she hadn't opened her bedroom door at the most inopportune time, Ms. Snidely wouldn't have lost her balance and stumbled. If she hadn't stumbled, she wouldn't have dropped the Yorkie.

Dammit. Klutzy Sadie strikes again.

And here she had been so sure she was going to be the perfect waitress and make a perfect impression on the reviewer at dinner tonight.

Sadie sighed. The best-laid plans.

Her spirits plummeted as she got down on all fours to crawl into Lulu's doghouse, unmindful of the fact that her barely clothed derrière was sticking up in the air.

Lulu had BonBon cradled in her paws and little BonBon was madly licking Lulu's face, obviously in the throes of true love.

"Here, BonBon," Sadie said in a high-pitched singsong and rubbed her thumb against her first two fingers in a "come to me" gesture.

BonBon bared his teeth and growled with a voice much too large for his small stature. It was like hearing a man's voice coming out of a little girl's body. The disconcerting sound startled Sadie so much she jumped and ending up banging her head on the top of the doghouse.

"Ouch." She caressed her aching noggin.

"BonBon, where's my BonBon?" Ms. Snidely wailed like a fire engine from somewhere behind her.

Sadie reached in and grasped BonBon. The tiny terrier sank his sharp little fangs into Sadie's flesh, but she refused to let go of him. Maybe there was some way she could salvage this disaster. Being martyred over Ms. Snidely's dog seemed a small price to pay to redeem Jake's reputation.

She backed out of the doghouse, BonBon held triumphantly in her hands.

Ms. Snidely rushed to scoop up the Yorkie and began cooing to him in baby talk. The woman didn't even say thanks.

Rude witch.

Sadie stood, dusted dirt off her knees and raised her head.

And then she spotted Jake.

Her heart tripped.

He grinned at her. "You saved the day."

"No biggie." She shrugged nonchalantly, but his grateful smile warmed her to the very tips of her toes.

THE DAY STARTED OFF badly and went downhill from there. It had taken a lot of tall talking to pacify the rather humorless Ms. Snidely. Opting for damage control, Jake had promised her he'd keep Lulu chained for the remainder of BonBon's visit and then he'd showered her with lavish compensations.

Coupons to Long Bear's sundries store. A free guided hike in the Tongass Rain Forest. A bottle of his most expensive wine. When he promised to kick in the money for her upgrade from coach to first class on her flight back home, the woman had finally seemed mollified enough to give Henri's cooking a fair shake.

But the unfortunate episode with BonBon had only been the start of his troubles.

The shipment of filet mignon for the Beef Wellington hadn't arrived and Henri was ready to split a gasket over the last-minute changes to his menu.

Unknown to anyone, for almost an hour Linc had gotten himself locked in the freezer and was on the verge of hypothermia when they found him. Jake had been forced to give Linc the rest of the day off, and that left him short a bartender.

One of the busboys had left the box of candles he'd bought to add romantic ambiance to the restaurant sitting near the stove and Jake ended up with a slab of multicolored wax.

The dishwasher broke. The credit card machine

was on the fritz and his best summer waitress picked that moment to tell him she was leaving town two weeks earlier than expected to help her sister with her new baby.

To top it all off, there was Sadie. He couldn't— no matter how hard he tried, no matter how important it was for him to keep his mind on the business at hand—stop thinking about her.

And looking at her. And aching to touch her.

He visualized her doing a striptease for him. Peeling off those so-skimpy-I-can't-believe-it's-called-clothing baby-doll pajamas, shaking her very fine booty, tossing her luscious red mane, undulating that taut belly.

Heat swamped him. Holy smokes! Where was the volunteer fire department when you needed them?

He eyed her from his place behind the bar as she took orders from a group of local men. As she teased and joked with them, their faces lit up. Jake tasted the bitter flavor of jealousy when she laughed at something Marvin Kemp said and rested her delicate arm on the guy's shoulder.

It also galled him to notice the men were wearing their dirty work clothes, completely ignoring his attempts to make the Paradise Inn a shirt-and-tie kind of place. None of the townsfolk, except for Kay, Cammie Jo and Meggie, seemed to share his vision for a more sophisticated Bear Creek.

"What's the special of the day?" Marvin asked Sadie.

"Goat cheese and rosemary tarts with shaved prosciutto and Armagnac macerated figs."

"Ewww!" said one of the men.

"What's that?" asked another. "I don't like eating anything I can't pronounce."

"Why is Jake going fancy on us?" inquired the third fellow. "We liked the Paradise the way it used to be."

"Just bring a round of cheeseburgers and onion rings," Marvin instructed her. "And a pitcher of beer."

"Cheeseburgers are no longer on the menu, Marv. Neither are onion rings. I'm sorry." Sadie shook her head.

"Ah, come on honey, you trying to tell me you can't go back there and sweet-talk the cook into broiling up a couple of patties?" Marvin said persuasively. "I know he's bound to have ground beef stashed away somewhere."

Jake held his breath to see what she would do.

Sadie smiled beatifically. "You're absolutely right, Marvin. I'll do that."

She turned and flounced toward the kitchen. Two seconds later, Jake heard a string of French expletives erupt from behind the swinging doors. He hurried to intervene and burst into the kitchen to find Henri waving a soup ladle at Sadie.

"Mais non!" declared the chef. "I will not make zee cheeseburgers. I have told you and told you."

"Now, Henri," Sadie spoke soft and low. "There's no reason to get testy. It's nothing personal. They just happen to like hamburgers."

"Then let them go to zee Hamburger Hut."

"They don't serve beer at the Hamburger Hut."

"Beer." Henri glowered. "Such a common drink."

"How about if I just throw a few meat patties on the grill. You don't have to have anything to do with it." Sadie made a move for the stove.

Henri leaped in front of her and shook the soup ladle under her nose. "Touch zee grill and you die."

Adrenaline pumped through Jake's veins. Not that he believed Henri would actually harm Sadie, although the wild look in the chef's eyes suggested otherwise, but he would not have the man threatening her. No matter how good a chef he might be.

He stepped between Henri and Sadie.

"Put down the soup ladle," Jake commanded. "Before somebody gets hurt."

"Fire her!" Henri said. "She is trying to usurp my authority in zee kitchen. I cannot work under such conditions as zeeze."

"You're overreacting." Jake feared the man's eyes might bug right out of his head.

"Overreacting? You zink I'm overreacting?"

"I know you are. And I won't have you menacing my wait staff with kitchen utensils."

"Bah! Zat woman is an incompetent imbecile. It is very clear why you hired her."

Jake froze. An eerie calm settled over him. He did not anger easily but when he did, Katie bar the door.

"Yes?" he said in a measured tone. "Share your theory with me, Henri. Why did I hire Sadie? I'm all ears."

Henri cast a disparaging glance at her. A glance that had Jake fantasizing about punching the chef's lights out.

"Because you want to have zee hot love with her."

"You will apologize to Miss Stanhope this instant for your unkind remarks."

Defiantly, Henri lifted his chin. "I will not."

Jake took a step closer toward the man and smacked his fist into his palm. He couldn't believe he was doing this. He was the kind of guy who joked and cajoled. He didn't get into fights. He danced around confrontation, but this obnoxious little Frenchman had insulted his Sadie and he wasn't going to stand for that.

His Sadie? Where on earth had that come from?

"Apologize."

"Non." Henri tossed his soup ladle into the sink and jerked at the ties on his apron. "Zat is it. I am out of here."

"Jake, it's all right. Henri doesn't have to apologize to me." Sadie's face had gone chalky white and the sight of her fear escalated his controlled rage.

"Sadie," Jake said tightly. "Stay out of this."

"But Jake, you can't let him leave. Ms. Snidely's coming to dinner and she's already disinclined to give us a favorable review because of what happened between Lulu and BonBon."

Us. Why that word should cause a strange hitch in his gullet, Jake had no idea. But it did.

"You can't quit," Jake said to Henri.

"Oh no? Just watch me."

"You can't quit, you temperamental prima donna, because I'm firing you."

7

————

"JAKE!" Sadie pressed a hand to her mouth in disbelief over what he'd just done. "You can't fire Henri."

The rest of the kitchen staff stared wide-eyed, as if worried they might be next.

"Don't let the door hit you in the butt on the way out," Jake called as Henri stormed off. "On second thought, never mind, let it smack you a good one."

She grabbed Jake by the shoulders. "Go after him. Apologize. Get him back here. ASAP."

"No way. He insulted you."

"We need him, Jake. And I've been insulted by far better men than he."

"Not within my hearing distance." Jake glowered.

"Your pigheaded gallantry is touching, but kind of dumb under the circumstances." Sadie shook her head. "Who's going to cook for Ms. Snidely?"

Jake blinked and then paled, as if realizing for the first time the consequences of his actions.

Sadie glanced at her watch. "She made reservations for eight and it's five-thirty right now. That doesn't give us much time for elaborate preparations."

"Oh boy."

"Oh boy is right."

"Well, I'm certainly not going after Henri. Not after the way he spoke to you."

"Is that the reason, Jake, or are you just too stubborn to swallow your pride?"

"I'm not begging him."

"Not even for the sake of the restaurant? Come on, a four-fork rating in *Yodor's* is what you've been dreaming of."

"I think it's a lost cause."

Sadie sank her hands on her hips. "Jake Gerard, I never figured you for a quitter."

"Sometimes it's better just to let things go."

"What does that mean?"

"Maybe I'm not meant to make a success of the Paradise. Maybe it's a sign my mother was right. I shouldn't get hitched."

"Baloney. I don't believe you're giving up so easily."

"It's not your worry, Sadie."

"The heck it's not. You fired Henri over me. What are we going to do about this?" She was ready to grab him by the neck and shake some sense into him.

Then something profound dawned on her. She was just as invested in the restaurant as he was. She wanted it to succeed. For Jake's sake. He deserved all the happiness in the world. He deserved a wonderful wife and kids.

Even if she wasn't fated to be that wife.

A golf-ball-size lump of emotion formed in her throat. An emotion she couldn't identify but didn't want to prod too hard. Once opened, she feared it would fill her entire body with a wistful longing for something she couldn't have.

Jake settled his hands on his narrow hips. "I've got an idea. It's a long shot, but maybe Quinn would be willing to help out. He's a pretty good cook. No gourmand by any stretch of the imagination, but he can make a wicked salmon chowder. I'll just go on over to his house and see if I can persuade him."

Perspiration beaded his forehead and that's when Sadie recognized that he was literally sweating this, even though he had been clinging to his philosophical whatever-fate's-got-planned-for-me stance.

He glanced at the kitchen help. "Back to work, everyone. Do whatever you were supposed to be doing to prepare the evening meal."

The helpers jumped to do his bidding.

"Good luck," Sadie told him, but she wasn't relying on luck. If he was too proud or too macho to beg Henri to stay, she wasn't. Unwittingly, she'd instigated this mess and she was going to fix it. The minute Jake departed, she left the restaurant in search of Henri.

Twenty minutes later, she was back, cursing the egotistical Frenchman under her breath. She'd tried reasoning with him, but when he said he wanted sexual favors in return for his cooperation, Sadie had told him to stuff himself.

Yuck. She shuddered. What a creep.

Jake hadn't returned. Sadie took a look at the revised menu Henri had prepared.

> *Broiled oysters with arugala puree and champagne sabyon.*
> *Foie gras sautéed with blueberries.*
> *Herbed salmon flamed in gin.*
> *Gratinee of asparagus.*
> *Curried carrots.*
> *Luxembourg salad.*
> *Chocolate soufflé.*

She read over the ingredients. Fancy schmancy names, but the dishes didn't really sound *that* complicated. Perhaps she could try her hand at preparing some of them. What would it hurt? It wasn't like she could make things any worse.

Sadie tied an apron around her waist and the next thing she knew, she was elbow-deep in cream and seafood and butter. Stunned, she watched her own hands performing intricate tasks. Pureeing, sautéing, flambéing. It was as if she had possessed these complex skills her entire life. Whipping up this intricate meal was almost as easy as breathing.

This self-discovery surprised and delighted her. Where had she learned to do such things? Surely not stripping on a cruise ship. But if she'd worked as a cook, why couldn't she recall it?

And Sadie wasn't the only one impressed with her newfound abilities. The kitchen staff was staring at her as if she'd stepped off a lime-green flying saucer and greeted them with a hearty, "How's it hanging, earthlings?"

She was so busy concocting the meal, she didn't even notice when Jake came back into the kitchen.

"Sadie," he said sharply, "what are you doing?"

She didn't even glance up from beating the egg whites for the chocolate soufflé. She smiled to herself as the white peaks grew stiff and glossy. Yum.

"Sadie."

She waved an irritated hand at him. Didn't he know how hard it was to make a great soufflé?

"Shh, man," one of the busboys whispered in awe, and nudged him in the side with an elbow. "Watch her go."

Jake's mouth flapped open in awed surprise. He didn't get it. How could the world's worst waitress be so darned accomplished with a wire whisk?

She put the soufflé into the oven, then turned to him, grinning happily, a dollop of flour decorating her cute little nose. He was still staring, open-mouthed, unable to believe what he was witnessing.

"Here," she said, spooning something from a pan and popping it onto his tongue. "Tell me what you think. Does it need a little more black pepper?"

His lips closed around the juicy tidbit. His tastebuds came alive with flavor. Oysters, cream, lemon, champagne.

"Mmm, mmm." He moaned with pleasure. He hadn't realized how hungry he was until that heavenly mouthful. He had been too worried to eat all day. His stomach rumbled for more. "This is absolutely awesome, Sadie."

"Thank you."

"Where did you learn how to cook like this?"

She shrugged.

"Come on, don't be shy. You're better than Henri, and he studied at the Cordon Bleu."

Truth was, he was giddy with relief to learn she could whip up an elegant spread like this one. He didn't really regret canning Henri, especially after the way he had treated Sadie, but he admitted to a momentary panic at the thought of getting a big fat one-fork rating in the *Yodor's* guide.

Sadie blushed prettily at his compliments, looking as pleased as a kid who'd just learned to ride her bike without training wheels.

"Honestly, I don't know. It just came to me. Weird, huh?"

"It's way more than weird. You've been hiding your light under a bushel."

"Did you find your friend Quinn?"

"No. He wasn't home. But who needs him when I've got you? Can I have another bite? Please?"

She laughed and fished another oyster from the pan. She held her palm under the spoon to catch any spillage and leaned in close to him.

Jake shot her a glance from his peripheral vision. She looked incredibly lovely in profile, with her flame-colored hair caught back in a purple scrunchie. She held the oyster just out of his reach, teasing him. Her face was flushed with the headiness of victory and she was breathing a little too quickly.

In that moment, she seemed so domestic, so accomplished, so in control. She was exactly what he was looking for in a wife. When he needed her, she'd not only pitched in and risen to the occasion, but far exceeded his expectations. This was much more than pretending to be something she wasn't simply to get him to sleep with her.

Jake was confused. What were Sadie's motives? *Something's fishy in Denmark.*

She waved the oyster under his nose. "Umm, smell."

He clamped his mouth around the spoon and at the same time grabbed her around the waist and pulled her close.

"What's going on?" he murmured, after he'd swallowed the oyster. "You're up to something, and I want to know what it is."

God, she felt so good in his arms, all soft, curvy woman.

She wriggled. "I'm cooking a dinner for a food critic from *Yodor's,* is what I'm doing. Now let me go, before I burn the asparagus."

Their gazes met and that now familiar electric spark arced between them. If they weren't in the kitchen surrounded by his inquisitive staff members, he would have certainly kissed her. Thank heavens for some sort of impediment. He couldn't seem to control himself where Sadie was concerned.

"Hey," one of the waitresses pushed through the swinging doors from the dining room into the kitchen. "She's here."

"She who?" Jake asked, so distracted by Sadie he had momentarily forgotten about Ms. Snidely.

"The food critic."

"Oh, her." He let go of Sadie's waist and hurried out to greet his guest.

The woman wasn't any easier to please at the

restaurant than she had been earlier, and she'd even brought Brigadier BonBon. Jake wasn't about to tell her the dog couldn't sit in the dining room with her.

She complained about her table. It was too close to the window. He moved her. She fussed about the wine. It was too dry. He brought her another bottle. She griped about the other diners, who certainly were not attired correctly for a gourmet establishment. It ate at Jake's craw, but he apologized for the unsightly appearance of his many friends and neighbors.

She kept on bitching about it until, in exasperation, Jake marched over to the B&B and returned with enough coats and ties to outfit his male customers. He had to do some tall talking to persuade a few of the fellas to put them on, and ended up comping everyone for their meals. It made Ms. Snidely momentarily happy, although in his estimation his patrons looked pretty silly sitting there in work boots, jeans and dinner jackets.

Remember what this is all about, he reminded himself. He forced a smile so fake he thought his face might crack when she pronounced the lighting too harsh.

And Ms. Snidely's sensibilities were quickly offended again. She didn't like the linen tablecloths. Too much starch. It irritated BonBon's sensitive behind. Jake had to grit his teeth to keep from telling her that if she didn't let BonBon sit on the scratchy tablecloth, his behind wouldn't get itchy.

Jake's earlier euphoria at discovering Sadie could cook like Julia Child dissipated. He worried that even Sadie's culinary talents could not impress this sour prune of a woman.

"You know, if Henri Renault were not your chef I would never have agreed to come to this godforsaken wilderness. How you managed to lure him here is beyond me, but I love his artistry with food. I dined at The Chateau Maison in Seattle when he was head chef there. I cannot say enough good things about his sublime talent."

Uh-oh. Jake wasn't about to tell her that Henri would not be rustling up her evening grub.

"I can't wait to be surprised by what he's created tonight."

"The menu was planned with you in mind," Jake said, and prayed that she wasn't allergic to oysters or anything else on the menu. "I'll bring your first course."

Jake held his breath until Ms. Snidely sampled the oysters and pronounced them divine. She carried on about the foie gras. BonBon seemed to like it too, scarfing up a good twenty dollars' worth of the stuff. She moaned with pleasure over the herbed salmon, had a fit over the Luxembourg salad and said she could die a happy woman after eating Henri's superb chocolate soufflé.

That's when Jake could no longer resist. He told her Henri had not prepared the meal. The surprised expression on her snobby face was priceless.

"What do you mean? No one else can cook like this."

"I'm afraid they can."

"You tricked me, young man."

"You said yourself the food was sublime."

She frowned, but grudgingly replied, "The chef must have been Henri's understudy."

"Nope."

"Well, then, may I meet this chef and congratulate him on a job well done."

"Not a him."

"What?"

"The chef. She's a woman."

Ms. Snidely looked more taken aback.

Jake was enjoying this. He half expected her to spit out that last bite of soufflé, wipe off her tongue with her napkin and go, "patooey, patooey, patooey," as if she'd just swallowed a chunk of Snow White's poisoned apple.

"Tell her I would like to see her, please." Ms. Snidely waved her hand.

"All right." Jake bowed, then grinning, he hurried to the kitchen to tell Sadie the food critic wanted to compliment her.

Sadie threw back her shoulders, held her head high and sailed into the dining room. Before she got to Snidely's table, she was stopped by many of the restaurant regulars, who expressed delight over their delicious meals.

She absorbed their accolades, feeling herself warm from the inside out at her success. Why hadn't she realized before now what a good cook she was? Food was definitely her calling.

"Simply marvelous," gushed one woman.

"You've got a gift," said her companion.

"And you're not too good to fry up a hamburger," someone else said.

Their praises rang in her ears. Proudly, she stopped at Ms. Snidely's table.

BonBon bared his teeth and barked at her.

Miserable mutt.

"Oh," Ms. Snidely said. "It's you. Could you get me some more coffee?"

"She's not your waitress," supplied Mack, who was sitting at the table kitty-corner from Ms. Snidely's.

Cammie Jo pointed to her heaping bowl of pasta and mouthed, "to die for."

Ms. Snidely blinked. "*You're* the chef?"

"Yes, ma'am."

"*You* cooked this meal?"

"Uh-huh."

Ms. Snidely shook her head. "Unbelievable."

Sadie shrugged.

"My dear, you cook like a dream."

"Thank you. Thank you very much."

"But I don't understand why are you wasting your God-given talents in a dead-end place like this one. I was going to ask Henri the same question. Take my advice. Leave this hellhole," Ms. Snidely sniffed audibly, "and these uncouth, rough-necked Alaskans and find a suitable place of employment."

Sadie stared in disbelief. "Excuse me?"

"I'm going to give this establishment a four-fork rating based solely on your culinary skills. Believe me, there's nothing else about this place I can recommend. Not the service, not the atmosphere, not the clientele and not that unctuous owner."

Unctuous? The witch was calling Jake unctuous?

Anger pushed through Sadie. How dare this woman insult her new friends, the Paradise and Jake? She gritted her teeth against the impulse to scratch the woman's eyeballs right out of her skull.

Every eye in the place was trained on them. Silence descended. Sadie cleared her throat. "Pardon me, but I don't appreciate it when people insult my customers."

Ms. Snidely looked down her nose at the people gathered around their tables. "You work in a dump like this, honey, that's the risk you take."

Okay. That did it. No more Miss Nice Girl. She'd been pushed to the limit and she was fresh out of patience.

Without stopping to consider the consequences of her actions, Sadie reached over, scooped up Cammie Jo's pile of pasta, smiled sweetly at her and said, "Hope you don't mind me borrowing this. I'll get you another bowl in a minute."

Without further preamble, she upended the spaghetti on Ms. Snidely's pointy little head.

Snidely shrieked.

BonBon yelped.

Been there, heard that, Sadie thought wryly.

"You, you, you..." Ms. Snidely sputtered and shoved spaghetti from her eyes, the bowl still balancing precariously on her head.

"Uncouth Alaskan?"

"Oh!" Ms. Snidely jumped to her feet and scooped BonBon into her arms. "I hope you're married to this job, sister, because no one in the lower forty-eight states will dare to hire you when I get through with your reputation.''

Married?

''And if you think I'm giving this dive a rating any higher than one fork then you've got some serious rethinking to do.''

Sarah blinked and stared disoriented at this strange, rail-thin woman covered in pasta and spaghetti sauce, who was practically hopping up and down, she was so mad. The woman stormed out the door, slinging pasta in her wake.

The restaurant patrons broke into applause. Someone, she thought it might have been Mack, let loose with a catcall. Then everyone in the place began to chant, ''Sadie, Sadie, Sadie.''

She looked over and saw Jake stalking toward her, anger flashing in his eyes.

Oh God, how could she face him? How could she face anyone after this? Choking back her tears, Sarah spun on her heels and fled the diner.

SARAH RAN to her bedroom at the B&B because she didn't have anywhere else to go. But even here, she found no refuge from herself. Spread across the quilt was a pair of thong undies and a red micromini skirt so sheer and clingy, a lady of the evening would think twice before wearing it.

Confused, Sarah picked up the foreign garments and examined them. Did these belong to her? But how? She would never wear such outrageous clothing.

Just like you would never dump spaghetti on

*someone's head, or make out with a man you
barely knew in a deserted restaurant?*

Groaning, Sarah slumped onto the bed. Apparently, she would do just about anything.

Something was terribly wrong with her. She did
all kinds of wild and impulsive things that she
never remembered doing. Like buying this hooker
skirt when she was supposed to be saving her salary for a plane ticket back home. She flung the
offending garment across the room. Gak!

She had to be losing her mind. That's all there
was to it. Maybe she should go ahead, swallow her
pride and call Papa. Or at the very least, try again
to contact Kim and Lizzy on the cruise ship. She'd
already tried a couple of times and the ship-to-
shore connection hadn't gone through. She
couldn't help but wonder why her friends hadn't
come looking for her.

Before she could decide who to call, there was
a gentle knock at her door.

"Sadie?"

Jake.

Oh no. She dived under the covers and snatched
them up over her head. She wouldn't blame him
if he throttled her on the spot. She deserved every
bit of his wrath.

Jake knocked again. "Sadie, honey, I know
you're in there. Gus saw you fly upstairs. Can we
please talk about what happened?"

Hmm. He didn't sound mad. Sarah peeked out
from under the covers. Maybe it was just a ploy
so she'd let him in. Once he got close enough,
that's when he'd pounce.

The doorknob jiggled, and she realized in sudden desperation she'd neglected to turn the lock behind her. She leaped out of bed, lunging for the lock, but she wasn't quick enough. The door swung open and she found herself nose to chin with Jake. Ulp.

She quickly backpedaled and banged the calf of her leg against the four-poster bed. She braced herself for a good bawling out.

But instead of castigating her, Jake slowly closed the door. "Are you all right?" he asked. The expression in his eyes was one of tender concern.

That's when she completely lost it and to her utter chagrin, burst into tears.

Jake crossed the short distance between them, scooped her into his arms and sat on the edge of the mattress with her clutched tightly to his chest.

"It's all right, sweetheart." He pressed his lips to her ear and murmured softly.

"No, it's not."

"Shhh. Don't cry." With a crook of his finger, he brushed a glistening tear from her cheek and his heart lurched painfully in his chest.

"Stop being so nice to me. I ruined your chances of getting a four-fork rating. Heck, I ruined your chances of even getting two or three forks."

He couldn't help smiling at her. She looked so despondent. "What? You want me to yell at you?"

She nodded somberly.

It was all he could do to keep from chuckling.

She was serious. "What's the point in that? It wouldn't change anything."

"I deserve a protracted blessing out."

"No, you don't."

"Go ahead. Scream away. Rant and rave. Holler and yell. Really let me have it. Fire me. I wouldn't blame you one bit."

"You're not being fired."

"Why not? I dumped spaghetti on the *Yodor's* food critic."

"To tell you the truth, Sadie, I was inches away from doing it myself."

"Really?"

"Who needs approval from the Wicked Witch of *Yodor's?*"

Sadie giggled, and the sound warmed his heart.

It was true, Jake realized. Sadie's feelings were more important than the financial success of the Paradise. He didn't need *Yodor's* coveted rating to make the Paradise a good place to eat. He needed Sadie and her culinary skills. He needed his friends and the locals. The tourist trade was nice, but not at the expense of his regulars. And that's what he'd been doing. Turning off his loyal customers by trying to make the Paradise something it wasn't.

Just like you've been trying to be something you're not. The ideal husband material.

And that was something else he'd realized on the walk over here from the diner, as he kneaded his great-great-grandfather's gold nugget beneath his fingers.

He'd been using the Paradise as an excuse. He didn't need a fancy restaurant in order to get married. Rather than getting angry with Sadie, he found himself wondering just why he was erecting roadblocks between himself and matrimony when supposedly that's what he really wanted.

He wasn't ready to dig that deeply into his own psyche. Jake was not the sort to kick over rocks to see what kind of critters skittered out or rattle closet skeletons.

"Anybody else would fire me," Sadie said. "You can't keep me on simply because you're attracted to me."

"That's not the reason I'm keeping you on."

"I'm not exactly the world's best waitress."

He peered down into her face and just melted. He felt all soft and squishy and romantic inside.

Uh-oh. Last time he felt this way Mrs. Renny had played him for a sucker. But Sadie wasn't Renny. Yet how much did he really know about her?

He reached out and brushed a lock of hair from her forehead. "Nope, you're not the world's best waitress. In fact, I'd say you were on the fast track to claiming the title as world's worst waitress."

"So why aren't you canning me?"

"Because you are one hell of a cook."

"You're giving me a new position?" Her face lit up.

"Yep. You just got Henri's job."

"Do I get his salary, too?"

"Don't push your luck," he growled playfully. They grinned at each other.

Her body felt soft yet solid in the crook of his

arm. Her fanny was pressed tight across his lap and certain parts were beginning to take notice.

If Jake bent his head just a few inches he could kiss her sweet mouth. He drew a shaky breath. He'd come here to comfort Sadie, not to take advantage of the situation. He had planned to reassure her, not arouse her.

And she was aroused. No mistaking the tightening of her nipples beneath the material of her blouse. Those nipples and Mr. Friendly, what a ménage-à-trois.

Her lips parted. He could see the tip of her pink tongue and he had to clench his teeth to keep from groaning. She wanted to be kissed as much as he wanted to kiss her.

"I'm glad you're feeling better," he said, fighting against every impulse in his body that urged him to kiss her. Kiss her and do a whole lot more than that.

But, he feared that if he got started, neither one of them would be able to stop.

Gently, he eased her from his lap and settled her on top of the quilt. "Don't fret over this incident with Ms. Snidely. You stood up for your friends, and you stood up for me. I admire you, Sadie Stanhope. You're one gutsy gal. A bit impulsive perhaps, but I wouldn't have you any other way."

Then he leaned over and lightly brushed his lips across her forehead before turning and walking to the door.

Sarah's pulse boom, boom, boomed in her ears like a whole chorus of snare drums as she watched Jake saunter from the room.

He wasn't firing her. And he told her he admired her.

Sarah felt a strange clutch in her belly. But it wasn't the real Sarah he admired, rather, the wild, impulsive, micromini-skirt-wearing Sadie.

Why was she having these memory lapses? Why was she assuming the persona of Sadie, a woman too much like her long-dead mother? Was this some kind of repressed wish fulfillment?

She had to face the fact that she had spent her life trying to be what her father wanted her to be. She'd rushed wholeheartedly toward being the perfect daughter. But those unrealistic expectations had obviously caused her subconscious to short-circuit and go searching for her hidden identity. She also had to deal with the idea that she had been holding her father back from a life of his own as much as he'd been sheltering her.

Everything in her world had changed. Everything.

What would happen if she were to just come out and tell Jake the truth? That she seemed to have developed some bizarre split personality that she could not control? Would he think she was nuttier than a box of trail mix?

It was a legitimate question. One she could not even answer for herself. She shook her head in despair. It was as if she was under some kind of spell. A feminine Dr. Jekyll and Mr. Hyde. But of course, she had not ingested any magical potions that she could recall.

And then the truth hit her. Slapped her hard, in

fact, with the reality of the situation. Bingo! She knew now what was happening to her.

People had been saying trigger words. She cast her mind back to the costume party on board the *Alaskan Queen,* when she was hypnotized. She struggled to piece together the disjointed fabric of her memory.

Sarah blew out her breath, at once relieved and embarrassed. Relieved to know what was happening to her but embarrassed to think how she must have behaved as Sadie.

Her heart sank at the recollection of the Polaroid picture Lizzy and Kim had taken of her when she was dancing provocatively on the cruise ship. Briefly, she closed her eyes against the shame flaming through her. She was no better than her mother.

No wonder Jake kept looking at her like she was a real hottie. No doubt that's the way she'd been acting. Sarah groaned and pulled the pillow over her head. He thought she was some kind of loosey-goosey vixen.

And then another thought occurred to her. A thought that sent her blood racing through her veins in a heated rush. Her mouth went dry.

What if she'd already made love to him as Sadie?

Sarah gulped. No. It couldn't be. Even in a hypnotic trance she would have remembered *that.*

Her mind conjured up a million naughty visions of her and Jake in bed, a tangle of arms and legs and sheets. She imagined them making love on the floor, in the bathtub, on a soft spot of ground under the pier where the ships docked.

Sarah Jane Stanhope, this is so unlike you. You stop having erotic fantasies this instant.

But oh, no. Her mind simply refused to stop spinning. She pictured her hands running over the contoured planes of muscular chest. She visualized his palms skimming her sensitive flesh. She conceptualized their joining and her temperature shot up a full ten degrees.

Sarah fanned herself with a hand.

"I want to make love to Jake Gerard."

Okay, there. She'd said it. She wanted him, but she was too chicken to do anything about it. She'd never made an advance toward any man. She was too nervous, too shy, too darned scared to make the first move.

Maybe you are, but Sadie's not, whispered a wicked little voice in the back of her head. What if you seduced him as Sadie?

How?

"Why, honey," Sadie's voice crooned in her head. "You've got to get him to say *hot sex.*"

8

IT TOOK TWO DAYS for Sarah to work up the courage to put her plan in action. On Sunday night, she realized it was now or never. Soon, her father and friends would discover she was missing. Soon, her adventure would come to an end. She didn't want to leave Bear Creek without making love to Jake.

After the restaurant closed and everyone else had gone home, she strolled out to the bar, determined to see this through. If she could get him to say "hot sex," then as Sadie, she would be spending the night in his bed, come heck or high tide.

It was Linc's night off and Jake was wiping down the mahogany wood of the bar with a hand towel lightly spritzed with lemon furniture polish. He stopped what he was doing and crooked a grin at her. An instant thrill raised the hairs on her arms.

"Everyone else gone?" he asked.

"Uh-huh." She hesitated, then said, "Linc was teasing me the other day about calling Bloody Marys Dirty Harrys. How come you didn't tell me I'd made a mistake?"

"You were just so adorable, I couldn't bring myself to break it to you."

"Well, I hated looking like a dooh-dooh, so I've decided to learn all the bar drinks."

"That's a tall order, Sadie. You're a chef now, no reason to worry about drink orders."

"It's a source of personal pride."

All right. How to continue? She paused a moment.

"Linc made me this new drink. It was so delicious, but I forgot the name of it. I hated to admit it to him since he already teased me about the Dirty Harry incident." She was making this whole thing up as she went along.

"What's in the drink?"

"I'm not really sure."

"That narrows it down." Jake chuckled.

"Some kind of liquor." This was going badly, she was coming off like an idiot.

"Most bar drinks generally have some kind of liquor in them." An amused expression crinkled the corners of his eyes.

Just wait until I get you to say "hot sex," buster, and Sadie comes back around. She'll show you amused.

"Umm, I think it was something 'sex.'"

Jake's grin widened. "That sounds like Linc. Giving you a sexy drink."

"I believe it had an H in it, too."

"Sex at My House? Amaretto, raspberry liqueur, pineapple juice."

"Nooo, that doesn't sound quite right." Just hearing him say the name gave her the shivers.

"Sex Appeal? White rum, coconut rum…"

She was shaking her head before he finished. "That's not right."

"Sex on Ice?"

Ooh handsome, with you I'd have sex anywhere. On ice, on the stove, in the freezer.

"Nope."

"Sex in the Shower?"

Hmm. "I don't think so."

"Sex in the Red Zone?"

"No."

"There are many versions of Sex on the Beach. Was it one of those?"

Frustrated, she shook her head again. This ploy wasn't working at all.

"Then there's the always-popular Sex on My Face."

"Jake!"

"Am I embarrassing you?"

"No."

"Liar."

"Okay, so I'm slightly embarrassed."

"I don't know about you, Sadie."

"What do you mean?"

"Sometimes you're bold and brassy and brave and at other times you're as prim as a schoolmarm."

"I'm not."

"You are. The two faces of Sadie Stanhope."

He had no idea how close to the truth he was. This was her opportunity to come clean about the hypnosis, but if she did, would she ever get him in bed?

She decided to make a joke of the whole thing. "Are you calling me two-faced?"

"Oh, no ma'am. I'm just a bit flummoxed by

your changeable nature, and I find myself wondering if you've got a twin sister or something."

"I think it has coffee in it," she said desperately. "The drink, I mean."

"Coffee?"

"And maybe whipped cream."

"Not an Irish coffee?"

"No."

"Wait a minute. I've got it." Jake snapped his fingers.

At last. Sarah braced herself, waited for the magic words. *When you turn into Sadie you're going to remember this. You're going to seduce Jake.*

"A Hot Shot. Coffee, Galliano, whipped cream."

Hot shot? He said "hot shot," not hot sex.

Argh! Sarah clenched her hands into fists. "The hot part sounds right, but I still think sex was in there somewhere."

"Well honey, I think Linc has been pulling your leg. As far as I know there's no drink called a 'hot sex.'"

Hot sex.

The words reverberated around the vacant tables and booths.

Sadie felt all warm and soft and sexy and ready for anything.

Yeah, baby.

"Why don't you make me one of those?" Sadie rested her arms on the bar.

"What?"

"Hot sex." She wriggled her eyebrows at him.

"You're not talking about the drinks anymore,

are you?'' Jake's pulse was racing like a three-year-old thoroughbred sprinting across the finish line at the Kentucky Derby.

She wagged her head and gave him a come-hither glance that threatened to sear his shorts to his backside. The next thing he knew she was rounding the corner and coming behind the bar.

He was in serious trouble here and he knew it. Sadie wanted him and he wanted her. Up until Friday night, he'd been able to tell himself he couldn't pursue her because she was too much like him to make a good wife.

And he hadn't been willing to engage in a simple fling on the grounds that he was cleaning up his act. But in the wake of the disaster with Ms. Snidely, he'd come to the conclusion that maybe he didn't really want to get married after all and he'd been using the restaurant as an excuse.

Mr. Friendly was voting for hot sex.

So was Sadie.

Rising onto her toes, she pressed herself against him. A soft groan of pure feminine approval resounded in her throat at the unmistakable evidence of his arousal.

''Can we go back to your place?'' she whispered huskily.

Can we?! In a twinkling, Jake turned off the lights, locked up and ushered Sadie back to the B&B. His heart was going ka-ching, ka-ching, ka-ching.

He wanted Sadie and she wanted him. As long as they both went into this with their eyes open, there was nothing wrong with that. By the time they reached his room, his stomach was trussed up tight as a sheep shank knot and he was breathing as heavy as a prank caller.

With a start, he realized that for the first time in his entire sexual history, he was actually nervous. Usually when it came to making love he was very self-confident, but something about Sadie felled him like a western hemlock.

He slipped a breath mint from his pocket and popped it into his mouth. He wouldn't let fear of halitosis stop this from being a memorable experience.

You need more than a breath mint. Come on. Think romance.

But his mind was numb, he couldn't seem to do anything but stare at her. She was standing in the middle of his bedroom looking far more lovely than he'd ever seen her look, wearing her simple white blouse and short black skirt. She gave him a grin so seductive his knees almost buckled.

Candles, dumb-dumb. Candles and champagne and soft music. Hop to it. The lady's waiting.

He went to the bureau drawer, fumbled among his holey socks and found a couple of candles and a book of matches he kept on hand in case of power failure. He lit the candles. Sadie switched off the overhead lights.

She was even more beautiful by candlelight.

"Let's have some music." He moved to the bedside table—placing himself within a few feet of her—and flicked on the radio to a romantic oldies station. The midnight-smooth voice of Johnny Mathis poured into the room.

He raised his head.

Their eyes met.

Sadie stepped closer.

"I could go get us some champagne," he suggested.

"Before you run off, I just want you to know, I'm not wearing any underwear."

Jake sucked in air at the full impact of her words. The mint was propelled backward in his mouth and slapped against his tonsils.

He coughed. The mint went down the wrong way.

He tried to cough again but no sound came out. How embarrassing. He raised a finger to indicate she was to give him a minute.

Sadie's forehead creased in concern. "Jake? Sugar Bear, are you choking?"

He shook his head, lying because he didn't want to look like a dufus in front of her.

"Er…maybe it's just the candlelight, but I think you're starting to turn blue."

He pounded himself on the chest.

"You *are* choking! Hang on. Lemme give you the Heimlich maneuver."

He wanted to make a joke about how he would gladly take the licking part but he found it a little difficult cracking wise remarks with a disk of cinnamon candy lodged in his throat.

She jumped behind him and slid her arms around his waist at the same time the candy melted enough to slip down his throat.

"It's all right…" he started to say, but he was

interrupted when she squeezed him just under his rib cage with a hearty thrust.

"Oof."

"Jake? You okay?" She peered around his shoulder at him.

Gratefully, he sucked in air and then finally said, "Yeah, Nancy nurse. Thanks."

"You really scared me."

Me, too.

"Do you want to just call it a night?" she asked.

"Do you?"

Damned if his knees weren't all shaky. Why was he so nervous, so clumsy, so very un-Jake-like? Where was the smooth operator who'd once occupied his body?

Gone. Vanished. Outta here.

Without the shield of his suave reputation, he felt totally exposed. Like the fraud he was. He knew now why he had always kept relationships light.

He hated getting hurt.

Maybe he should put a stop to this whole endeavor before things got out of hand. Except Sadie was giving him adoring looks like he was the best invention since long weekends.

"I think you should just kiss me. No preamble."

"You sure about that? You saw what I do to breath mints. You're taking a big chance on me."

"It's a risk I'm willing to take."

"You're a brave, brave woman." He leaned in close. Gosh, she smelled so good. Like rosemary and basil, chives and garlic and pure, sweet woman.

"Or foolishly impulsive, depending on your point of view."

"From here I'd say the view's pretty great."

He glanced into her laughing eyes, her rich pink lips curled into a tantalizing smile, her hands still wrapped around his waist. A Mack truck loaded with sexual desire slammed right into his lower midsection. The expression on his face must have changed because her eyes dilated and her body tensed.

"On the whole, I prefer daringly adventuresome." He dipped his head to hers.

"Not impetuously scatterbrained?"

"Nope."

Their lips were almost touching.

She caught her breath.

He dropped a kiss on that curvy indention between her nose and the bow of her upper lip. Then he rubbed her nose with his.

"Eskimo kisses," she said. "That's what my mother used to call them."

"Oh?"

"Uh-huh."

Her eyes fluttered closed. He kissed her eyelids.

"Hmm, I like that," she murmured. "My mother called those butterfly kisses."

He nibbled her ears. "What's this called?"

"Come on, Jake. My mother never nibbled my ears."

He chuckled. "I suppose not. How about we name it?"

"What about paradise nibbles?"

"Works for me." He slid his mouth down to her chin.

Sadie sighed.

When he flicked out his tongue to touch the throbbing vein at the spot where her neck intersected with her jaw, she moaned.

His skin was on fire, blazing with scary intensity. Damn. They were just getting started and he was already a human torch, burning, aching, flaming for her. He wanted her. Over him. Under him. Long, racehorse legs wrapped around him. She was firecracker-hot and ready to explode in his hands.

Mr. Friendly rose to the challenge. He'd never been so horny, so full of lust. Oddly enough, these feelings were unlike anything he had ever felt before, and Jake had a whole lot of experience with lustful feelings. This desperate sensation throbbing through his veins had an urgency, a hunger that was totally alien…a delicious fervor that shattered common sense to smithereens.

Clearly he had given up any notion of getting married and settling down. He had fallen under Sadie's magnetic spell, and nothing else seemed to matter except their being here together in his room. He was his old rash, impulsive self again and he didn't regret it for a minute.

"You Sexy Thing" came on the radio.

Sadie stepped back from him, and his arms felt terribly bereft. He reached to pull her back into his embrace, but she shook her head and in that moment, he knew what she was aiming to do. The realization thrust him headlong into a whole new level of arousal.

Holy cow, holy cow, holy cow. All his dreams were about to come true.

Slowly, she began undoing the buttons on her blouse. Mesmerized, Jake perched on the edge of the bed and watched Sadie perform her striptease.

Sadie had never felt so alive, so cherished, so desired. The expression in Jake's eyes produced a strange tugging sensation deep within her. She loved that he wanted her. She yearned to please him any way she could. She rolled her left shoulder forward, let her blouse slip a notch, revealing a peek of skin.

The musical group sang of believing in miracles.

Jake sat transfixed, his gaze never leaving her.

She rotated her hips. *Chaka-boom-chaka-boom-chaka-boom-boom-boom.* Tossing her head, she pulled her hair up off the nape of her neck with both hands and twisted her fanny toward the floor, legs gyrating in time to the music.

She got caught up in the dance, savoring Jake's overt appreciation, enjoying the movement of her own body, relishing her feminine power. In one slowly seductive movement, she stripped off her silky blouse and twirled it over her head like a cowgirl spinning a lasso.

The radio crooned that she was a sexy thing.

Jake apparently concurred, because he was humming along with the song, his eyes locked on her chest, which was now clothed in only a skimpy white bra.

Sadie winked and then turned her back to him. She reached around and inched the zipper of her skirt down a notch.

Jake inhaled sharply.

Glancing over her shoulder, she made certain he wasn't choking again before she angled him a coquettish smile.

"More?" she asked in a husky, breathy whisper.

He nodded. Vigorously.

She slipped the zipper down just a little bit farther. "Do you see anything you like?"

"Oh, yeah."

Poor man, he was practically drooling.

Sssss, hissed the zipper.

The skirt pooled to the floor, she stepped out of the circle of material and slowly turned back around to face him. She wore black stockings with a red garter, white satin thong panties and her chaste white bra.

If Jake were a cartoon character, his eyes would be bugging right out of his head. Oooga! Oooga!

"You told me you weren't wearing any underwear," he croaked.

"I'm not, now." She smiled wickedly, peeled off her panties and unhooked her bra. "Am I?"

Jake slapped a palm across his chest as if to keep his heart from jumping out.

"Come here," he commanded.

She wasn't the sort of girl who needed to be asked twice. In a split second, she was standing beside the bed with his legs wrapped tightly around her waist.

"I gotcha," he said, "and you're not getting away. There's no escaping Stalag Jake."

"As if I wanted to escape." She laughed. "You

just better make sure you know who you're taking prisoner.''

He rocked back onto the bed and pulled her down snug on top of him. The minute his lips touched hers, the tower of anticipation that had been all day in the making toppled inside Sadie and she collapsed. Had she ever wanted a man to make love to her so badly she literally ached?

She wriggled against him and a low moan of feminine delight escaped her startled lips at the unmistakable evidence of his full-blown arousal. His arms spanned her waist, and she reveled in the magnitude of his strength. She inhaled his masculine, outdoorsy smell, felt the hot hunger of his lips as his tongue explored the outline of her mouth.

Time ceased to exist. His kisses rendered her senseless. One minute his mouth was gentle and coaxing, the next fiercely demanding. She liked both moods, both sides of him.

His hands skimmed her back, then came to rest on her bottom, which he kneaded and stroked and pressed more firmly against his solid arousal. Pure molten lava flowed beneath her skin, burning her, stinging her, thrusting desperate desire and pulsating passion through the core of her body.

She wanted, no, *needed* to feel his bare flesh against hers, taste the salt of his skin, inhale the scent of his essential maleness.

Her fingers cried out to strum his naked nipples. Her tongue strained to sip his flavor. Her nose tingled to be filled with the smell of him.

In a heated daze, she grabbed for the front of his shirt, fingers fumbling madly at his buttons.

Roughly, she shoved the material aside and laid her hot palms against the equally fevered flesh of his taut abdomen.

His hormones were as unruly as hers. He ripped off his shirt and went for the snap of his jeans.

"Let me help," she cried and shifted positions in order to assist him in shucking off the restrictive denim. She tossed his pants across the room.

He combed his fingers through her hair, then looked deeply up into her eyes. "You are the sexiest woman I've ever known."

"From what I've been told about your reputation with the ladies, that's quite a compliment."

"My reputation is exaggerated," he said.

"It doesn't bother me that you've been with lots of women."

"Not all that many, really. I just like to flirt a lot. It doesn't mean anything."

"I know." She touched her index finger to his chin. "But I'm not asking to be your wife. You don't have to promise me happily ever after. This is just about sex. No big deal."

But why then, did it feel like such a gigantic deal?

And why did she suddenly feel so impossibly sad? Did she want more from him?

Sadie shook her head. No. He'd made it clear on numerous occasions that she was the wrong kind of woman for him.

From the radio came the opening notes of a familiar oldies tune, "Going to the Chapel." She knew the song. Her heart skipped a beat when she realized the word *married* was mentioned in the song. Not once, but numerous times.

Fear zipped through her. When the singers uttered that word would it trigger her transformation back into stuffy old Sarah? As Sarah, she knew she couldn't go through with indulging in a one-night stand.

She had to shut the radio off before she heard the trigger word, before she was propelled into the fuddy-duddy personality that had kept her from really living for the last twenty-four years.

Frantically, she rolled off Jake, scrambled across the bed and lunged for the radio dial.

"Come back here, you," he teased and grabbed her around the waist.

"No, please, you don't understand." She squirmed, she wriggled, but she knew she wasn't going to get away from him in time.

"I get it," Jake said. "You want to wrestle."

He flipped her onto her back.

She struggled to get away but he pinned her, spread-eagled, against the quilt. He sat on her legs, staked her arms up over her head.

Their gazes locked.

Sadie was breathing heavily, her ears straining to catch the words of the song.

Oh, no. Oh, no. Here it comes. She cringed.

"Married," the singers warbled.

And then, she was prim Sarah again.

9

"SADIE, ARE YOU ALL RIGHT?"

Sarah panted, terrified and yet wildly exhilarated to find herself underneath this powerful masculine man. Startled, she glanced up and down the hard length of his body.

He was exquisite beyond words. And she, sheltered, overprotected Sarah Stanhope, was in bed with a potent stick of human dynamite. Sadie had gotten her this far, but now Sadie was gone and she was all alone with the man of her dreams.

She'd never been so anxious. Or so blasted turned on.

He watched her like a cat at a mouse hole. In one smooth movement, he flipped them over again so that she was on top once more, her legs straddling his waist.

"Sadie?" he repeated, his gaze searching her face.

"Fine," she said, when at last she found her tongue. "I'm fine."

"I thought for a moment there that I might have hurt you."

"Nope."

Part of her wanted to leap out of bed and run away. But another part of her—the part that had been wishing and hoping and praying for this moment since the day she'd met him—was too hot and hungry and wound up to even think about going anywhere.

And yet the notion of making love to him had her insides quivering with fear of the unknown.

Just pretend to be Sadie. Do what she would do and you'll be fine.

Yet how did she know what Sadie would do? The woman was a figment of some hypnotist's imagination.

"Are you having second thoughts?" Jake murmured. "Because it's allowed."

She drew in her breath and said in a very shaky voice, "No. No second thoughts here."

He cradled his palm against her cheek. "Sweetheart," he said, his voice hoarse with strain.

Her nipples pulled tight at the sound and her belly tingled. He was gorgeous, all sinewy muscles, hard ridges and firm angles. Completely masculine. Totally male. Nothing at all like the soft city boys of her acquaintance.

With tentative fingers, she reached down to touch the velvet head of his manhood. She felt the heat of his pulse beating there, matching the fretful rhythm of her own heart.

She'd never touched a man's appendage before and she found the experience enlightening as well as erotically stimulating. The softness of him surprised her. Who would have suspected it could at once be so hard and yet so velvety smooth?

Apparently the contact was good for Jake as well. He groaned and closed his eyes.

Her other hand wanted to explore uncharted territories. She traversed her way across his firm backside, the iron muscles of his thighs, the tender area between his bottom and his erection.

Jake gasped, and the strangled, erotic sound gave her the courage to go on. He seemed to like what she was doing.

Liked it a lot if the increased swelling in his shaft were any indication. She kissed his chest, then laved his nipples with her tongue. His appreciative noises increased in urgency and tempo.

He wanted more, and she intended on giving it.

Her lips trailed lower, kissing the swirl of hair from his nipples to his navel and beyond. He rested his hand on her head and then gently, inexorably guided her to where he wanted her to go.

Overwhelmed with a desire to please him, Sadie did what he wanted. But in her naive, innocent enthusiasm, she didn't lead up, didn't tease or taunt. She simply drew him deep into her mouth. As deeply as she could.

Jake hissed through clenched teeth, sounding exactly like a tire going flat.

He tasted of forbidden fruit. She swirled her tongue up and down him, enthralled by how much this was turning them both on and by how very natural it seemed.

"Wicked," he moaned. "You're so wicked."

This was Sarah he was talking about, not her wild alter ego. Couldn't he tell the difference?

Could she?

That disquieting thought disturbed her, but not for long.

"My turn." He panted. "To torture you. Come here."

As she moved over, he pulled her into the curve of his arm and kissed her, while his fingers went to work below her waist, gently stroking and kneading the inside of her thighs until her entire body throbbed.

"How's this feel?" he asked.

"Umm."

"And this?"

"Heavenly."

"Then I'm not doing something right. It's suppose to feel devilishly good."

"Ah, Sugar Bear, believe me, you're doing everything right."

Why did it sound as if Sadie's voice was coming out of her mouth? Sarah would never say such a bold thing. Was she channeling the imaginary seductress?

"You are so beautiful. I can't believe I'm in bed with you."

With the tip of one callused finger, he stroked her slick feminine flesh. Up and down, around and over her most sensitive nerve endings.

"I've been wanting to do that for days," he confessed.

"Oh my."

He continued to strum her body like a musical instrument. She was amazed at the noises slipping from her throat as his sly fingers played her.

If she made love to Jake, there would be no going back. She could never be the woman she'd been before coming to Bear Creek. She sat perched precariously on the verge of a personality shift, an amalgam of uninhibited Sadie and repressed Sarah.

But who was she really?

And which personality was it that Jake wanted?

She was both frightened and awed, not knowing who she would be once this was over, unable to guess at what the future might hold for her and Jake.

Was this just a one-night stand? Could it be something more? Did Jake want it to be more?

Did she?

The power of his hands and lips, as they did erotic things to her, robbed her of breath and the will to think.

Suddenly, Jake pulled away from her. Was he having second thoughts? Her gaze went immediately to his face.

''What's wrong?''

''I've got…we need…''

''Yes?''

''Protection. I'll be right back.'' He vaulted off the bed and darted into the bathroom.

''Huh?''

Dazed, Sarah stared after him, not realizing what he was talking about until he returned a minute later wearing an orange, glow-in-the-dark condom. She slapped a hand over her mouth to suppress her giggles.

''Making fun of me, are you?'' he asked, leaping headlong back onto the quilt beside her.

''A fluorescent condom?''

''I didn't want you to risk losing me in the dark.''

"Like *that's* going to happen." She reached for him.

And then he simply took over. Slowly, thoroughly and with tender loving care, he dove into their lovemaking at a fevered pitch. He left no part of her unexplored. He lavished her with moist licks and heated kisses from the top of her head to the tips of her toes. Her body throbbed and writhed beneath his clever hands. Throbbed and ached and begged for release.

Then, when Sarah thought she could not stand one second more of this masterful torture, he separated her legs and gently tried to enter her.

And met with a firm resistance.

Jake gasped and his gaze flew to her face.

"You…you're…a virgin?" He stared at her, incredulous.

Sarah nibbled her upper lip with concern. "Is that a problem?"

"I…I…" He was obviously stunned by her revelation, his mouth hanging open in surprise. Jake speechless? This was unheard-of. "I never would have guessed."

"Do you mind terribly?"

"Mind? Mind? Woman, are you nuts? It's every man's dream to bed a virgin."

"It is?"

"Double A right."

"You've never been with a virgin before?"

"No, and if I'd known you were one, I would never have started this."

"Why not?"

"Because your virginity is special. You need to give it to someone special."

"You are special, Jake."

"Really?" he asked huskily.

Slowly, she nodded.

Jake gulped, felt himself falling into something deep and wildly exciting. Was it possible that this woman he thought uninhibited and free and impulsive was not like that at all? Underneath her blasé facade, could she really be the steady, reliable, sensible woman he needed?

He scarcely dared hope, but the discovery of her virginity rattled him to the soles of his feet.

"Stop thinking so much, Jake, and just make love to me," she whispered.

His mouth captured hers. They kissed for a long, heart-stopping moment and then slowly, inch by careful inch he slid into her warm, willing body.

When she whimpered, he stopped moving.

"Am I hurting you?" he asked anxiously.

"It's a good kind of pain," she murmured. "Keep going."

He savored every second of their journey together. Kissing her tenderly, ruffling her hair with his fingers, whispering sweet nothings into her ear. Telling her how beautiful she was, how manly she made him feel.

Her eyes lit up at his compliments and he realized that for the first time he meant these words. He had expressed similar sentiments to other women and perhaps at the time he believed them, but he'd never experienced the true meaning of connection until his body was joined with Sadie's.

"I love the way you feel inside me," she said. "Filling me up, making me whole."

His heart lurched. He cupped her face in her hands and kept moving soft and slow even though he was aching to thrust fast and hard. He was in control here, not his errant member.

His eyes never left her face. She stared up at him and they looked at each other until they seemed to blend into one body, one mind, one soul.

SARAH WOKE, stretched, smiled. Her body ached sweetly, telling her she possessed muscles she'd never known existed. Last night had been pure heaven. She reached across the bed for Jake. Her hand touched nothing but sheet. She raised her head, looked over to where the big, sexy man had lain next to her last night. His side of the bed was empty.

Maybe he'd just tiptoed off to the bathroom.

"Jake?" she called.

No answer. No bathroom sounds from the adjoining room.

Her spirits sank to her ankles. Her smile evaporated.

What had she expected? Tender professions of love? Heartfelt promises of happily-ever-after? As Sadie, she'd made it quite clear to him that she was only passing through. Why did she feel cheated?

Especially since she'd been the one doing the cheating.

She had allowed him to take her to bed, thinking that she was wild, lighthearted Sadie. It wasn't his fault if last night hadn't been anything more than a fun time. That's what Sadie had told him she wanted.

And apparently, it was what Jake wanted as well.

But now he was gone. *He couldn't stand to wake up next to you,* Sarah thought.

She bit down on her bottom lip to keep from crying, but it was a hopeless gesture. Tears stung her eyes. She should have been honest with him. The minute she realized that truth about her hypnotized state, she should have told him what was going on. Instead, she'd misled him, using his attraction to Sexy Sadie to get him into bed.

No wonder he'd run out on her.

Sighing, Sarah sat up, clutched the covers to her chest and brushed her disheveled hair from her face.

That's when she saw the note pinned to his pillow.

With fingers trembling and a pounding heart, she reached for it.

Dear Sadie,
Thought I'd let you sleep in, don't worry about coming in until noon. Last night was fabulous. Can't wait until tonight.

Jake.

Her hopes rose on shaky wings. He hadn't just run out on her, he'd gone to work. Like any responsible business owner. She exhaled and realized belatedly that she'd been holding her breath. Time to get dressed and go tell him the truth. Time to see what he said when he discovered his Sexy Sadie was none other than Staid Sarah.

THE BELL over the door jingled merrily and two attractive young women stepped across the threshold into the B&B. Jake looked up from behind the front desk.

"Morning, ladies." He smiled in greeting.

The taller of the two, a brunette with a soft Southern accent, stepped across the hardwood floor with her hand extended.

"My name's Lizzy Magnason," the brunette said. "And this is Kim Bishop." She indicated the petite blonde beside her with a flick of her wrist.

"Nice to meet you. How can I help you?"

"We're looking for a friend of ours. We just found out she walked off the *Alaskan Queen* when it was docked here ten days ago."

"And you just now realized she was missing?" Jake arched an eyebrow. With friends like these, who needed complete strangers?

"It's a long story," the blonde interrupted. "We thought she was having a rendezvous with some guy in his stateroom. We didn't discover what had happened until the cruise ended in Anchorage yesterday."

"We called her father, of course, and he's frantic," Lizzy added. "He's flying out on his private jet from San Francisco, but we were hoping to find Sarah before he gets here. We were thinking that somebody in town might have seen her. Maybe she's even staying here?"

"We're really worried," Kim said. "Although our friend is very smart, she's also naive about the ways of the world."

Jake's gut roiled. Before he even asked the question, he knew what the answer would be.

"What's your friend's name?"

"Sarah Stanhope, but she might be going by the name of Sadie. See, we were playing parlor games during a costume party and Sarah got hypnotized on the ship, but she left before the hypnotist had a chance to deprogram her. The problem is, under the influence of this Sadie persona, she acts really wild and seductive. In fact," Lizzy dropped her voice an octave, "she thinks she's a stripper."

Jake was finding it hard to breathe. The room suddenly seemed far too warm and far too small. His head throbbed with the pain of this new information.

"Sarah's about five-six, beautiful red hair, blue eyes. Have you seen her?" Lizzy asked.

Oh, he'd seen her all right. Every bare inch of her.

Jake nodded, unable to speak. His mind raced a million miles a minute. Suddenly, everything made sense. Why Sadie was sometimes quiet and reserved, at other times giddy and flirtatious. He'd thought her moody and mercurial when all along she'd been under the influence of hypnosis.

Who had he made love to last night? Sweet-natured Sarah or this false persona, flashy-trashy Sadie?

Wincing, he closed his eyes. Considering she'd performed a striptease, it had to be Sadie. It was she who had gleefully surrendered Sarah's virginity. Not Sarah herself. In fact, would Sarah even remember what had happened between them?

This was too confusing. He couldn't process it all. Jake kneaded his brow with his fingers and opened his eyes.

Just in time to see Sadie, or was it Sarah, coming down the back corridor to the lobby. Her hair was twisted on top of her head, her blouse buttoned up tight, sensible shoes shod her feet and a anxious expression rode her mouth.

She had to be Sarah.

Nervousness assailed him. Nervousness and fear. All the things he'd planned on telling her this morning about how completely right she felt for him flew right out the window. How could he tell her he'd fallen in love with her, when he didn't even know who she was?

"There you are," she said to Jake.

At the very same time Lizzy and Kim spotted her.

"Sarah!"

The next few minutes erupted into chaos as the three best friends squealed gleefully and launched themselves into each others' arms.

"Omigosh, what are you doing here?" Sarah asked.

"Harvey lied. He claimed you were sleeping with him and we were gullible enough to believe him," Kim said.

"That jerk. Yesterday evening, when we found out that he'd been fibbing and you'd gone ashore in Bear Creek, we were frantic, crazed with worry.

We chartered a plane and got here as quickly as we could.'' Lizzy hugged Sarah tight.

"I'm fine. Really."

The three women chattered like chipmunks, with Lizzy and Kim explaining about the hypnotism, while Sadie told them about her week and a half spent in Bear Creek working as a waitress and then a chef. They seemed to forget Jake was standing there, cut adrift, left out of the conversation.

The very earth had shifted out from under him. All morning he had been making plans, trying to find a way to convince Sadie to stay in Bear Creek and work for him to give them both time to see where the relationship was headed. Now there was this new discovery. She wasn't the woman he thought she was. No down-on-her-luck stripper, but the privileged heiress to a fortune.

"Sadie," he said, taking her by the arm after the excitement had died down. "Can I see you in private, please?"

She turned those big blue eyes on him, and he felt a clutch of fear all the way to his bones.

"Give me a minute," she told her friends. "I'll be right back."

"Sure. No problem. Now we know you're safe. Take your time." Kim nodded.

"Oh, Sarah," Lizzy said. "We forgot to tell you."

Sarah turned back around to look at her friends. "What?"

"We called your father as soon as Harvey confessed. He's on his way." Lizzy glanced at her watch. "In fact, I wouldn't be surprised if he arrives at any minute."

Her father was coming. Here. To Bear Creek.

Sarah wasn't sure she was ready to face him, but Jake wasn't giving her much time to think about that. As he dragged her toward the backyard, he seemed really upset. His mouth was screwed into a disapproving line, his eyebrows dipped into a deep V. She had never seen him like this. Stern and vexed.

He hadn't yet shaved and his beard stubble gave him an ominous appearance. She gulped.

"Okay," he said, once the back door shut behind them. "Out with it."

"Out with what?"

"This whole hypnosis thing. How long have you known you were switching back and forth from yourself to this Sadie person?"

She looked at him and got a funny little stabbing sensation in the center of her heart. She had hurt him and she had certainly never meant to do that.

"Jake, I..."

"How long?" he asked gruffly.

"Since the night that I dumped the pasta on Ms. Snidely's head. Sadie did the dumping; I was remorseful."

"Why didn't you tell me? I would have understood."

"Would you have? Really? You'd already told me you'd had enough of flaky women. If I said that I was toggling back and forth between my real self and this made-up personality, wouldn't you have thought I was a kook?"

He said nothing, just blew out his breath with a heavy huff. "Do you remember what happened between us last night?"

She ducked her head. "Yes. Of course."

He cradled her chin in his palm, lifted her face up to his and forced her to look him in the eye. His gaze was troubled.

"Who did I make love to last night? Was it Sadie or Sarah?"

How was she supposed to answer this?

"Which one did you want me to be?" she asked softly.

Her heart broke right into two pieces when she saw the answer reflected in his hazel eyes. Sexy Sadie was the one he wanted. Not Sensible Sarah.

"I told you before that you can't be what *I* want you to be. You have to be yourself. So here's a better question, sweetheart. Just who in the hell are you?"

10

FAIR QUESTION. The only problem was, Sarah
didn't know the answer. Not any more.

All her life she'd been a good girl, devoted to
her father, doing the right thing, living up to the
Stanhope name. No one could question her ethics
or claim that her mother's tempestuous blood
pulsed through her veins.

But somewhere in the back of her subconscious
lurked a rebelliousness that had seized on the opportunity the hypnotist presented when he turned
her into Sadie.

Somewhere deep inside Sarah lurked a wild
woman.

And for the last twenty-four years she'd been
both ashamed and terrified of that person.

She opened her mouth to tell Jake about her confusion over her identity, when a sudden rapping
sound drew her attention to Kim and Lizzy poking
their heads around the back door.

"Sarah," Lizzy said. "I hate to interrupt, but
your father just arrived and he's got some woman
with him."

Some woman? Sarah's tummy clenched. Was it
the woman who had answered his phone?

She glanced over at Jake again. He had his arms

crossed over his chest, an unreadable expression on his face. He was shutting down, closing her out, creating a barrier between them.

Could she blame him? No doubt he was feeling hurt and disappointed and confused.

But no more confused than she.

"Go talk to your father," he said. "Maybe he can help you find the answers you're looking for."

Jake was right and she knew it, but was she ready for this? Sarah sucked in her breath. Her eyes met his. "Will you come with me?"

He nodded, and relief washed through her. He hadn't written her off completely.

Not yet anyway.

Nerves atwitter, heart ajitter, Sarah turned and mounted the back steps with Jake right behind her.

Lizzy and Kim marched ahead of her into the lobby of the B&B. She halted when she saw her father seated on the plush leather sofa. An attractive, well-dressed woman who appeared to be a few years younger than his own fifty-eight years sat beside him holding his hand.

Sarah might have turned and ran if Jake hadn't been blocking her exit.

"Sarah!" her father cried, and sprang to his feet, arms out thrust.

In that moment her fears vanished.

"Papa," she cried, and ran to him.

His grip was strong, but he was trembling all over.

"Darling," he said. "We were so worried about you."

We. As in him and his new woman. That single

word took the joy right out of their reunion. Sarah stepped back from the circle of her father's arms and eyed his companion.

The woman had risen to her feet. She extended her hand. "I know this is an awkward way to meet, Sarah, but I'm Margery Kowling."

"Dr. Margery Kowling," her father said proudly, looking at the woman with deep affection. He draped an arm nonchalantly around her shoulder. "She's a cardiologist. We met at the vinegar festival. We've been dating on and off since then."

The annual festival had been six months earlier. Her father had been seeing Margery behind her back for six months? Why had he felt the need to slip around? Why hadn't he told her?

Reluctantly, Sarah shook Margery's hand and the woman smiled such a genuine, friendly smile. Sarah immediately felt guilty for holding a grudge.

"Nice to meet you, Margery."

"Your friends told us what happened to you. The hypnotism, getting left by the cruise ship." Margery nodded at Lizzy and Kim. "It must have been a disconcerting experience for you."

"To say the least."

"We need to find that hypnotist and get you deprogrammed as soon as possible," her father said to Sarah. "We need to get things straightened out before making the trip home."

"He's probably still in Anchorage," Lizzy said. "Kim and I'll go call the cruise line and see if we can locate him."

It was all coming to a close. Her time in Alaska.

Her wonderful adventure as first a waitress and then a chef. Her father had come to take her home.

But she didn't want to go. She wanted to stay.

What did Jake want? Sarah glanced over at him. He stood with his back against the front desk, his complete attention focused on her. He smiled and that gave her courage.

"Why didn't you call me right away, darling?" her father asked. "You know I would have sent the jet."

"I know and I did try to call, but when Margery answered the phone, I didn't know what to say to her. Or to you. It occurred to me that I'd been standing in the way of your romantic life. I didn't want to spoil your good time, so I decided to stay in Bear Creek until I could earn the money to come home. I realized I had been depending on you far too much."

Her father took her hands in his and guided her to sit down on the sofa on his right side. Margery perched on his left. It felt odd to see him with a woman. Many times as a child, she had wished he would remarry so she could have a mother, but he had rarely dated. As time went on, she'd become accustomed to it being just the two of them.

Too accustomed, apparently.

"No, darling," her father said gently. "I was the one leaning too hard on you. Margery has helped me to see that. She told me that a lot of my cardiac problems could be related to emotional stress. I took her advice and started seeing a counselor."

"You've been going to a shrink?"

He nodded. "For the past four months. And it's the best thing I've ever done. Should have done it years ago. My blood pressure is finally in the normal range without medication, and I feel more alive than I've felt in years."

She had to admit he did look good. If Margery was responsible for the luster in his eyes and the starch in his step then who was she to complain?

"Why didn't you mention this before now?" she asked. "And what's all this about emotional stress?"

Her father looked to Margery and she nodded. "It's time to tell her everything, Charles. She has a right to know."

"Tell me what?" Sarah looked from her father to Margery and back again.

"I didn't tell you that I was going to counseling, because I wasn't ready to face what I had done to you." Papa shook his head.

"You didn't do anything to me. You've been a wonderful father."

"If only that were true."

"But it is true," Sarah protested, feeling uneasy.

"No, it's not. All these years I was terrified you would grow up to be like your mother. That you would find me much too dull and leave me, just as she did. I kept you tied to the business. I never allowed you to fully express yourself. I convinced you to work in my business rather than become a gourmet chef like you wanted. I'm afraid I even exaggerated my heart condition. You were getting to be the same age your mother was when she took off. I used my mild heart attack to bind you even tighter to me. I'm very ashamed of what I've done.''

"But you've got nothing to be ashamed of." Sarah squeezed his hand. "I loved taking care of you. And I'm nothing like my mother."

Except that is, when she was Sexy Sadie.

"You look just like her, Sarah, and she wasn't a bad woman. In fact, she was wonderful. So alive, so vivacious, so uninhibited."

She studied her father. She'd never heard him speak this way about Maria. "And she was a frivolous, feckless woman who abandoned us to pursue her acting career."

Her father shook his head. "That's not true."

"What?"

"Your mother didn't leave. My parents chased her away."

"Gramma and Grandpa Stanhope?"

"Yes."

Silence wedged itself between them like a gigantic white elephant.

"Are you going to explain?" Sarah asked him at last.

She was so focused on her father she forgot all about Margery and Jake being in the room. All she could think about was the sound of her mother's voice humming "Sexy Sadie" and rocking her to sleep. She remembered her mother's smile and the color of her eyes. Blue. Just like her own.

"Your mother was much younger than I. A girl really, when we married. And she was trying hard to break into acting. Her zeal and idealism were what attracted me to her and I suppose that I represented security to her. She had a very tumultuous life. Your grandparents were against the marriage from the beginning, but I was so enchanted with Maria I couldn't see that we were mismatched in so many ways. She needed someone younger, more flexible.''

"Don't blame yourself.''

"But I was to blame. I was so involved with the vinegar business, I didn't see how unhappy she was after you were born. Not that she didn't love you, Sarah, but she missed her old life. One day when you were about three years old and I was working, she took you with her to visit some of her acting friends. They were laughing and drinking wine and having a good time and she thought you were napping in the back room. But you climbed out the window and the police found you wandering the streets and took you to the station. Luckily, we had taught you your name and address. My parents came to pick you up, but they never forgave Maria.''

Sarah sucked in her breath. Her hands trembled; her heart ached. "But she hadn't meant for any harm to come to me and none did.''

Her father paused a moment, then took a deep breath and continued. "There's more. In order to make ends meet, your mother had once worked as a stripper. She was very ashamed of her past, and she never told me about it. But my parents found out, and on top of the other incident, they decided she was unworthy of their son. They told her she was a worthless mother. They convinced Maria that you and I would be better off without her.

They told her if she caused trouble they'd make sure she never got another acting job.''

"No," Sarah whispered, hurting for the sad young woman who'd been her mother.

"Yes. She left in the middle of the night. I hired a private investigator to go after her, but by the time he found her, she was seriously ill from pneumonia and I never got to speak to her. I didn't find out the real truth of what happened until many years later when your grandmother confessed to me on her deathbed. After seeing how miserable I was without your mother, she regretted what she and my father had done.''

"But why didn't you tell me this before?" Sarah asked, wondering how different her life might have been if she'd had this information growing up.

"Because I was afraid you would admire her and try to emulate her. And while she was a wonderful woman, I was fearful of losing you. Whenever you showed the least signs of exuberant behavior, I squelched it in you. I never let you fully express yourself. Anything that smacked of your mother, I tried to stomp out.''

"Papa." She laid a hand on his shoulder. "Don't judge yourself so harshly.''

"I've come to grips with my role in what happened, thanks to Margery and my counselor." Her father smiled at his new lady friend before turning back to look at Sarah. "And I've also come to realize that I've cheated both of us by holding on to you so tightly. It's time to let go and allow you to stand on your own two feet.''

Eleven days ago, before she'd met Jake and

started working at his restaurant, the thought of leaving her father's home and abandoning her job in the family business would have been unthinkable. It was all she'd ever known.

If she was glib Sadie, she would shrug and say, "That's how the cookie crumbles."

But she wasn't Sadie.

Sarah stared down at her father's hand, which was clasping her own. She felt oddly cut off from her emotions, as if there was an internal wall between her heart and her head.

Who was she, if she wasn't prim-and-proper heiress to a vast vinegar empire? If she wasn't her father's devoted daughter, his dutiful nurse?

He'd found happiness with Margery, that much was clear, and he was ready for his life to change.

Was she?

Was there, after all, a bit of her mother buried deep inside a place she'd tried to cover over, but never forgotten?

Something fluttered in her chest. A quickening sensation, as if she was finally, fully awakening. She'd been sleepwalking through her existence—never truly experiencing life—for a very long time.

All these years of resisting her natural inclinations to dance and sing and have fun. All this time she'd spent trying so hard not to be like her mother. But Maria had been a modern woman, ahead of her time. She had been mistreated and misunderstood by Sarah's grandparents.

Hypnosis had been the catalyst. The key that turned the lock and allowed the long suppressed

"Sadie" to leap from her dungeon and into the light of day.

Three things had irrevocably changed her.

Her father's confession.

Being hypnotized.

And making love with Jake.

Jake.

Her heart clutched to realize she'd forgotten all about him in the wake of her father's revelation. She raised her head, seeking his saucy wink and brave reassurance that everything was going to be okay.

Pulse accelerating, she glanced around the room for him.

But he was gone.

THIRTY MINUTES LATER, she'd searched both the B&B and the diner, but he was nowhere to be found. When had he left the conversation between her and her father? How much of Papa's confession had he heard?

Concerned, she walked down Main Street. She saw Cammie Jo and Mack, Quinn and Kay. She greeted Caleb and then later, Meggie. There were lots of tourists milling about, but there was no sign of Jake.

Sarah's hopes sank.

And then she saw him. Sitting on the dock in a lounge chair, watching the cruise ships pull into port.

"Hey," she said, and sat down cross-legged on the dock beside his chair.

"What are you doing out here? I thought you'd be with your father."

"I wanted to talk to you. Gus arranged for Papa and Margery to take a room at the B&B." She stared across the dock at the cruise ship tying up. "It's weird, when your father has a girlfriend."

He reached down and took her hand. "You'll adjust."

"You really think so?"

"You're one tough cookie, Sarah. I know so."

"Sadie's the tough cookie," she said softly. "Not me."

"You underestimate yourself."

Purple mountain peaks rose up in the distance, pristine in their breathtaking majesty. The breeze was cool on her skin. Cooler now in the middle of August than it had been on the day she arrived, wearing nothing but Sadie's sexy bustier.

She wanted to talk to him about what had happened the night before. How wonderful their lovemaking had been, how much it meant to her, but she didn't know where to start.

Plus, she couldn't seem to concentrate. All she could think about was the pressure of his long, masculine fingers interlaced with hers and the warmth of his palm. She recalled in blinding detail how that same bold hand had greedily roamed her body the night before. Her tender thighs would not let her forget.

"What are you doing out here?" she asked after a long moment.

"Watching the ships roll in."

"Don't tell me, you're gonna watch 'em roll away again."

"I just might." He smiled at her.

"Are you sure you're not just avoiding me?"

"Not sure at all," he admitted.

"I've been thinking," she said. "Maybe I won't let the hypnotist deprogram me."

Cocking his head, he looked at her pensively. "Why not?"

"I'm scared," she confessed. "What will happen to me when Sadie's gone?"

"You'll be the old you again."

Jake shrugged nonchalantly, but inside, he was worrying about the very same thing. He had as much riding on the outcome as she did. Because, he'd realized back there in the B&B while she was talking with her father, exactly how he felt about her.

He was in love.

But was he in love with Sarah or Sadie?

The answer? Both of them.

It was the amalgamation of these two personalities that had captured his imagination. She was everything he'd ever wanted. At once carefree and stable, frivolous yet sensible, impulsive yet cautious. On the one hand, she could fly with him to the stars, but on the other, she was the anchor he secretly longed for.

What would happen when the hypnotist removed the suggestion of Sadie from Sarah's subconscious? Would that flirtatious, fun-loving babe be gone? Would Sarah pack up and follow her father back to San Francisco? Would they both disappear from his life forever?

Despite the bright sunshine, the world suddenly seemed a much darker place. The only thing in his past that could compare to this feeling of despair was when he'd lost his parents. How could this woman have come to mean so much to him in such a short period of time?

He had no answer, but he knew it was true. Without her, he was less of a man.

"I don't want to be my old self again," she whispered. Tears misted her eyes. This was clearly very hard for her. "I don't want Sadie to go away."

He shifted in his chair so he could peer straight into her face and reassure her in a way he could not reassure himself. She needed him to be strong for her.

"You won't lose Sadie. She's a part of you. She always has been." He tapped her chest over her heart with his two forefingers. "I've heard it said that someone will never do something under hypnosis that they wouldn't have done in the first place. Everything that you did as Sadie was a reflection of the part of your personality you've been repressing for too long."

"You really think so?" She sniffled and wiped at her eyes with the back of her hand.

"Abso-friggin'-lutely." He grinned and hoped like hell that he was right.

"YOU ARE GETTING very sleepy."

It was later that evening when Sarah shifted in her chair at Jake's B&B, surrounded by the hypnotist, her father, friends and Lulu. It was hard trying to concentrate with an audience, but she didn't have the heart to tell a single one of them to leave. They were all important to her, each in their own special way.

"Please try to concentrate," the hypnotist scolded. "Keep your eyes on the watch."

She wanted this. She really did. Because without it, she would never know for sure who she really was.

To thine own self be true.

The phrase popped into her head. Ah, good advice if you knew who thine own self happened to be. It was a tad more difficult when you'd spent the last week and a half alternating between wild and free and staid and restricted.

"Focus. That's it. Allow your eyelids to close naturally."

Go ahead. Let go. Let it happen.

She inhaled deeply several times, allowing her body to go loose and limp.

"When I snap my fingers, you will awaken. You will no longer be Sexy Sadie. The words 'hot sex' and 'married' will no longer trigger a transformation in your personality."

Okay, okay. She was ready.

The hypnotist snapped his fingers.

Sarah blinked and looked around at all the people she loved.

Everyone held their collective breaths, waiting.

"Hot sex," said the hypnotist.

Sarah rose from her chair and began to perform a striptease.

The hypnotist looked panic-stricken. "Wait a minute, this isn't supposed to be happening. I de-programmed you."

She stopped and grinned. "You might have taken away the trigger words, but you can't take away Sadie. Jake was right. She was inside me all along. Your hypnosis just gave her an excuse to come out. Without it, I would never have been brave enough to embrace my adventuresome side. And for that I thank you."

Everyone cheered.

Her father hugged her close and whispered, "I'm so proud of you."

Margery shook her hand.

Lizzy and Kim squealed with glee. "At last, you'll stop spending your weekend balancing the books on vinegar accounts."

Quinn and Kay, Cammie Jo and Mack, Meggie and Caleb all congratulated her on facing her fears.

And then she turned to Jake.

"I want to thank you for everything you've done for me. You gave me the opportunity to express myself and you never once judged me harshly."

What was this? Were his eyes misty?

"Excuse us, folks," he said, took Sarah by the hand and led her from the room.

"Where are we going?" she asked, suddenly nervous again.

"Shhh." He ushered her into his bedroom and closed the door behind them.

"Are we going to have hot sex?" She winked boldly. "Because I'm ready."

"Hold that thought, sweetheart, but first there's something else I want to discuss with you."

"What is it?" she whispered. Her heart rolled in a low, lazy somersault.

He pulled something from his pocket. A gold nugget on a key chain. He took the nugget off the chain, placed it in her palm and curled her fingers around it. "My father gave me this piece of gold before he died. It belonged to my great-great-grandfather, who found it during the Alaskan gold rush."

"No kidding?" Sarah opened her palm and stared down at the smooth chunk of gold. It glinted brightly in the light.

"The nugget was a reminder. To be true to myself and not to compromise, no matter what."

"I'm not sure I understand."

"All these years I kept telling myself that I was not husband material. That I was too much like my dad. That if I got married I'd either have to reconcile giving up a part of myself or I couldn't be the man the woman I loved wanted. I feared hurting her in the same way my father broke my mother's heart."

He took her by the hand and led her to the bed. He sat down and patted the spot on the quilt beside him.

"I realize now that's why I've always been attracted to the no-strings-attached kind of woman, like Sadie. I figured it was better for me to get my heart broken than for me to hurt them."

"Do you still believe this?"

He shook his head. "Through knowing you, I've come to see things differently."

"Oh?" Sarah held her breath, and waited for him to continue. What was he leading up to?

"See, I was wrong about the kind of man I was. I thought I was being true to myself when I was chasing adventures, having a good time, hanging out with the ladies."

"That wasn't the real you?"

"No. I was trying to live up to my father's reputation. I thought when he gave me this nugget he was telling me to be like him and, that's what I tried to be."

"So what changed your focus? Why did you go in on that ad with your friends?"

"When all of them decided they were going to get married, I felt left out, lonely. I'd just gotten hurt by a woman who neglected to tell me she was married."

"Ouch."

"Yeah. I realized I did want to get married. I wanted a family, but I was also still scared I couldn't live up to the responsibility. I convinced myself the only way to prove I had really changed was to provide a financial bottom line. So I bought the Paradise and tried to make it into something it wasn't. Just like I'd been trying to make myself into something I wasn't all these years. I had adventures because I thought that's what Gerard men did. I indulged in casual affairs because I thought it was expected. But now I really understand what my father was trying to tell me when he gave me that nugget. He was telling me to be me.''

''And what is that, Jake?''

''Eager, eligible and Alaskan.''

''Meaning?''

''You're what I need in order to be true to myself.''

Omigosh, she thought she was going to faint.

''Are you sure, Jake? We've known each other less than two weeks. And for most of that time, it's Sadie you've been attracted to.''

''We can take things slow if you want, but I know I've never felt like this about anyone, Sarah. No one gives me goose bumps the way you do. No one keeps me on my toes the way you do, either. We've got chemistry, darling, and you can't deny it.''

''No, I can't. But mix the wrong chemicals and *ka-blewy*—there goes the neighborhood.''

''Ah, but mix the right chemicals and you create something new and wonderful.''

''What are you saying, Jake?'' Her breath was coming in short, fast gasps and she was feeling mighty panicky. Was she ready for this?

''I'm a lucky, lucky man to have had you in my life even for just a few days.'' He rubbed her shoulder with the flat of his hand. ''But I want more and I think you do, too.''

Sarah went completely still under the gentle pressure of his firm palm. Oh! Oh! She felt light-headed and giddy and well…just plain happy.

''I love you, Sarah.''

She stared at him, slack-jawed and bug-eyed.

She'd hoped for this. Hoped and wished and dreamed. But to actually hear him say the words knocked the breath from her body. She couldn't speak. Her tongue didn't work.

"This is the part where you tell me that you love me, too." He looked a little uneasy, as if he were a lion tamer who had just stuck his head in the lion's mouth and realized belatedly that she wasn't *his* lion.

"Jake...I...I...I..." she stammered.

"You're shocked. I caught you off guard. Well, let me tell you something, sweetheart, it caught me off guard, too. One minute I'm thinking you're Sexy Sadie and there's no way you'll fall for me. And then I find out you're this wealthy heiress. I felt certain you wouldn't fall for a regular Joe like me."

"That's screwy."

"I can't help the way I felt. But then I was holding this damned nugget and I thought, what the hell! If there was ever a time to be true to myself, it's now. So dumb as it may seem, here I am, laying it on the line. I love you, Sarah Stanhope."

Jake studied her face, his heart in his throat. Oh God, what if she said she didn't love him in return? What if she said something truly awful, like she just wanted to be friends?

But he wasn't sorry he'd taken the risk. He loved her and he knew it. She was the one he'd been waiting for. They went together like lox and bagels, like summertime and ice cream, like a skydiver and his parachute. If she couldn't see that, well then...what?

"Cut me some slack, Sarah. I'm dying here."

"Oh, Jake," she said, and damned if her eyes weren't misty.

But was it a good kind of misty, as in—hell, I love you too, big boy. Or was it a bad kind of misty, like—I'm so sorry you've made a terrible fool of yourself, dimwit, now I'm going to have to be the bitch and break your heart.

A single tear slid down her cheek and panic sliced him to the bone.

"Come on, no crying. Please. I didn't mean to make you cry." He felt himself beginning to freak out. He shoved his hands in his pockets, frantically looking for a handkerchief he knew wasn't there.

"I'm not crying," she denied, sniffling harder.

"Yeah, and it don't get cold in Alaska in the wintertime."

Another tear plopped down her cheek. In desperation, he grabbed the corner of the quilt and dabbed at her eyes. "Hush, now. It's okay if you don't love me back, I understand."

"You ninny, I do love you. Jeeze Louise. What does it take for you to figure that out, man? For a building to fall on you?"

"You love me?"

She gave him a watery smile. "Abso-friggin'-lutely."

"Marry me, Sarah. Let's spend the rest of our lives together."

"What about Sadie?"

"What about her?"

"How does she figure into this equation?"

"Other than the fact that it's going to be one hell of a wedding night?"

"Oh, you." She poked him in the ribs.

"Is that a yes?"

"Yes, yes, yes, a thousand times, yes."

And then she was in his arms, kissing him with an intensity that took his breath. She poured her heart and soul into that kiss and he loved her all the more for it.

"Mmm," Jake groaned. "I love how you taste, the way you laugh, the incredible things you do to Mr. Friendly."

"Mr. Friendly?"

He drew her into his lap and Sarah's eyes widened. "I believe you two have already met."

"Oh, *that's* Mr. Friendly."

"Indeed. But that's not all I love about you. I love how you're at once sweet and sexy. I love how you stick up for the people you care about, how you throw yourself into your work heart and soul. I love the way you cut your food into a million small pieces, I love the way you snore..."

"I don't snore."

"Honey, you snore."

"Well, then, thank you."

"For what?"

"Being the kind of guy who likes a woman that snores. For being so damned good in bed, for being so macho and adorable and completely male." She paused to give him Eskimo kisses and butterfly kisses and paradise nibbles. "But mostly, thank you for loving me, just the way I am. Split personality and all."

"Hey, babe, we've all got our quirks."

"You too?"

"But of course."

"Are you going to tell me what they are?"

"I'm more than ready to show you. But first, you've got to say the magic words."

"Magic words?"

"You know what they are."

Boldly, Sarah winked at him and murmured, "Hot sex."

"Anything you want, babe." Jake grinned, sat her to one side of the bed, got to his feet and then *he* started stripping.

Epilogue

"THE SECOND MEETING of the Wild Women City Girls Club will now come to order," Kay said. "Current business on the agenda, induction of our newest member."

"Hear, hear." Meggie and Cammie Jo applauded.

"Put your left hand on this copy of *Metropolitan* magazine."

Sarah complied, grinning.

"Sarah Jane Stanhope, forever after to be referred to as Sadie, do you swear to uphold the rules and regulations outlined in our handy-dandy City Girls Guide to Wilderness Life?"

"I do."

"Okay, now put your right hand on this black bustier." Kay held out the skimpy garment Sadie had worn on the day she'd shown up in Bear Creek.

Giggling, Sadie did as she was told.

"Do you swear to maintain your City Girl essence even while living amongst bears and moose and snow deep enough to get lost in?"

"I do."

"Do you also swear to act sassy when the need

arises in order to keep your Alaskan man on his toes?"

"But of course. How do you suppose I caught him in the first place?"

"Good point," Cammie Jo said.

"I never had to swear to that clause." Meggie nibbled her cucumber sandwich.

"Don't worry," Kay said, "you will. Just as soon as you catch your man."

"As if! I'm done with men," Meggie said.

"Famous last words," Kay muttered.

"I heard that."

"Back to the matter at hand." Cammie Jo interrupted their good-natured squabbling.

"Yes," Kay said. "All right then, Sadie, we now pronounce you officially wild."

They draped a feather boa around her neck, kissed her cheek, then dumped a glass of champagne over her head.

"Hey, hey, what's going on over here?" Jake sauntered in from the kitchen.

Sadie beamed at him and licked champagne from her lips. "Hey Jake, I'm a member of the Wild Women City Girls Club."

"Heaven help us, as if you need any encouragement to be wild." He untied his apron from his waist and gently toweled her head.

Sadie looked up at Jake, her heart filling with love for him.

His gaze met hers and the same emotion shimmered in his eyes. Reaching down, he took her hand and hauled her to her feet. Right there in front of all the other wild city girls, he kissed her.

"Oooh." Cammie Jo sighed.

"Isn't that sweet?" Kay said.

"Mush, pure mush." Meggie shook her head.

"Skeptic." Cammie Jo and Kay threw bread sticks at her.

But Sadie wasn't paying them much attention. She only had eyes—and lips—for the man before her. The man who had changed her life in so many wonderful ways. He'd given her the courage to face her past and make peace with it. Because of Jake, she was a whole woman, no longer staid on the outside and sexy on the inside, but everything all at once.

"What say we close the restaurant an hour early," Jake growled low in his throat. "Go on home and give your friends something to talk about."

"Hey, I've got a man of my own to set tongues a-waggin' with," Kay said.

"Me, too." Cammie Jo jumped up from her chair and grabbed her purse. "Mack should be getting home right about now."

Then at the same moment everyone realized that Meggie had no one. They all looked at her.

"Oh please, no pity. I've been married. It's not what it's cracked up to be."

"Not when you don't have the right person," Cammie Jo said. "But when you do it's heaven."

"Don't despair, Meggie," Kay chimed in. "Three bachelors may be down, but there's still one to go." She opened the copy of *Metropolitan* magazine that Sadie had taken her oath on and tapped a finger on Caleb's picture.

"Caleb? Are you guys nuts? He's just a kid."

"Only two years younger than you," Kay pointed out.

"Two and a half, to be exact. And, in case you've forgotten, he's my ex-husband's step-brother." Meggie shook her head.

"Oh yeah. There is that."

"Bummer."

Meggie shifted in her seat, trying to look nonchalant, but in that moment, they could all feel her pain. "Well," she said. "Guess I better be going."

"Me, too." Cammie Jo followed her to the door.

"Welcome to the club," Kay said, and shook Sadie's hand. "I'll be writing up your story in *Metropolitan*. A special Christmas issue, just in time for your wedding."

"Thanks, Kay."

"Don't mention it." Kay winked and then went after Meggie and Cammie Jo.

"I feel bad for Meggie," Sadie said to Jake once her friends had gone. "And Caleb, too. I wish everyone could be as happy as we are."

He held her tightly against his shoulder. "Don't worry. Until I met you, I didn't really believe in happily ever after, but now I know it's true. Meggie will find someone. And so will Caleb," Jake said. "I'd stake my life on it."

"You're sure?"

"As surely as the sun comes up in the morning."

"Watch what you say, wild man. This is Alaska. Sometimes the sun doesn't come up at all."

"And those are the days you spend cuddled up in bed."

"I can hardly wait for winter." She grinned.

"No need to wait. There's always the freezer." Then Jake Gerard scooped the woman he loved into his arms and carried her into the rest of their lives together.

* * * * *

Will Caleb and Meggie find romance?
Be sure to watch for their story,
coming only to
Harlequin Blaze in Fall 2002.

HARLEQUIN®
Duets™

"**EXCELLENT! Carol Finch has the ability to combine thrilling adventure and passionate romance into her long line of masterful romances that entice readers into turning the pages.**"

"**A winning combination of humor, romance....**"

–Romantic Times

Enjoy a
DOUBLE DUETS
from bestselling author
Carol Finch

Meet the Ryder cousins of Hoot's Roost, Oklahoma, where love comes sweepin' down the plain! These cowboy bachelors don't give a hoot about settlin' down, but when a bevy of strong-willed women breezes into town, they might just change their minds. Read Wade's and Quint's story in:

Lonesome Ryder?
and
Restaurant Romeo
#81, August 2002

HARLEQUIN®
Makes any time special ®

Who was she really?

Where Memories Lie

GAYLE WILSON

AMANDA STEVENS

Two full-length novels of enticing, romantic suspense—by two favorite authors.

They don't remember their names or lives, but the two heroines in these two fascinating novels do know one thing: they are women of passion. Can love help bring back the memories they've lost?

Look for WHERE MEMORIES LIE in July 2002— wherever books are sold.

Harlequin invites you to experience the
charm and delight of

A brand-new continuity
starting in August 2002

HIS BROTHER'S BRIDE
by *USA Today* bestselling author
Tara Taylor Quinn

Check-in: TV reporter Laurel London and noted travel
writer William Byrd are guests at the new Twin Oaks
Bed and Breakfast in Cooper's Corner.

Checkout: William Byrd suddenly vanishes and while
investigating, Laurel finds herself face-to-face with
policeman Scott Hunter. Scott and Laurel face a painful past.
Can cop and reporter mend their heartbreak and get to the
bottom of William's mysterious disappearance?

HARLEQUIN®
Makes any time special ®

Princes...Princesses...
London Castles...New York Mansions...
To live the life of a royal!

In 2002, Harlequin Books lets you escape to a
world of royalty with these royally themed titles:

Temptation:
January 2002—*A Prince of a Guy* (#861)
February 2002—*A Noble Pursuit* (#865)

American Romance:
The Carradignes: American Royalty (Editorially linked series)
March 2002—*The Improperly Pregnant Princess* (#913)
April 2002—*The Unlawfully Wedded Princess* (#917)
May 2002—*The Simply Scandalous Princess* (#921)
November 2002—*The Inconveniently Engaged Prince* (#945)

Intrigue:
The Carradignes: A Royal Mystery (Editorially linked series)
June 2002—*The Duke's Covert Mission* (#666)

Chicago Confidential
September 2002—*Prince Under Cover* (#678)

The Crown Affair
October 2002—*Royal Target* (#682)
November 2002—*Royal Ransom* (#686)
December 2002—*Royal Pursuit* (#690)

Harlequin Romance:
June 2002—*His Majesty's Marriage* (#3703)
July 2002—*The Prince's Proposal* (#3709)

Harlequin Presents:
August 2002—*Society Weddings* (#2268)
September 2002—*The Prince's Pleasure* (#2274)

Duets:
September 2002—*Once Upon a Tiara/Henry Ever After* (#83)
October 2002—*Natalia's Story/Andrea's Story* (#85)

 **Celebrate a year of royalty with
Harlequin Books!**

Available at your favorite retail outlet.

HARLEQUIN®
Makes any time special ®

Visit us at www.eHarlequin.com

HSROY02